"YOU DON'T HAVE TO DO ANYTHING YOU DON'T WANT TO." He spread a blanket on the road and motioned me to sit. "But I don't believe you want to be just another person, doing the same thing every generation. You have more power than anyone, Ana. It's up to you whether or not you use it."

"I don't feel very powerful." My hands hurt, I could barely feed myself, and Sam kept rescuing me. "I feel like the smallest, most insignificant person."

"Small, maybe. Definitely not insignificant." He sat next to me, and we watched the empty road. "Everyone knows who you are."

BY JODI MEADOWS

Incarnate
Asunder

INCARNATE

JODI MEADOWS

 KATHERINE TEGEN BOOKS
An Imprint of HarperCollins Publishers

Katherine Tegen Books is an imprint of HarperCollins Publishers.

Library of Congress Cataloging-in-Publication Data

Meadows, Jodi.

    Incarnate / Jodi Meadows. — 1st ed.

      p.   cm.

    Summary: After 5,000 years of the same souls being reincarnated, Ana,
a new soul, is born and on her eighteenth birthday sets off on a mission to
learn the truth about her existence.

    ISBN 978-0-06-206076-1

     [1. Fantasy. 2. Reincarnation—Fiction. 3. Identity—Fiction.]
I. Title.

PZ7.M5073In 2012   2011022931

[Fic]—dc23   CIP

                                                AC

Typography by Joel Tippie
12 13 14 15 16 CG/RRDH 10 9 8 7 6 5 4 3 2 1
❖

First paperback edition, 2013

For my mom,
who encouraged me to follow my dreams
and never freaked out when I called
and asked how to treat concussions, broken limbs,
or second-degree burns.

INCARNATE

330th Year of Songs, Week 3

What is a soul, but a consciousness born and born again?

    With the rise of new technology, we know souls can be measured as a series of vibrations, which Soul Tellers map out on machines. Each sequence is unique. Each sequence is the same as it was in its previous incarnation, no matter how different the body may be. I have been reborn a hundred times, and I remember every generation.

    Souls are sentience, an essence born into a new body when the old one dies.

    There have always been a million souls, but now we're a million minus one. Five years ago, the temple flashed dark on the night Ciana died. This evening, when Li gave birth to our daughter, we expected Ciana's reincarnation. Instead, truths on which we'd built society were irrevocably made uncertain.

    Soul Tellers took the newborn's hand and pressed

it on the soul-scanner, and the vibration sequence searched for a match in the database.

There was no match, which means this soul has never been born before. So where did it come from? What happened to Ciana's soul? Has it been replaced? Might others be replaced?

Is this new soul even real?

—Menehem's personal diary

1
SNOW

I WASN'T REBORN.

I was five when I first realized how different that made me. It was the spring equinox in the Year of Souls: Soul Night, when others traded stories about things they'd done three lifetimes ago. Ten lives. Twenty. Battles against dragons, developing the first laser pistol, and Cris's four-life quest to grow a perfect blue rose, only for everyone to declare it was purple.

No one bothered talking with me, so I'd never said a word—not ever—but I knew how to listen. They'd all lived before, had memories to share, had lives to look forward to. They danced around the trees and fire, drank until they fell over laughing, and when the time came to sing gratitude for immortality, a few glanced at me, and the clearing was so eerie quiet you could hear the waterfall crashing on rocks a league south.

Li took me home, and the next day I collected all the words I knew and made a sentence. Everyone else remembered a hundred lifetimes before this one. I had to know why I couldn't.

"Who am I?" My first spoken words.

"No one," she said. "Nosoul."

I was leaving.

It was my eighteenth birthday, only a few weeks after the turning of the year. Li said, "Safe journey, Ana," but her expression was stony, and I doubted she meant it with any sincerity.

The Year of Drought had been the worst of my life, filled with accumulated anger and resentment. The Year of Hunger hadn't started much better, but now it was my birthday and I had a backpack filled with food and supplies, and a mission to find out who I was, why I existed. The chance to escape my mother's hostile glares was a happy benefit.

I glanced over my shoulder at Purple Rose Cottage, Li standing tall and slender in the doorway, and snow spiraling between us. "Good-bye, Li." My farewell misted in the frigid air, lingering when I straightened and hitched my backpack. It was time to leave this isolated cottage and meet . . .

everyone. Save the rare visitor, I knew no one but my snake-hearted mother. The rest of the population lived in the city of Heart.

The garden path twisted down the hill, between frost-covered tomato vines and squash. I shivered deeper into my wool coat as I began the march away from the woman who used to starve me for days as punishment for doing chores incorrectly. I wouldn't complain if this was the last time I ever saw her.

My boots crunched gravel and slivers of ice, which had fallen from trees as morning peeked between mountains. I kept my fists in my pockets, safe in tattered mittens, and clenched my jaw against the cold. Li's glare stalked me all the way down the hill, sharp as the icicles hanging from the roof. Didn't matter. I was free now.

At the foot of the hill, I turned toward Heart. I'd find my answers in the city.

"Ana!" From the front step, Li waved a small metal object. "You forgot a compass."

I heaved a sigh and trudged back up. She wouldn't bring it to me, and it was no surprise she'd waited until I got all the way down before reminding me. The day I'd gotten my first menstruation, I'd run from the washroom shouting about my insides bleeding out. She'd laughed and laughed until she realized I actually *had* thought I was dying. That made her guffaw.

"Thank you." The compass filled my palm, and then my front pocket.

"Heart is four days north. Six in this weather. Try not to get lost, because I won't go looking for you." She slammed the door on me, cutting off the flow of warm air from the heater.

Hidden from her sight, I stuck my tongue out at her, then touched the rose carved into the oak door. This was the only home I'd ever known. After I was born, Menehem, Li's lover, left beyond the borders of Range. He'd been too humiliated about his nosoul daughter to stay, and Li blamed me for . . . everything. The only reason she'd taken care of me—sort of—was because the Council had made her.

After that, still stinging from Menehem's disappearance, she'd taken us to Purple Rose Cottage, which Cris, the gardener, had abandoned and Li had given a mocking name when no one thought the roses were blue. As soon as I was old enough, I spent hours coaxing those roses back to life so they'd bloom all summer. My hands still bore scars from their thorns, but I knew why they guarded themselves so fiercely.

Again I turned away, tromped down the hill. In Heart, I would beg the Council for time in the great library. There had to be a reason why, after five thousand years of the same souls being reincarnated, I'd been born.

Morning wore on, but the chill hardly eased. Snowdrifts lined the cobblestone road, and my boots flattened the film of white that developed over the day. Every so often, chipmunks and squirrels rustled iced twigs or darted up fir trees, but mostly there was silence. Even the bull elk nosing aside snow didn't make a sound. I might have been the only person in Range.

I should have left before my quindec, my fifteenth birthday and—for normal people—the day of physical adulthood. *Normal* people left their parents to celebrate that birthday with friends, but I didn't have those, and I'd thought I needed more time to learn the skills everyone else had known for thousands of years. Served me right for believing every time Li said how stupid I was.

She'd never have that chance again. When the cottage road ended, I checked my compass and took the fork that led north.

The mountain woods of southern Range were familiar and safe; bears and other large mammals never bothered me, but I didn't bother them, either. I'd spent my youth collecting shiny rocks and shells that had wormed to the surface after centuries. According to books, a thousand years ago, Rangedge Lake flooded this far north in rainy seasons, so now there were always treasures to hunt.

I didn't break to eat, just nibbled on cellar-wrinkled apples while I walked, leaving a trail of cores for lucky critters to find. Stomach sated, I tugged my shirt collar over my nose, making breath crawl across my lips and cheeks. With my throat and chest full of warm air, I sang nonsense about freedom and nature. My footfalls kept cadence, and an eagle cried harmony.

I'd never had formal music training, but I'd stolen theory books from the cottage library and, a few times, recordings of the most celebrated musician in Range: Dossam. I'd memorized his—sometimes her—songs so I'd have them after Li discovered my theft; the beatings had been worth it.

Gradually, the cloud-diffused sunlight sank toward the horizon, silhouetting the snowy peaks on my right. Odd, because I was going north, so the sun should have set on my left.

Perhaps the road had snaked around a hill and I hadn't noticed. The mountains were filled with tricky paths that looked promising until they stopped at a small lake or canyon. When plotting roads through the wilderness, engineers had been careful to avoid those things, but they still had to be mindful of steep hills and mountains. Curves, both sharp and shallow, were to be expected.

But when I left my backpack on the cobblestones and climbed a cottonwood to get a better view, I couldn't find a place where the road turned back. As far as I could see through the twilight gloom, the road carved a path through firs and pines, straight past Rangedge Lake, which marked the southern boundary of Range.

Li had tricked me.

"I hate you!" I hurled the compass to the ground and squeezed my eyes tight, not even sure who I should be angry at. Li, who'd given me a bad compass, or myself, for trusting her to offer even that much kindness.

I'd wasted an entire day of walking, but at least I'd noticed before passing beyond Range. The last thing I needed was to run into a centaur—quite possible this far south—or sylph, which haunted the edges of Range. They didn't usually come in, thanks to heat-detecting traps placed throughout the forest, but I'd often dreamt of them as a child, and I wasn't always convinced the shadows and warmth were nightmares.

Whatever. Li would never know about her victory if I didn't tell her.

Full dark settled as I climbed off the cottonwood; only thin moonlight penetrated the clouds. I fished through my backpack until my hand closed around the flashlight, gave the tube a few sharp twists, and set up camp by that white glow. There was a fast-running stream just off the road, and thick conifers sheltered a clearing barely big enough for my sleeping bag.

I swept snow out of my way and laid the bag on the ground. It was large enough to zip over my head and leave sprawling room. I didn't have a tent, or need one; it'd take too long to warm up, since Li hadn't given me a heater. Not that I'd expected such decency. Still, when I crawled inside, I quickly grew as toasty as if I'd been in the cottage.

Maybe, once I learned where I'd come from and whether I'd be reborn, I could live in the wilderness of Range forever. I didn't need anyone else.

As the flashlight grew dim, I hummed the melody of my favorite sonata, sound muffled against my ears. The bag was stuffy, but it was better than waking up with a mouthful of snow. My eyelids grew heavy.

"Shh."

I snapped awake and stiffened, clutching at my flashlight, not ready to turn it on, not ready to dismiss the idea.

"Hushhh."

A deep groan came from across the stream. No twigs cracked under footfalls, however, and no branches rustled. All was quiet, except water tumbling from rocks. And the whispers.

The murmurs continued; someone else had decided to make their camp here, and somehow missed seeing my sleeping bag.

Fine. I'd leave. I wasn't ready to deal with anyone so soon after Li. She'd always said people wouldn't like me because of what I was, and I didn't want to explain to anyone why I was on the very edge of Range. Leagues and leagues of human territory, most people holed up in Heart, and someone had to stop here of all places.

The intruders' tones never changed as I slipped my arms

into coat sleeves and pushed my belongings inside my backpack. Years of avoiding Li's notice had been useful for something after all. Frigid air snaked in as I unzipped the bag and crawled out.

Someone moaned. Now I really wanted to leave.

I rolled the sleeping bag, stashed it away in my backpack, and crept toward the road by snow-reflected moonlight, just bright enough that I could make out trees and underbrush. No tracks from my visitors, though. I must have slept for a little while, because the sky was clear and black, with a dusting of stars like snow. Wind rattled tree limbs.

"Shh." The whispers followed my retreat.

Heart speeding, I twisted my flashlight on and swung the beam toward the burble of water on rocks. Snow, dirt, and shadows. Nothing unusual, except disembodied voices.

As far as I knew, only one creature moved without touching the world. Sylph.

I fled down the road, snow crunching under my boots and icy air shivering into my lungs. Moans became shrieks and laughter. While the heat on the back of my neck might have been terror-fueled imagination, the sylph were gaining. I'd survive a graze of their burning touch, but anything more would kill me.

There were ways to capture them long enough to send them far into the wilderness, but I didn't have the tools. There was no way to kill a shadow.

I ducked into the woods. Branches slapped my face and caught on my coat. I tore myself free every time, pushing deeper into the forest. Only hissing hinted how close the sylph were.

Freezing air stung my eyes, and the flashlight was already dimming; it had been Li's spare because it was old. My chest burned with cold and fear, and a cramp jabbed at my side. Sylph keened like wind whistling in a storm, closer and closer. A tongue of invisible flame landed on my exposed cheek. I yelped and pushed harder, only for my bag to snag on a tangle of pines. No amount of yanking freed it.

Sylph melted snow as they formed a dark circle of cacophony and wind. Tendrils of blackness coiled toward me, and the burn on my cheek stung.

I slipped my arms from my backpack and darted between the shadow creatures, a rush of heat on my face like leaning into an oven. They shrieked and pursued, but I could move in tighter quarters now that I was unencumbered. Trees, brush, fallen logs. I dodged and jumped, fighting to keep my thoughts together, focused on getting past the next obstacle rather than the snow and cold, or the fiery death that chased me.

Perhaps I could lead them to one of the sylph traps. But I didn't know where they were. I didn't know where *I* was.

My flashlight went dark. I thumped the butt and twisted the tube until weak light revealed bright snow and trees.

Sylph moaned and wept, closing in as I avoided a snow-covered fir. Heat billowed on the back of my neck. I hurtled over a log and skidded at the edge of a cliff overlooking the lake. Snow slipped under my boots as I threw myself to my knees to stop before falling over the rim. My flashlight wasn't so lucky. It clattered from my mittened hands and plummeted into the lake with a splash. Three seconds. A long drop.

Wind gusted up from the water as I climbed to my feet. Sylph floated by the woods, seven or eight of them, creatures twice my height made of shadows and smoke. They glided forward, melting snow as they trapped me between them and a cliff over Rangedge Lake.

Their cries were of anger and hopelessness, ever-burning fire.

I glanced over my shoulder, the lake a stretch of darkness and nothing behind me. If there were rocks or chunks of ice, I couldn't see them. Drowning would be a better end than burning in sylph fire for weeks or months.

"You won't have me." I spun and leaped off the cliff. Death would be fast and cold; I wouldn't feel a thing.

2
WATER

A SCREAM ECHOED. Mine.

I inhaled and slapped my hands over my mouth and nose. Water slammed into my boots and up my sides, covering my face. Pressure swept the air from my chest and throat in a flurry of bubbles. Cold soaked my coat, dragging me deep.

Mittens didn't work like fins, and my boots were too heavy to let me kick. With the numbing cold, I barely felt the chunks of ice that thumped against my flailing limbs as I scrambled to the surface. Gravity felt the same in all directions underwater, but even as I thought I'd gotten turned around, icy wind stung my face.

I spit water and gasped. I tried to push myself to the nearest shore, but my arms were too heavy to lift with my clothes all waterlogged. The weight drew me under again, leaving only seconds for me to fill my lungs.

No matter how I struggled, I couldn't find my way back to the surface. I grabbed on to a lump of ice and tried to haul myself up, but it sent me spinning instead. A glow drew my gaze: the flashlight, drifting to the bottom I couldn't see.

I kept my mouth sealed shut, but my chest spasmed as my lungs yearned for fresh air where there was none. If the freezing temperature didn't kill me first, the water would. I couldn't move.

My thoughts grew icy and splintered. My heartbeat echoed in my ears, slowing under cold and depth and lack of oxygen. No matter how I tried to reach up, I couldn't *find* up, and I couldn't convince my arms to move. The water became darker as I followed my flashlight to the bottom of Rangedge Lake.

All the air I'd trapped in my lungs escaped, bubble after bubble.

Water gurgled next to me, swirling where it should have been still. As my toes tapped the bottom, light drifted beyond my eyelids and something wrapped around my middle. I shot upward. The grip on my waist tightened and dragged me through black water.

The slow thud of my heart grew ever more distant. My chest jumped, as if that would trick me into inhaling. I couldn't keep holding my breath. My lungs would explode if

I didn't let something in to ease the pressure.

I couldn't stop myself. I breathed water and gave in to the cold.

Time drifted in an icy haze. Water moved around me, inside me, and everything grew obsidian-smooth and dark.

I was on my back.

Something pounded on my chest. A rock. A fist. Anger. Chill and wet pressed on my mouth, and heat blew in. The beating on my chest resumed and a bubble formed inside me, grew, and forced its way up.

A dark and dripping face floated in my vision a heartbeat before I choked up lake water. It seared my throat like fire, but I coughed and spit until my mouth was dry. I fell to my back again as the shivers came, rattling through me like the cottage windowpanes in a storm.

I was alive. The freezing wind was colder than the lake, but I could breathe. Someone else's air filled me. I forced my eyes open, hardly able to believe anyone would bother to rescue me.

The ice and encroaching blackness must have damaged my vision, because I saw a boy's concerned expression shift to relief. Maybe it was my fading consciousness that made him appear to smile. At me.

Then I was gone, lost in dreams.

Wool blankets brushed my face. My bulky coat and boots were gone, and I was dry, lying on my side. My toes and fingers tingled as the numbness retreated. Already I was sore from my impact with the water, but the only thing that really *hurt* was the graze on my cheek. Blankets trapped me in a pocket of warm air. Foggy thoughts trapped me in this dream of safety.

Something solid pressed against my back. A body breathed in time with me, steady in and out, until I broke the unity by thinking about it. An arm was slung over my ribs, and a palm rested on my heart as if to make sure it continued beating, or to ensure that it didn't fall out. Breath warmed the back of my neck, rustling hairs across my skin.

Just as I began to drowse further into my dream, a deep voice behind me said, "Hi."

I held my breath, waiting for the dream to change.

"It's been, what, four thousand years since anyone thought midwinter swimming was a good idea? It's an awful way to go. Did you just want to see if that had changed?"

My eyes snapped open as my situation crystalized. I jumped, legs tangled in the blanket, and my elbow bumped a small heater. The tent seemed to close around me. Only a tiny lamp illuminated the space, but it was enough to show me the zipped door. I lunged for it.

The boy caught my waist and pulled. I dropped to my butt, dragging the zipper with me. Winter air poured inside as I wiggled from his grasp and threw myself into the waiting night. Snow sparkled in moonlight, deceptively peaceful with its smothering silence.

Wool socks protected my feet until I got to a line of trees across a clearing, and then pine needles and pebbles stabbed through the snow. I didn't care. Didn't stop. I ran anywhere, as long as it was away from sylph and the strange young man. There was no telling what he wanted, but if he was anything like Li, it wouldn't be good.

Winter caught up with me as I rounded a tower of boulders and stubby trees. Goose bumps crawled up my bare arms. I wore only a thin shirt and too-big trousers—neither were mine.

Freezing air hit the back of my throat with each ragged breath. I stumbled down a staircase of rocks and packed dirt, intent on running again, but the lake stretched wide under moonlight, right in front of me. Wavelets glinted as they lapped the shore and my toes.

I staggered backward, images of ice and a dimming flashlight on the backs of my eyelids every time I blinked. The cliff where I'd fallen—no, jumped—hung over the lake a ways to my right, silhouetted against bright starlight and snowy mountains. I should have died.

Maybe Li had paid that boy to rescue me. It wouldn't be the first time she used me like a cat playing with a mouse until it nearly died of fright.

Pine needles rustled and snow swished underfoot. Light bled across the waves in front of my feet. I spun around. The boy held a lamp shoulder high, his gaze beyond me. "After I worked so hard saving you, I'd appreciate if you didn't try to kill yourself again."

I clenched my jaw against chattering teeth. Tremors racked through me as I searched for escape, but he was blocking the only path. I could try beating him up, or swimming to another shore where he couldn't follow. Both were unlikely to work, especially since getting back in the freezing lake was the last thing I wanted. He'd probably just save me again.

He must have been strong, dragging me from the bottom like that. Stubble darkened his chin and he towered over me, but he looked my age. Tan skin, wide-set eyes, and shaggy, shadowed hair. Those must have been his arms around me underwater, and his breath that filled me when I had none of my own.

"You might as well come back." He offered his free hand, long fingers slightly curled in welcome. "I won't hurt you, and you're shivering. I'll make tea." He didn't quite hide his shivers, either; no coat or gloves meant he hadn't taken the extra time to dress for cold before following me. Perhaps his concern was genuine, though I'd thought Li sincere when she reminded me about bringing a compass. "Please?"

My other option was freezing to death, which seemed

less appealing now that I was definitely alive. I would watch him, though, and if he did anything Li-like, I'd escape. He couldn't make me stay.

I followed him through the woods. Didn't take his hand, just hugged myself and was glad he'd brought that lantern, and that he'd paid attention to where I'd run.

The forest was black with shadows and white with snow-drifts. Fir and pine trees shuddered under the weight of a million snowflakes. I jumped at noises, straining to hear the whispers and moans that had driven me into the lake to begin with.

My cheek still throbbed where the sylph had touched me and was hot to my bare fingers. It didn't feel blistered, though; doubtful it would kill me. I was lucky it hadn't got-ten me more than that. Large sylph burns were said to grow and consume the entire body over time. Li had warned me it was a painful way to die.

We reached the tent. Outside, a small horse snorted and eyed us from underneath half a dozen blankets. When we didn't do anything alarming, he tucked his head down to sleep.

My rescuer held open the tent for me. Our boots and coats hung by the door, still damp. Blankets on the left, a small solar battery heater in the center, and his bags on the other side. There was just enough room for one person to stretch out, two if they were friendly . . . or staving off hypothermia.

He'd known exactly how to save my life, while I would have panicked in his position. I'd panicked enough in *my* position.

"Sit." He nodded at the blankets and heater.

I didn't lower myself gracefully so much as collapse into a trembling heap. My entire body ached. From cold, from hitting the water. From the fiery shadows chasing me through the woods.

If he'd known I was the nosoul, he wouldn't have knelt and helped me sit up. He wouldn't have pulled a blanket tight around my shoulders and scowled at the burn on my cheek. But he didn't know, so he did. Which meant maybe he wasn't one of Li's friends after all. "Sylph?"

I cupped my hand over the burn. If it was obvious, why was he asking?

He retreated to his bags, filled a portable water heater, and flipped the switch. When bubbles rose from the bottom of the glass, he produced a small box. "Do you like tea?"

I forced a nod and, when he wasn't looking, held my hands toward the space heater. Hot waves prickled across my skin, but the cold burrowed deeper than that. In my feet especially, from running outside. The wool socks—which must have been his, because I could have fit my hands in there too—were damp with snow.

He poured two mugs of boiling water and dropped in tea leaves. "Here." He offered one. "Give it a minute to finish steeping."

Nothing he did was threatening. Maybe he *had* saved me out of the goodness of his heart, though he'd probably regret it if he knew what I was. And now I felt stupid for dragging both of us into the cold night again.

I took the offered tea. The ceramic mug was dimpled from either long use or poor craftsmanship, and a choir of painted songbirds decorated the side. It was nothing like Li's stark, serviceable belongings. I wrapped my hands around the mug to soak up the warmth, breathing in steam that tasted like herbs. It scalded my tongue, but I closed my eyes and waited for my insides to stop shivering.

"I'm Sam, by the way."

"Hi." If not for the risk of melting my insides to puddles, I'd have gulped down the tea all at once.

He peered at me, searching for . . . something. "You're not going to tell me who you are?"

I frowned. If I admitted to being the nosoul, the *thing* born instead of someone named Ciana, he'd take my tea and kick me out of the tent. This wasn't my life, Li had sometimes told me. She hadn't revealed Ciana's name then, but I knew I'd replaced someone. I'd overheard her gossiping about it once. Every breath I took should have belonged to someone whom everyone had known for five thousand years. The guilt was crushing.

I couldn't tell this boy what I was.

"You didn't have to chase me outside. I'd have been fine."

He scowled, shadowed lines between his eyes. "Like you were fine in the lake?"

"That was different. Maybe I wanted to be out there." Stupid mouth. He was going to know if I couldn't control my stupid mouth.

"If you say so." He wiped the inside of the water heater dry and stuffed it back in its bag. "I doubt you wanted to die. I was filling my canteens when I saw you jump. You screamed, and I saw thrashing as if you were trying to swim. When you reached the lake a little while ago, you startled like a mouse realizing there was a cat in the room. What were you doing in the woods? How did you run into sylph?"

"Doesn't matter." I scooted closer to the heater.

"So you aren't going to tell me your name." A statement, not a question. He'd start guessing soon. He could rule out all the people who I definitely didn't behave like, all the people reborn in the wrong time to be eighteen right now, and all the people my age he'd seen in the last few years. "I can't remember offending anyone so much they wouldn't trust me with their name. At least not recently."

"You don't know me."

"That's what I said. Did you get water in your brain?" It only half sounded like a joke.

I didn't know of a Sam, but considering the meager collection of books in the cottage library, that wasn't a surprise. I didn't know about a lot of people.

I gulped the rest of my tea and lowered the empty mug, mumbling, "I'm Ana." My insides were warm now, and I wasn't drowning. When he kicked me out, I'd be no worse off than before, as long as I could find my backpack.

"Ana."

Shivers crawled up my spine when he said my name. And what a name. When I'd gotten the nerve to ask Li why they chose that, she said it was part of an old word that meant "alone" or "empty." It was also part of Ciana's name, symbolizing what I'd taken from her. It meant I was a nosoul. A girl who fell in lakes and got rescued by Sam.

I kept my face down and watched him through my eyelashes. His skin was flushed in the warm tent, with steam from the tea. He still had the full cheeks of his apparent age—close to mine—but the way he spoke held authority, knowledge. It was deceptive, the way he looked like someone I could have grown up with, but he'd actually lived thousands of years. Hair fell like shadows across his eyes, hiding whatever he thought while he studied me in return.

"You're not—" He cocked his head and frowned. I must have been as easy to read as a sky full of rain clouds. "Oh, you're *that* Ana."

My stomach twisted as I pushed off the blanket, torn between anger and humiliation. *That Ana.* Like a disease. "I'll get out of your way now. Thank you for the tea. And for saving me." I moved for the door, but he held his arm across the zipper.

"That's not necessary." He jerked his head toward the blanket again, no room for argument in his tone. "Rest."

I bit my lip and tried to decide if, as soon as I fell asleep, he would contact Li, tell her he'd found me in a lake, and I wasn't capable of caring for myself yet.

I couldn't go back to her. Couldn't.

His tone gentled, like I was a spooked horse. "It's all right, Ana. Please stay."

"Okay." Gaze never straying from his, I lowered myself again, back under the blanket. *That* Ana. Nosoul. Ana who shouldn't have been born. "Thank you. I'll repay your generosity."

"How?" He was motionless, hands on his lap and eyes locked on mine. "Do you have any skills?"

Nerves caught in my throat. This was one of the few things Li had explained, and she'd explained often. There were a million souls in Range. There'd always been a million souls, and every one of them pulled their weight in order to ensure society continued to improve. Everyone had necessary talents or skills, be it a head for numbers or words, imagination for inventions, the ability to lead, or simply the desire to farm and raise food so no one would starve. For thousands of years, they'd earned the right to have a good life.

I hadn't earned anything. I was the nosoul who'd taken eighteen of Li's years, her food and skills, pestered her with questions and all my *needs*. Most people left their current parents when they were thirteen years old. Fourteen at most. By then they were usually big and strong enough to make it wherever they wanted to go. I'd stayed five extra years.

I had nothing unique to offer Sam. I lowered my eyes. "Only what Li taught me."

"And that was?" When I didn't speak, he said, "Not how to swim, obviously."

What did that mean? I'd figured out how to tread water when I was younger, but everything was different in the winter. In the dark. I frowned; maybe it had been a joke. I decided to ignore it. "Housecleaning, gardening, cooking. That sort of thing."

He nodded, as if encouraging me to go on.

I shrugged.

"She must have helped you learn to speak." Again, I shrugged, and he chuckled. "Or not."

Laughing at me. Just like Li.

I met his eyes and made my voice like stone. "Maybe she taught me when not to speak."

Sam jerked straight. "And how to be defensive when no offense was intended." He cut me off before I could apologize, though my mouth had dropped open to do so; I didn't really want to leave the warm tent, especially now that the herbs and overall exhaustion were taking effect. I grew drowsy. "Do you know anything about the world? How you fit in?"

"I know I'm different." My throat closed, and my voice squeaked. "And I was hoping to find out how I fit in."

"By running through Range in your socked feet?" One corner of his mouth tugged upward when I glared. "A joke."

"Sylph chased me and I lost my backpack. I planned on walking to Heart to search the library for any hint of why I was born." There had to be a reason I'd replaced Ciana. Surely I wasn't a mistake, a big *oops* that cost someone her immortality and buried everyone else under the pain of her loss. Knowing wouldn't help the guilt, but it might reveal what I was supposed to do with my stolen life.

"From what you've said, I'm surprised Li bothered teaching you to read."

"I figured it out."

His eyebrows lifted. "You taught yourself to read."

The tent was too hot, his surprised stare too probing. I licked my lips and eyed the door again, just to remind myself it was still there. My coat, too. I could escape if I needed to. "It's not like I created the written word or composed the first sonata. I just made sense of what someone else had already done."

"Considering how other people's logic and decisions are rarely comprehensible to anyone else, I'd say that's impressive."

"Or a testament to their skills, if even I can figure out how to read."

He gathered the empty mugs and put them away. "And the sonata? You figured that out as well?"

"Especially that." I covered my mouth to yawn. "I wanted something to fall asleep to, even if it's only in my head."

"Hmm." He dimmed the lamp and shifted bags around the tent. "I'll think about repayment, Ana. Get some rest for now. If you want to find your bag and go to Heart, you'll need all your strength."

I glanced at the blankets and sleeping bag, wary in spite of exhaustion. "Like before?"

"Janan, no! I'm sorry. I thought we knew each other. I didn't mean to make you uncomfortable."

"It's okay." He was probably wondering how he'd managed to find the only nosoul in the world when chances were so much higher of him rescuing someone he already knew. He was showing me more kindness than anyone ever had, though; I should try to reciprocate. "There isn't much space. I'll face the wall if you'll face the other way. That way neither of us is cold."

"Don't be silly. I'll face the wall." He motioned me closer to the heater. "We'll discuss other issues in the morning, and that's"—he checked a small device—"in three hours. Get some rest. It sounds like you've had a difficult day."

If only he knew.

3

SYLPH

MOVEMENT AROUND THE tent dragged me to the edges of consciousness.

Water murmured, a switch clicked, and something unfamiliar swished, like powder falling into ceramic. A heavy, bitter scent flooded the tent as Sam stirred water into a mug.

"Wake up. Time to go." He touched my shoulder.

I gasped, fighting the way my mind conjured a similar image of him leaning over me, only a few hours old. The dark hair had been dripping, and the broad hands urging my heart to beat again.

Like an idiot, I stared at him until I saw only the present. Last night became a memory again. "Oh." I'd been staring too long. "It's just you."

"Yes." His tone was chalk-dry. "Just me." Before I could apologize for insulting him somehow, he sat back. "Drink your coffee. We're leaving in twenty minutes. That gives us enough time to pack and load Shaggy. We'll eat breakfast while we walk."

"Shaggy?" I sat, blankets knotting around my legs, and reached for the nearest mug of dark liquid. Then I answered my own question with a smirk. "The horse? Creative name."

"His full name is Not as Shaggy as His Father, but that's a mouthful." Sam's grin turned into a grimace when he tried his coffee. "Drink up. It's not worth lingering over, trust me."

I inhaled steam as I took a careful sip to test the temperature. Hot and bitter, with a strange sweetness to it, like honey. I gulped down the entire mugful. "I like it." My skin felt warm enough to glow. "Li never let me drink coffee. She said it would make me short." And it was too expensive to waste on a nosoul, but I didn't need any more of his pity.

"Li was tall last time I saw her. What happened to you?" He suffered another taste and held the mug toward me.

"Apparently Menehem was short and I'm unlucky." I eyed the coffee, judging whether he'd yank it back at the last second. If he did, he'd spill it on me. Better to ask. "You don't want that?"

"A companion on a caffeine high will wake me up just as well, without the aftertaste." He set the mug between us. I snatched it up and drank before he could change his mind.

"Wait until you try real coffee, grown in special greenhouses in Heart. You'll never want to drink this chemical imitation again."

I couldn't help but be intrigued. Something better than this? I looked forward to finding the greenhouses he described.

"Now pay attention to where everything goes. I'll pack this morning, but if I'm going to help you get to Heart, you're going to do your share."

I stared. Why would he help me? Weren't we supposed to talk about how I'd pay him back for saving me last night? Now that he'd offered, however, I couldn't bear if he took it back. He seemed— Well, he seemed like he didn't hate me, and he'd rescued me. Not that the latter meant anything, since he'd assumed I was someone he already knew. Not Ana the nosoul.

"That's fair." I cleaned the mugs and water heater. Everything went into the pouches I'd watched him store things in last night. "What else?"

He went outside to feed Shaggy, leaving me to roll blankets and check the tent floor for anything that had escaped its bag.

Only one thing. A brass egg the size of two of my fists together. A thin silver band circled the middle, covering a seam where you turned it. And to keep your grip on the slick metal, the top half of the egg had shallow grooves.

It was pretty, if you didn't know it was for catching sylph.

34

Sam walked in as I turned the sylph egg over in my palms, inspecting the delicate latch that held the flat lid on one end. "You only carry one of these?"

"I wasn't planning on leaving Range." He crouched in front of me and closed my fingers over the device. "You hang on to it."

My first instinct was to decline. Did he think I was afraid? I didn't deserve to be coddled or given special things. I'd done well enough last night. No, I'd ended up in the lake.

I tried not to let my relief show. "Thanks."

"Get your coat and boots. We'll take down the tent while Shaggy eats, then drop our things off at my cabin. It's only a few hours south, so we can sleep there tonight. Your bag shouldn't be too hard to find."

Considering I didn't even know where it was? Maybe it wouldn't be hard for someone who knew every inch of the world.

I followed him outside. Morning hovered on the other side of the mountains, bathing the clearing in shades of indigo. Ospreys and smaller birds took flight, dark against the clear sky.

My first full day of freedom from Li.

I helped Sam pack the tent and load Shaggy, trying to memorize where everything went so he'd know I wanted to earn his help. It annoyed me that he'd just assumed I needed help, like a poor little nosoul couldn't even get to the city on her own. But it bothered me more that he was right.

"Is the cabin the reason you're out here?" I couldn't fathom why anyone would willingly traipse about the wilderness in the middle of winter. Maybe this body was insane. Madness didn't carry along with the soul, according to Cris's books. There was a physical component to it, which geneticists and the ruling Council had mostly removed from society by allowing only certain people to have children, but every now and then there were surprises.

Sam took Shaggy's lead and tugged him west. "Yes." We walked, and he never answered my unspoken question of why. Not that I'd expected it. "You and Li were staying in Purple Rose Cottage, right?"

I mm-hmmed.

"It's been, what, eleven years?"

Maybe not insane, just stupid. "Eighteen. She moved us when I was still an infant. I thought everyone knew all about the nosoul."

He winced. "You shouldn't call yourself nosoul. New doesn't mean you don't have a soul. The Soul Tellers would have known the day you were born."

Like he knew anything about it.

"Why did you decide to leave yesterday?"

He sure was nosy. Instead of answering, I watched a family of weasels scramble into the brush as we approached;

they continued their play hidden in a tangle of snow-covered branches.

Sam was still waiting for a reply.

Fine. He should know exactly what kind of thing he'd offered to help. "It was my birthday. I decided it was time to find out what went wrong."

"Wrong?" He sounded appalled.

I struggled to stay calm, keeping myself deep inside my coat, and my eyes on the ground. "When I was young, I overheard Councilor Frase telling Li that a soul named Ciana was supposed to be reborn. It had been ten years since she died—twenty-three now—and that was the longest it had ever taken someone to come back. And she didn't." I could barely say it, but he'd asked. "She's gone because of me."

He didn't disagree, and his gaze was far off, like he saw worlds I didn't. Couldn't. Lifetimes, anyway. What if he and Ciana had been friends? "I remember the night she died. The temple went dark, like it was mourning."

I said the first thing I could think of that didn't have anything to do with Ciana. "When is your birthday?"

"I don't—" He flashed a smile, uncertainty evaporating from his voice. "Yesterday. I think that puts us at the same age."

Sure, physically. Counting from the 330th Year of Songs. But his soul had been around the 329 before that, and all the years between. "I think you're missing about five thousand years in that math."

Silence was, apparently, his favorite response. He gave me a breakfast bar, thick with oats and dried fruit, and continued leading Shaggy down the road. Sunlight reflected off snow, making my eyes water. I pulled on my mittens and hood.

I strode ahead, though he could easily catch up with his long legs. It was nice that he didn't try to outpace me like Li would have, though maybe it was just because of the pony, and being mindful of hooves on slick ground.

Pine boughs draped across the road, heavy with shiny snow. I ducked around them, underneath them, but still got powder on my coat. I brushed it off.

"That Li's coat?" He maneuvered around the trees without difficulty.

"I didn't steal it."

"That wasn't the question."

I shrugged.

"What about those boots? Passed down as well?"

What was his problem? I stopped and turned on him, but there were no words sharp enough for what I wanted, so I mumbled, "A nosoul doesn't need her own things," and ducked my face.

"What was that?"

"I said"—I glared up at him—"a nosoul doesn't need her own things if she's only going to live the one life."

"Newsoul." His expression was a mystery. Li's tended to range from anger to loathing, and though his eyebrows were drawn in and that was definitely a frown—he didn't look like he was about to lock me in my room for a week. "And don't be ridiculous. You should have your own things. Your body is still unique, and not only do these old things not fit you, they're . . . old. They're falling apart."

Old. He should know. "Doesn't matter. She's not part of my life anymore. Ever again." I started back in the direction we'd been going. "I'm not going to waste time being angry about things I can't control. If I only have one life, I should make the most of it."

Sam and Shaggy caught up with me. "Wise."

"Just what Li insisted every time I said I hated her." Maybe he wasn't like Li, but he certainly wasn't like me. Then again, no one was. I was alone. "She said I shouldn't waste my time hating her, or Menehem, or anyone else. That's her wisdom. I just happen to agree."

He hesitated, and his voice lowered like he didn't want the wind to hear. "The last time I felt like this much of a jerk was when I told Moriah his idea for keeping time by using gears rather than sun on a slab of stone was stupid. And then I found out he'd built a huge clock in the Councilhouse and was unveiling it later."

Okay. I could forgive him. A little. "Don't worry about it."

He sounded more cautious when he spoke again. "Does

it scare you, knowing you might not come back?"

"Not especially. Death seems so far away." Last night notwithstanding.

I climbed onto a snow-covered stump, careful of the slickness beneath my boots. That was where I spotted my backpack, a brown and gray thing trapped in a tangle of pine boughs. I hopped off the stump, trotted into the brush, and retrieved my bag. Before I could put it on, though, Sam loaded it onto Shaggy, like he didn't think I was strong enough to carry my belongings.

Or maybe he was just being nice, because I *did* ache after my leap into the lake. "Thanks," I muttered. "So, would you be scared if you knew this was your last time?"

We walked in silence while he pondered and the sun reached its zenith. I hummed, echoing melodies made by shrikes and wrens. The sky was a perfect, clear blue over the mountains, hardly a cloud in sight. Last night might have been only a bad dream, except for the presence of Sam, who kept eyeing me like I might do something crazy.

After we crossed a river bridge and shadows stretched away from the lowering sun, Sam said, "I'd live differently, I suppose."

It took me a second to realize he was answering my question. "How?" I liked it better when I could make him uncomfortable, rather than the other way around.

"If I knew there wasn't much time left, I'd get things done more quickly. See more places, finish all my projects. I wouldn't waste time daydreaming or starting new things. Seventy years isn't that long."

Seventy years sounded like eternity to me. I couldn't imagine being seventy years old. "But that's not being afraid."

"I'd be afraid of what would happen after. Where would I go? What would I do? I don't want to stop existing." He didn't move, just halted on the path, his back toward a clearing and an iron-fenced yard of stones. His gaze stayed on mine, like there was something I was supposed to read in his expression, but he just looked tired to me. "That's probably the most frightening thing I can imagine."

My hood slipped back when I shifted my weight, my face still turned up to his. "At least you'll never have to worry about that." I shivered against chill and the thought of having only one lifetime. The sylph burn on my cheek stung.

Thought made a crease between his eyes. He looked ready to say something when a stray shadow in the clearing caught my attention.

I stepped back, the word like an avalanche. "Sylph."

Had he brought me here to feed me to it?

"What?" His voice dripped with confusion.

A surprise to him, too. Okay.

I peeled off my mittens and dragged the sylph egg from

41

my coat pocket. I felt like a girl made of ice as I shoved past him, into the clearing. "Move." I would have revenge for the mark one left on my cheek last night.

The sylph moaned, a shadow twice my height and blacker for the white all around it. Steam hissed beneath it where its fires had melted snow. I twisted the sylph egg and thrust it at the shadow.

"Stop!" Sam cried, at the same time as hooves pounded the ground and a tendril of shadow shot out of the sylph. The egg flew from my hands, and I screamed at the heat on my fingers. I stumbled backward as the sylph loomed over me like burning night.

I was on the ground before I realized, Sam rolling with me—away from the sylph. Our knees and elbows jabbed each other, only somewhat dulled by cloth. I sat up and lifted my red, peeling hands.

Soon I would die.

"Watch out!" Sam shoved me off him as the sylph lunged again, shrieking.

I caught myself, but swayed with pain too sharp to comprehend. Then I jerked back into reality when Sam shouted.

"Get behind the fence!" He scrambled out of the sylph's way.

Iron. Right. I sprinted toward the graveyard, but Sam was still near a copse of snow-smothered trees. He'd saved me and I couldn't just let him—

The sylph grew thicker, darker than midnight, and a giant, dragonish head pushed out from one side like it was trying to escape a bubble. It snapped at him, and Sam became expressionless. As if he was somewhere else. Somewhen else, like I'd felt when I saw the lake again last night.

No, I had to help him. My new sylph burns would kill me, anyway.

I searched through the steaming snow and gathered up the sylph egg. From the corner of my eye, I saw Sam return to himself—return to now—and begin pelting the sylph with snowballs. The dragon head disappeared, but his snowballs melted within seconds of passing through the shadow.

"Ana!"

Ropes of shadow forced Sam to dodge and duck. The clearing reeked of ash. The sylph attacked Sam again, trapping him against a tree.

My hands closed around the egg; I could barely feel with my sylph-scalded hands. It was slick, almost too slippery to grip, but I gave the device a final twist and flipped up the lid just as the sylph lunged for Sam with a dissonant shriek.

I thrust the egg into the burning shadow, and smoke streaked into the brass when I dropped it. Heat raced through me, and my entire world grew too hot to live in. I felt like a legendary phoenix must, consumed in its own fires so it could be reborn.

But I wasn't a phoenix.

Just a nosoul with blackened hands.

Across the sylph egg stood a young man who looked my age, but wasn't. He might have said my name again. I couldn't hear through the rushing in my ears as I ran to the nearest snowdrift and shoved my hands inside.

I would not cry. Would not.

A moment later, Sam knelt in front of me. "Hey."

"Go away." I clenched my jaw, trying not to look at the pitying expression he wore. He knew about the sylph burns, surely. He knew how they'd spread and engulf me, and soon I'd be dead. Probably forever. At least I was near a grave-yard.

"Let me see your hands." He spoke softly, as if that would change my mind. "Please."

"No." I scooted away and pressed my hands into a new patch of snow. They burned no matter how much snow I packed onto them. If I pulled them out, they'd be black and flaking, like charcoal. The singe on my cheek echoed the sensation. "Leave me alone."

"Let me help you."

He wasn't going to listen. He didn't care what I wanted. "No! Just go away. I don't need you. I wish you'd never found me." I was hot and cold and so tired of everything hurting. For someone who'd died a hundred times, he had a poor grasp of the situation. "In the last two days I've been given a bad compass by my own mother so I'd go the wrong

44

way, attacked by sylph *twice*, burned, and nearly drowned in a freezing lake. You should have left me there. Everyone would have been happier to forget about me." I collapsed over myself and wept. "I hate you. I hate everyone."

Finally, he left.

4
FIRE

AFTER I'D CRIED myself out, hooves thumped the ground behind me, then stopped. Sam scooped me into his arms. Snow fell in clumps. I tried to hold on to it, but gripping hurt too much. When I dug my elbow into his chest, he just shifted me around and carried me through the cemetery's iron gate. "Go away." My throat hurt from cold and crying.

"No." He swept snow off a stone bench and set me down, then sat next to me. "You should have come in here when I told you."

I squeezed my eyes shut and hugged my legs to my chest, buried my face in my sleeves. The alternating hot and cold in my hands made drowning in the lake seem like a leisurely summer swim. "You don't listen, do you? Go away."

"Piffle." Icy hands closed around my cheeks as he turned my face to his. Couldn't make me meet his eyes, though; I kept my gaze down. "*You* don't listen," he said.

Why wouldn't he just leave? I was going to burn up, anyway, with fire creeping up my arms to consume me. My eyes ached with fresh tears. I hated crying.

"But if you'd listened," he murmured, "I'd be dead."

I looked up, and he looked earnest. Gentle features twisted into concern when I just sat there, hands shaking. Maybe they'd shake off.

"Thank you for saving me." He said it like he meant it, like I'd actually done something good and worthwhile. But now I was going to die a slow and fiery death. That didn't seem to bother him.

"You'd have come back." My brain and mouth weren't connected. This wasn't the time to be mean. I should apologize for screaming at him. "I mean I'm glad you're okay."

One corner of his mouth twitched up, and he wiped his thumbs under my eyes, avoiding the burn on my cheek. "Your hands must really hurt. Will you let me help?"

"That's not why I'm crying." Ugh. I'd meant to blame that on the snow. "I'm just mad at all this. Sylph. Li. You."

"Why me?" He released my face and reached inside a bag on his lap. Bandages, ointments, painkillers: it would have been nice if I'd seen those before. "As far as I know, I've only tried to keep you out of trouble."

"Exactly." I let my heels slip off the bench so I could sit normally; Sam held my shoulder in case I lost my balance, but I didn't, so I shot him a glare.

My hands were crimson and blistered, as if I'd held them in fire. Perhaps I'd avoided permanent muscle damage, because all my nerves dutifully sent panicked pain signals, but it didn't matter. The charred flesh and powdering bones of a large sylph burn would come eventually.

"It's your fault I'm going to die." I imagined the burns crawling up my wrists and arms until they consumed me.

"You'll die eventually, but not for a good long time, as long as you'll stop racing into danger every day."

I was *dying* and he had the nerve to mock me? I struggled to choose between angry replies, but all I managed was, "Li said sylph burns won't heal. They'll get worse."

Lines formed around Sam's frown as he removed a packet from his bag and ripped it open. "She lied."

"Oh." Of course she lied. She always did. Visions of my demise vanished. "So my hands?"

"Will heal to make more mischief. Now let's see them." He turned his palms up as if to hold my burned flesh, but didn't actually touch me. My hands did look gross, all red and blistering. "Shoving them in snow probably wasn't the best idea."

The radiating pain kept me from caring about his chastisement. I gritted my teeth to cage any sounds when he laid a piece of gauze over what was left of my skin. Something so delicate shouldn't hurt me so much, and I just wanted the pain to stop. Dizziness surrounded me, a black haze over my eyes and ears.

An eternity later, Sam's deep voice brought me back. "We're done."

I came to with tears freezing on my face, my hands wrapped in layers of gauze. Pain shot through my forearms. Even the pressure of bandages was too much.

"You were brave. We're done." He tugged my hood over my ears and smoothed my hair underneath. Chill tinged his nose and cheeks red as he fished a handful of pills from the medical kit. "These are for the pain. I don't have anything strong enough to do more than dent it, but it'll be better than nothing."

Five white pills rested on his palm, then went into my mouth one by one. He held a canteen to my lips and I drank.

"My cabin is on the other side of the cemetery. Can you walk?" Everything went back into his bag, and he hooked the strap over his shoulder. "The walls have iron in them, so no sylph will be able to get in." He spoke gently. "Range is dynamic. It wasn't always as big as it is now, and the boundaries can change season to season. This area hasn't always been safe from sylph, but I thought—" Deep brown eyes met mine. "I thought it was okay now. I'm sorry."

No point in apologizing for something he couldn't help. I

lurched up and lost my balance. He caught my elbow.

A dozen cobblestone paths twisted through the vast graveyard, leading to mausoleums with scrolled iron gates, limestone statues gazing at scattered headstones, and metal-framed stone benches. As the day warmed, snow melted off solemn statue faces like tears.

I could imagine what this place looked like in spring or summer, with vivid flowers or vines spilling from huge stone goblets, ivy climbing the walls and grave markers, or autumn leaves carpeting the paths. There was a melancholy beauty here, an old and exhausted silence. A few of the statues played instruments—a woman with a flute, a man with a harp—as if the sculptor had caught them between notes. A stone elk grazed on the far end, while a pair of chipmunks stayed trapped in a position of ever-tumbling together. The quiet was uncanny.

"What is all this?" I asked as we passed an iron trellis with tendrils of metal shaped into flowers and leaves. Frost glistened. "Who's buried here?"

Sam inclined his head. "I am."

I couldn't interpret his tone, but I'd feel sad if these graves were mine.

Raven-topped obelisks guarded the center of the cemetery, a slab of snow-covered stone with gold veins running through. Writing had been carved into the limestone, but ice and snow obscured the words. Sam led me around it.

"What's this one?"

"My first grave. The original materials were falling apart, as they do after a few thousand years. I didn't want to dig myself up, but I didn't want to lose track of it."

So everyone was responsible for their own cemeteries. "Why honor old flesh if you're coming back?" Focusing on anything but the pain helped, though every several steps, a dizzy spell forced me to pause.

"It's not so much honoring old flesh as acknowledging past lives, achievements. It's a way of remembering. After you live so long, it's easy to forget what happened when. Not everyone does as much with their cemeteries, and plenty do more. I don't know everyone's reasoning behind keeping one, only mine."

For a moment, I wondered what Li did with her former bodies. Probably left them where they fell. But I didn't have to think about her anymore.

"Are you afraid of forgetting your achievements?" I searched the frozen yard for a sign of what they might be, but I could only see death. "Can you tell me about them?"

"I keep journals. Most people do, and then give them to the Councilhouse library for archivists to copy and file. You can read them if you like." He guided me to another path that went all the way to the back gate, black metal on white and green and brown.

The promised cabin stood in the shelter of fir trees. It was smaller than Purple Rose Cottage, but there were curtained windows and a chimney. It looked cozy. "You like sleeping by your corpses?"

His chuckle misted on the air. "It's a long trip from Heart every morning, just to work on a statue."

"So you made all these?"

"Most of them." He pushed open the gate and let me through. "Last night was the final night of my journey here from Heart. I like getting work done in the winter. It's quiet. Peaceful."

"Sorry to disrupt your plans." The bandages around my hands weighed a thousand pounds.

He just shrugged. "There's plenty of time for that later. It's not every day I get to know someone new." He turned away, but not before I saw him wince. At least he knew he said stupid things. "Let's go inside."

"What about Shaggy?"

"He'll be waiting by the stall in the back. I'll get him settled." Sam pushed a key into the lock and opened the door.

While he took care of Shaggy, I explored the cabin. As expected, it was small and dusty, though what I first mistook for cracks in the wood panels were actually etched animals of Range: osprey, deer, eagle, bison, fox, pronghorn, and dozens of others.

It was an open room with a kitchen area to one side and

a sleeping area on the other, all heated—presumably—by a wood-burning stove near the middle. Only a small washroom had been sectioned off. In spite of the rustic appearance, the kitchen held modern conveniences like a coffeepot and sink, cupboards and a pantry, neither of which I could open without help.

Before I had a chance to feel too sorry for myself, I turned toward the front of the cabin and found the bookcases carved right into the wall. Hundreds of leather-bound volumes rested in the dim alcoves. I had no idea what stories or information they held. It didn't matter. I wanted to absorb anything they had to say.

No. My hands. I couldn't even imagine holding a book without pain flaring up my forearms.

5
HONEY

THERE WAS NO telling how long I stood in the center of the cabin, staring at the books I couldn't touch, surrounded by cold and dust and someone else's life. And his deaths right outside the door. As long as I didn't move, as long as I didn't think about anything but the point right in front of me—the spine of a red book—I didn't hurt.

"Ana."

My vision untunneled and the room snapped back into focus. So did the blaze in my hands and wrists. A groan rumbled through me.

Sam stood before me, concern dark on his face. "Come on. You're still in shock." He guided me to a chair by the now-lit stove and removed my boots and coat, taking extra care where the sleeves brushed my hands. "What can I do for you?"

I just wanted to stop hurting. Staring at the books had been better. I turned back to them, willing myself to get lost in my own numbness. The pain was too intense, more than I could possibly endure.

He crossed my field of vision, pausing in front of the bookcase. "You like to read."

Had I said that? Had he guessed? Either way, I didn't move from the chair. Eventually I *would* make it back into the nothing-state of no pain.

Sam chose a book and carried it to me, like I'd be able to do something with it. But he sat on the arm of the chair, next to me, and opened to the first page. "So I guess you know the fifteen years are all named after events or accomplishments that happened in the first few generations, before we'd created a formal calendar?"

I didn't move.

"Year of Drought, obviously there was a terrible drought. Followed by the Year of Hunger, when everyone starved to death the next year." He raised an eyebrow at me. "Yes? You know all this?"

I still didn't move. We were in the 331st Year of Hunger now. Maybe they'd rename it the Year of Freezing, Then Burning, And Mostly Running for Your Life. After me, of course.

"My second-favorite story is the Year of Dreams, when we began trying to understand the hot mud pits and everyone started hallucinating from inhaling the fumes around one of them." He flipped through the pages of the book, steady-handed, sure of himself. I tried not to be envious of his lack of burns. "Let's see. Year of Dance." He turned a few more pages. "Year of Dreams." His voice pitched lower as he read aloud. "'We set out on an expedition to make sure the geothermal features around Heart weren't immediately dangerous. Of course, we were quite surprised at what we discovered. . . .'"

He continued to read for another hour, changing his voice to match the mood of the passage. He was good at this, and I'd never been read to before. The way he spoke drew me in until finally I relaxed.

The pain eased.

I hovered in the misty place between waking and sleeping, half dreaming of a deep humming. Then the fire in my hands returned, and when I groaned and opened my eyes, the only sound was the scratch of pen on paper.

"Did I wake you?" Sam looked up from scribbling in a book.

Yes. "No." It didn't matter. My hands wouldn't stop hurting long enough for me to rest well.

I was lying on the bed, though I didn't remember moving. Had he carried me? He'd definitely pulled the blankets over me. My burns hurt too much to grasp the thick wool.

There was a terrifying thought. What happened when I had to use the washroom? I steeled myself and considered my hands; the left one wasn't quite as bad. I could suffer a little pain to salvage any remaining dignity.

Reassured, I glanced at Sam again, who'd gone back to writing in his book. "What are you doing?"

His pen hesitated over the paper, like I'd made him lose his place.

I shouldn't have asked. I knew better, but my hands—

"Writing notes." He blew on the ink, closed the book, and set everything aside. "Would you like to read more?"

"Only if you want." When he looked away, I tried to sit up. But every time I used my elbows to push myself, they jabbed onto the blanket. I kept pinning myself to the bed. Refusing to let a stupid blanket win, I kicked to move it downward. With it out of my way, I pushed again with my elbows. I'd miscalculated and the same problem—the blanket—threw me back down.

I slapped the bed to keep my balance—

An inferno surged through my arm and I screamed, clutching my hand against my chest.

Sam was at my side in an instant, arms encircling me.

Trapped. I yelled and fought to escape, but he wouldn't let go. Unable to use my hands to push, I tried to bite him. Mouthful of wool. An ugly sob escaped.

"I'm so sorry," he whispered, shaking like he could be

anywhere near as upset about this as me. "I'm sorry."

This wasn't trapping me. It was . . . hugging? I'd seen Li embrace her friends during the rare visit. No one hugged me, of course. Apparently no one had told Sam.

When he finished hugging me, he checked my palm for new damage. I'd been lucky. "Take these." He retrieved a handful of pills from a small table and offered water to wash them down. "Tell me if you need anything else."

I swallowed the pills. "Okay."

He met my eyes, seemed to search me. "You have to tell me. Don't make me guess."

I lowered my gaze first. "Okay."

He didn't believe me. It was the same expression Li used when she didn't think I'd actually cleaned the cavies' cages, or turned the compost pile. But he hadn't asked me to do chores, just wanted me to tell him if I needed anything.

Okay. If I *needed* anything, I would tell him.

"Do you want to read more?" he asked, after a few moments of sitting unnervingly close.

I nodded.

He sighed and freed me from the blankets. "This is already going to be a difficult recovery for you, but it doesn't have to be terrible. Tell me things you want, too."

Like that would ever happen.

Over the next few days, Sam told stories until his voice grew hoarse. He reminisced about learning stone carving, textile arts, glassblowing, carpentry, and metalworking. He'd spent lifetimes farming and raising livestock, learning everything he could.

He told me all about the geysers and hot springs around Heart, the desert lands southwest of Range, and the ocean beyond that. I couldn't even fathom the ocean.

I liked listening to him, and he'd stopped asking me to tell him if there was anything I needed. At least, I thought I was safe until he closed the book he'd been reading from and said, "I can't talk anymore."

He *did* sound rougher, but I tried not to feel guilty, since I'd never actually asked him to talk until he lost his voice.

"Will—" I swallowed and tried again. "Will you turn the pages so I can read to myself?" The weight of his regard settled like fog. "Please," I whispered.

"No."

My heart sank. I shouldn't have asked.

"Not until you tell me something about yourself."

No one wanted to hear what the nosoul had to say. All his stories had been so interesting, filled with people and events I couldn't have dreamt of. I had nothing that would compare. "I can't."

"You can." He studied me, like if he looked hard enough he'd find all the things I wasn't telling him. But I didn't have anything. "What makes you happy? What do you like?"

Why did he care? At least he didn't expect me to tell him about a grand adventure. And if I told him something I liked, he'd turn the pages so I could read more. A fair trade.

"Music makes me happy." More than happy. More than I could ever explain to him. "I found a player in the cottage library and figured out how to turn it on. There it was, Dossam's Phoenix Symphony." Easily, I could recall the way my stomach had dropped when the first notes played, and then I'd felt—swollen. Full. Like something inside me had finally awakened. "I love him, his music."

No, that wasn't right. A nosoul couldn't love.

I lurched to my feet and stumbled across the room, but there was nowhere to go, nowhere to run. Li would find me. She'd *know* what I'd said. She'd hit me and yell about how a nosoul couldn't love. I'd been stupid, careless with my words because the thought of music had relaxed me. I had to be careful. No more slips.

"I'm sorry," I whispered. "I didn't mean love."

Footsteps approached, making my heart thud against my ribs as I braced for the strike that never came.

"Ana." Sam stood within arm's reach but didn't touch me. Probably afraid I'd break down if he did. "Do you really feel that way? That you aren't allowed certain emotions?"

I couldn't look at him.

60

"You're not a nosoul. You're allowed to feel however you feel."

So he kept saying, and I wanted to believe him, but . . .

"I think we should talk about this."

My throat hurt from holding back tears. "I don't want to." His good intentions just made it more confusing.

He touched the small of my back. I jumped, but he was so gentle. "Someone without a soul wouldn't have risked her life to save mine, especially since—as you said—I'd just come back."

I stepped away. "I don't want to talk about it."

"All right." He hazarded a smile. "At least I learned something about you."

Flinching, I tried not to count the number of things he'd just learned: I claimed to feel emotions I couldn't, I jumped and ran even when no one was chasing me. . . .

"You like music." He smiled warmly. "I have my SED here. It can play music. I'm happy to let you borrow it, if you ask."

If I asked?

My confusion must have been evident, because he brushed a strand of hair from my eyes and said, "Say the words. Ask."

My hands and heart ached. I wanted to run outside and hide, never have to worry about this again. When to ask. When not to ask. Whether Li would appear and punish me for thinking I was allowed any sort of happiness. There was just *too much*, and it felt like drowning, like burning. But running away wouldn't help.

Sam had offered to take me to Heart, had spent the last few days speaking his voice raw, and would let me listen to music—if only I asked. Surely that wasn't too much to give him, a few words.

I swallowed knots in my throat. "Sam, may I please listen to music?"

"Of course. I'll find it for you." Tension ran from his shoulders, like he'd actually been worried I wouldn't ask. Like he cared.

Maybe he did.

Music pressed into my ears, filling me completely. A piano, a flute, and low strings I couldn't identify.

I'd never heard the song before, and I wanted to explain to Sam how much I appreciated it—how much of a *gift* this was—but I couldn't find the words. Instead, when he sat on the chair, I sat on the arm like he had the day he'd started reading to me.

With a mysterious smile, he pulled the SED from the harness at my waist and flicked on a screen. A dozen musicians sat in a half-moon, playing instruments I'd seen drawings of, but never the real thing. The stage projected their sound to a darkened audience, and to my earpieces.

Phoenix Symphony, my favorite. That must have been Dossam conducting from the piano. The books in the cottage library never had his—sometimes her—picture. Even this was difficult to see. The screen was small, and the image blurry. But I liked the way he caressed the piano keys and directed the other twenty members of the orchestra, as though physically drawing the music from them. Without him, there'd be only silence.

Mesmerizing.

"Li's didn't have video. I think Cris must have left it behind. Was it just old?"

Sam nodded. "Li probably had a newer one she didn't let you see. Everyone uses Stef's new design now."

I scowled at the piece of machinery, which probably fit perfectly in Sam's palm, but mine was too small. Not that I could pick it up right now. "Stef from your stories?"

"The same. He loves this kind of thing, but for a long time, no one used any of the technology he developed. Too annoying to carry around. Eventually he decided to put everything—image capturing, playback, voice communication, a billion other things—into one device."

"Clever."

"Tell him you think so, and you'll have made a friend for eternity." Sam grinned. "Better yet, tell him you like the name."

"SED? Why?"

"It stands for Stef's Everything Device." He paused while the music swelled against my ears, and while I smiled. "Now the Council makes sure everyone has a SED so they can be reached during emergencies. Stef may be a *little* proud of that."

"Deservedly so, because now I get music." I closed my eyes during a flute solo, wishing I could wrap the silvery sound around me, like armor. When the rest of the musicians started to play again, I twisted to face Sam, so maybe he could see in my eyes how much this meant to me. "*Thank* you."

"I still want to know more about you."

That again. Watching the musicians on the screen, I considered whether there was anything worthy of telling. But maybe he didn't care about worthy. Maybe, for some unfathomable reason, he just wanted to know anything. "Once, I found a jar of honey in the cupboard. I took a spoon and ate half of it. Li had never let me try any before." And she'd withheld meals for two days after.

"So you like sweet things. Did you ever get any more?"

"No, she hid it better after that. Up high." I stilled, realizing I'd just admitted to stealing from Li. "But don't worry. I was younger then and wasn't thinking. I wouldn't just take anything from you."

What I really meant was, please don't send me away.

"Besides," I added, turning my bandaged hands palm up, "I can't take anything without asking."

"Your hands will recover soon." He gave a sly half smile. "And in my house, you can have all the honey you want. I'm friends with the beekeeper."

64

"I'm going to Purple Rose Cottage," he said, our second week in the cabin. "We're low on painkillers and gauze."

"No!" I stood so quickly the SED dropped, cutting off the music. "Don't go there."

Sam knelt in front of me, retrieving the device. "Either I get supplies, or your hands go back to hurting all the time."

"Don't go. She'll know I'm with you and do something awful. Neither of us will be safe." Adrenaline flooded me, making me shake. "I'm willing to suffer the pain. Just don't go."

"I'm not willing to let you suffer." He reconnected the SED with my earpieces, and a dozen-person symphony began again. "I'll be back before nightfall."

And he was. I wasn't clear on how far the cottage was from his cabin—I'd never found this place during my explorations—but he returned well before dark. Maybe he'd run. I was just happy to see him again.

"Was she terrible?" I asked from where I sat on the chair with the SED. Now it played a piano song with a strange, bouncy rhythm.

He dropped the bag of supplies on the counter with a clatter of pills and a *thunk* of glass. "She wasn't there, but the door was unlocked."

"So you just took things?" That idea made me smile.

"You need them." He frowned toward the stove, in spite of our good fortune. Li wasn't there. She wouldn't come after me. He should have been relieved, but he just looked pensive. "I wonder where she went."

"Maybe she went to fight dragons and they ate her."

Sam just shook his head. "I do have good news."

Li's absence was great news. If that didn't count as good to him, I was eager to find out what *did*.

From the bag, he drew out a glass jar filled with golden-amber liquid. "I found where she hid the honey."

Emotions tangled inside of me, like vines. Carefully, I nudged the SED off my lap and onto the chair. The earpieces followed.

Sam watched as I moved, and as I walked toward him. "Ana?"

The way he said my name, I must have been some mysterious creature; he'd thought he'd known my habits, but now I threw my arms around him and hugged him as tight as I could. I shook with nerves—with touching someone voluntarily, and allowing him to trap me in his embrace—and I shook with warring confusion and gratitude.

Why would he do something so nice?

I didn't understand. If he'd been Li, he would have used my desires against me somehow, but every time I told him something about myself, he gave me something in return. Music. Honey.

Hugging him felt nice, safe almost, but it lasted too long. Not long enough. He pulled away first and began checking my hands. "Looking much better." One side of his mouth pulled up. "Think you can hold a spoon?"

"Maybe. Why?"

One eyebrow raised, he glanced at the jar of honey on the counter.

"You aren't serious."

"Only if you can hold a spoon." He gave me a look I couldn't decipher. Amusement? Challenge? It wasn't like Li's challenge look. "But if you can't . . ."

"Oh, I can. I'm just not sure whether you can keep up and eat your share."

He grinned and riffled through drawers for a pair of spoons. "We're going to make ourselves sick."

"It's going to be fun." I tested my right hand. Though it certainly didn't feel good, when Sam offered a spoon, I was able to hold it.

Soon, we were both perched on the counter, jar between us, and desperately trying not to dribble honey all over our clothes. He told stories, and listed all the things he thought we should do when we got to Heart, and I couldn't remember ever smiling so much.

6
BUTTERFLY

AT THE BEGINNING of the third week, we quit the cabin before dawn. The weather had warmed and the sky was deep sapphire as we made our way through the graveyard, the silence as delicate as hoarfrost. The predawn air was crisp, but pleasant. Elk pushed through the forest, while eagles and hawks called their territory boundaries at one another. I couldn't help but hum as we crossed the river bridge.

"You're chipper." Sam tugged Shaggy down a stair carved into the path; the pony snorted and swung his head toward the cabin again, and his warm stall with endless food.

"Yep." Finally, we were going to Heart, the great white city I'd heard about since I was a child. "The idea of learning what I am is"—I rolled my shoulders to keep the backpack straps from digging—"it's terrifying, because I might not like what I find out. But it's exciting."

"There's always the option of deciding for yourself who you are and what you'll become."

The sky turned paler shades of indigo as we walked. I couldn't ask him to understand the *need* to know what had happened, why Ciana was gone forever. He couldn't understand the guilt, knowing everyone wished I were her.

I tugged at the gauze. "For a year after Councilor Frase's visit, I convinced myself I was Ciana. I called myself Ciana in my head and told myself I'd somehow lost my memory between lives. I read everything in the cottage library about her, tried to imagine myself weaving and inventing ways to mass-produce cloth. It turns out I can barely imagine how that would work, let alone discover ways to synthesize silk to avoid the mulberry trees and worms. So there's that. Plus, the Soul Tellers are never wrong."

"Not these days, anyway."

"Oh?"

He chuckled. "The tests weren't always as accurate, but we figured it out when toddlers started cursing at the Soul Tellers. It took some doing to remember Whit was actually Tera and we should call him that. A few of us might have had faulty memories for the next few years, just to make him angry."

My grin appeared before I could hide it. "You're lucky you

have any friends left if you treat everyone so badly."

"That's why I had to go out and find a new one. The others all left me." He winked before I could wonder if he was serious. "When we get to Heart, I'll introduce you to anyone you want to meet. Even the friends I don't deserve."

"I can think of a couple." I blushed, remembering the confession about Dossam, but Sam kindly didn't say anything. That was part of a conversation I still wasn't ready to have.

We followed the path around spruce trees and rotting logs, down to the road, which would take us to Heart.

Just before midday, Sam came back to our earlier discussion as if we'd never left. "Seems to me you're in a unique position to be anything you want."

"I doubt that."

"You have the benefit of learning from others' experiences. You don't have to make the same mistakes we did in the beginning, or the ones we're still making." He led Shaggy to the side of the road and looped the rope around a low cottonwood branch, leaving enough slack for the pony to nose around in the sparse foliage. "And *who you are* isn't already cast in everyone's eyes. No one knows what to expect from you. Some would say society is in a rut. Stagnant. By virtue of being new, you have the power to shake us out of that."

He was crazy if he saw that in me. A nosoul couldn't do that. "What if I don't want to? De-stagnate you, that is."

"You don't have to do anything you don't want to." He

spread a blanket on the road and motioned me to sit. "But I don't believe you want to be just another person, doing the same thing every generation. You have more power than anyone, Ana. It's up to you whether or not you use it."

"I don't feel very powerful." My hands hurt, I could barely feed myself, and Sam kept rescuing me. "I feel like the smallest, most insignificant person."

"Small, maybe. Definitely not insignificant." He sat next to me, and we watched the empty road. "Everyone knows who you are."

That didn't sound like a good thing. I was *that* Ana. "Aside from you, no one bothered talking to me. Not even Li."

"Last life, no one could get him to shut up."

I almost corrected, "Her," but bit my lip. It was hard to remember that my mother, definitely a woman, had been male before. Different body. Different life. Instead, I said, "What about everyone else? Did Li forbid it? Or did they just not want to bother?"

Sam took a knife and a wedge of hard cheese from his bag and began cutting. "Honestly? I think people aren't sure it's worth getting to know you. It would be like you deciding if it was worth befriending a butterfly, even though it wouldn't be there in the morning."

It hurt to breathe. "What about you?"

"Surely you know by now."

I didn't, but I didn't want to admit it. "Nothing stopped

you from seeing me before. I could have used"—not a friend, that was too familiar—"someone to talk to me."

He gave one of those half smiles. "Li stopped me. We haven't gotten along in lifetimes. And I didn't know how she was treating you. If I had, I can't say I'd have been able to do anything, but I might have tried."

Might have. It didn't matter what he said about me being powerful. I was just a butterfly to everyone, and why would anyone in their right mind rescue a butterfly from being ignored by a cat?

He offered a slice of cheese, but I wasn't hungry anymore. "You have to eat."

"Says the boy who just told me I can do whatever I want." I flinched away—Li would have slapped me for that—but he just turned back to his lunch.

"Okay." He ate the entire meal by himself and didn't offer anything else. When he was done, he folded the blanket and slung the bag over his shoulder. "Time to go."

Part of me felt like I should apologize, mostly because I didn't want him to ignore me, but neither of us had actually done or said anything wrong. We'd just kind of . . . gotten mad. I sighed and fiddled with my bandages for the next mile before I rested my palm on his shoulder, gently so as not to irritate my healing skin. "Sam?"

He stopped walking. "Are you hungry now?"

I shook my head. "I'm glad you talk to me." In the cabin,

especially. Maybe he'd only rambled for hours to keep me from weeping in agony—maybe he'd only wanted to save his own ears—but he *had*, and he'd been careful and gentle. That meant everything. If only telling him that didn't mean *telling* him that. "I won't expect anyone else to be like you."

"No one knows if you'll be around very long. If people have been less than welcoming, that's the reason why."

"I'll be around my whole life," I whispered, not quite under the breeze in the forest, the pounding of my heart, and the beating of my invisible and incorporeal wings. "That's a long time to me."

He brushed a strand of hair off my face and nodded.

7
WALLS

AS WE BROKE through the forest, a white wall soared high into the air, like smooth clouds below the cobalt sky. It stretched in both directions as far as I could see, flowing like water on the dips and crests of the plateau that carried the city of Heart.

Gates of iron and brass guarded the Southern Arch into the city, but as wide as the entrance was, I couldn't make out anything beyond. Just darkness.

"Look up." Sam stood next to me, one hand twisted in Shaggy's lead, and the other shoved into his pocket.

His cheeks were bright with chill, but his smile was wide and relaxed. Stubble darkened his chin like shadows, and his lips were chapped from wind. It had been a long walk, and he'd chatted constantly. He'd pointed out ruins, mostly derelict cabins, but there were a few mysterious mounds of rock. We'd walked by five immense graveyards, which we'd stopped to look at while he told me stories about the people buried there.

Apparently I hadn't responded quickly enough. He glanced at me, his expression a cross between teasing and curiosity. "Not at me." He nudged me with his elbow. "Look at Heart. Look up."

Above the wall, an enormous tower jutted into the sky, taller than a hundred ancient redwood trees stacked on one another. It vanished into a cloud, white stone making that vapor look dirty in comparison. "What is it?" My chest felt too tight, like something squeezing and reminding me I was a nosoul. I resisted the urge to back away from it, lest it see me.

"The temple." Now he peered at me with concern, something he did too much. "Are you okay?"

Evidently he saw nothing wrong with the tower, felt nothing wrong. So it was probably a side effect of my newness. "Yeah, of course." I crossed my arms, mindful of my bandages. They were fewer today; the burns didn't hurt nearly as much. Generous application of lotion helped. "So it's a temple? For what?"

He started walking again, his gaze on the city. Or the temple. "It's an old legend. Many stopped believing in it thousands of years ago."

The reminder was a slap. He was *old*. He only appeared my age. "Why?"

"Because nothing ever happened, not once since we discovered Heart and made it our home."

I searched my memory for anything about that, but Li's library had been small. And if Sam had read anything about it in the cabin, it must have been one of the times I dozed off. "Maybe start from the beginning? What's your very first memory?"

"Si—" He smiled and flipped a strand of hair off my face. "Maybe later. To be honest, some of the earliest memories are lost, which is one of the reasons we started keeping journals. The mind can hold a lot, but after a while, less important things fade to make room. You don't have crystalline memories of everything in your life, after all. Or do you?"

I shook my head. There were some things I didn't want to remember, either. How many memories had Sam willingly given up?

"One of the things everyone agrees on is that we started out in small tribes scattered across Range. Some say everyone appeared there, fully grown. Others insist that only a few did, and the rest were born." He looked askance at me. "I don't remember that at all. That truth is gone forever."

"No one wrote it down?"

"We didn't have writing yet. We had language, but I suppose we didn't talk about it because we'd all been there. A lot of our early lives were focused on survival. It took time to learn what was safe to eat and what wasn't, that not all the hot springs were safe to drink or bathe in, and the geysers—remind me later to tell you about the time one erupted while Sine was standing over it." He started to grin, but other memories overshadowed whatever had been so funny about Sine's misfortune. "We also had to focus on staying away from dragons and centaurs and . . . other things."

"Sylph."

He nodded. "We drew pictures in the dirt or on walls, but those weren't permanent, and we couldn't always translate one another's—for lack of a better term—artwork. Things got lost and misinterpreted. I suppose we just gave up."

"Okay." As we neared the city, I could make out smaller metal tubes protruding from the southeastern quarter of the city. Antennae, perhaps, or solar panels. Maybe both. "So everyone was out wandering one day and you stumbled across Heart?"

"More or less. We fought over it for a while, before we realized how huge it is. There's more than enough room for everyone."

"Did that ever strike you as odd? That a city was waiting for you, complete with a temple right in the center?" I winced preemptively, but Li wasn't here to hit me for my curiosity. Either Sam didn't notice, or he was good at pretending.

"It should have, but we were so busy being grateful for shelter, we didn't think about it. By the time we did, if there'd been a trace of a previous civilization, we'd destroyed it simply by living there. People still search for evidence, but there's almost nothing in Heart."

"Almost."

"Well, there's the temple, which is actually where we discovered writing."

"But the books said—"

"That Deborl came up with the system? It's not entirely false, but not accurate, either. He deciphered it. He's always been good with patterns. There are words carved around the temple, which talk about Janan, a great being who created us, gave us souls and eternal life. And Heart. He was to protect us."

I stared at the temple protruding from the center of the city. "None of that was in Li's books."

"Deborl has taken the liberty of editing a few things." He tipped his head back, following my gaze. As we approached the city, the wall blocked more of the horizon. "At any rate, Janan never revealed himself to us, or helped during times of trouble."

"Like drought and hunger, or some of the other year names?"

Sam nodded. "Exactly. The Year of Darkness was named because of a solar eclipse that happened early on. It seemed the entire sun went out. And Janan wasn't there to help us when we were afraid."

Until recently, no one had ever been around to help me when I was afraid, so the betrayal didn't sit so sharply with me. But maybe it was different if someone promised, then didn't follow through.

"The temple doesn't even have a door. A few people firmly believe in Janan, and that he'll return one day to rescue us from the terrors of this world, but most of us decided a long time ago that he wasn't real."

"But if what's written on the temple is true—having souls, being reborn—doesn't that mean he's real too?"

"Maybe he was a long time ago. Some stories say he sacrificed his existence to create us, and that's why there's no door." The sky vanished as we came to a stretch of barren land that ran up to the city wall. Steam puffed from a nearby hole in the ground. A geyser? "When it came time to write new copies of histories, some things got left out because people decided they weren't real or important, which is why you've never heard about Janan."

"You've said his name, though. You use it as a curse?"

He grimaced. "Some felt betrayed when Janan never saved us from griffin or centaur attacks. It's been five thousand years, after all."

I'd probably give up waiting on someone after that much time too.

"It started out as a simple oath, not an imprecation, but it grew and became a habit some of us can't shake."

"The people who still believe in him probably don't like that."

Sam chuckled. "No, not really. Try not to pick up my bad habits if you want to stay on the Council's good side. Meuric *really* believes."

As I left the road, my boots crunched on the ground, an odd mix of ash and pebbles. Sulfur-reeking steam tickled my nose, but it blew toward the forest, leaving white deposits of rime on branches. I started toward the geyser—I wanted to look inside—but Sam touched my shoulder, silently reminding me of his cautions as we'd entered the immense caldera: the ground was thin in some places, and would crack and drop you in scalding hot mud before you could leap away.

Since he tended to keep silent when I did potentially stupid things like scramble up old rock walls to get a better view of our surroundings, I'd taken the warning about the ground seriously.

"So did *you* feel betrayed? About Janan, I mean." I drifted toward the wall, like I'd been heading that way all along.

"A little. I wanted to believe we were here for a purpose."

"I know that feeling." The wall bore no cracks or dapples of color, and was as hard as marble when I removed a bandage to feel if it was as smooth as it looked. The sun-warmed stone was frictionless on my tender palm.

"Wait," Sam said as I was about to withdraw. He stood unnervingly close. "Just a moment." Then his hand rested on the back of mine, fingers threaded between mine, carefully. "Do you feel it?" More a breath than a whisper.

Feel what? His touch? Heat radiating off his body? I felt it all over.

The stone wall pulsed, like blood rushing through an artery.

I jerked back, away from Sam, away from the wall. Sunlight hadn't warmed the stone; heat emanated from inside. "How did it do that?" I itched to scrub my hand on my trousers, but the new skin was too delicate to risk. Instead, I wrapped the bandage around it again, sloppily and likely to cut off circulation to my fingers.

His gaze followed my hands. "It's always done that. Why?"

"I don't like the way it feels." I edged away, not that I knew where I'd go. Just *away*.

He followed my not-so-subtle retreat, glancing between me and the geyser at my back. "Why?"

I stopped and ordered myself to breathe when the ground thumped hollowly under my steps; it was too thin to stand on safely. After weeks, I was finally at Heart, and now I wanted to run? No. I'd come here to find out why I'd been born, and I wouldn't let a stupid *wall* scare me away.

Sam offered his hands, still shooting worried glances at the ground. "Come on. We're nearly home."

His home. Right. Where I'd stay until the Council decided what to do with me. "Okay." I didn't take his offered hands.

Sam studied me a moment more, but nodded. "This won't take long. I can open the gate, but I suspect they'll want to log your entrance." He gave an apologetic smile, so I didn't complain about the unfairness. This time.

"Why do you keep them closed?"

He walked between the wall and me as we returned to Shaggy, who swished his tail and gazed longingly at the archway. "Mostly tradition. We haven't had a problem with giants or trolls in the last few centuries, but there were years we had to barricade ourselves in. Centaurs, dragons—all sorts of things used to attack, not to mention the sylph. Now the edge of Range is better protected, but just because they haven't tried in a while doesn't mean they won't again. We don't want to be unprepared."

There'd been drawings of battles in some of the cottage books, most involving liberal use of red ink. If I'd died in countless wars against the other inhabitants of the planet, I'd keep my doors shut, too.

The arch was tall and wide, and deep enough for ten people to stand abreast. Still creeped out by the pulse of the wall, I hugged myself and stayed in the center.

Beyond the iron bars, the archway opened into a wide chamber. "Guard station," Sam explained. "And this is a soul-scanner, so the Council knows who is coming and going.

There are a few around armories and places they don't think *everyone* should have access to. Normally you'd have to touch it, too, but I assume you're not in the database, so it wouldn't do anything." He pressed his palm on a small panel by the gate. It beeped, and a section of the gate swung open just as yellow light spilled across the floor and footsteps echoed.

A slender man, perhaps in his thirties, appeared. "Hey, Sam. Would have been here sooner, but Darce just gave birth to Minn—who's a girl this time—and a bunch of us had to keep Merton from getting revenge on him while he's still so young. Her. That might take some getting used to. Minn hasn't been a girl in ten generations."

Sam went first with Shaggy. I followed when the hooves were out of the way, and didn't even have time to take in the sparse furnishings before all eyes fell on me.

"Speaking of getting used to." The stranger glanced at Sam, then back to me. He wore loose-fitting pants and a heavy, button-up brown shirt. The afternoon was warm enough to make coats unnecessary. "Ana, right?"

As if there were a question. He'd known because I hadn't touched the soul-scanner, then started gossiping to make me feel excluded. I lifted my chin like I was about to come up with a brilliant retort, or like Sam might say something, but neither happened, and the stranger and I just watched each other, stares slowly turning into glares.

Shaggy broke the silence with a long sigh.

The guard turned back to Sam. "Still doesn't talk, hmm? Sad." He retreated to a wooden desk shoved against the city wall. A slim, flickering screen rested in the center—it was blank—and a few neat stacks of paper sat around that. He flicked on the lamp and leaned against the desk, casting shadows.

Sam hauled his bags off Shaggy, grunting between words; otherwise, his tone was congenial. "Actually, I think she was waiting for you to give her your name."

"Actually," I said, "I don't care." I took a bag from Sam, transferring it to my shoulder with minimal use of my hands. The one bandage was coming undone from where I'd been sloppy about rebinding it. "But I do talk, and have for quite some time."

Sam turned his head as though to hide his smirk.

"Well then, glad to hear. I'm Corin." The guard offered a palm, which I didn't take, just held up my bandages. "What happened to your hands?"

"Burned them."

"She rescued me from a sylph." Sam didn't mention how he'd rescued me from the sylph, too, and the lake before that, or how he'd been taking care of me for almost three weeks. It was nice of him to make me sound brave.

Corin whistled. "Impressive, but you know he'd come back, right?"

Eventually, sure, but not in time to save me from everyone

treating me like Corin was. I hefted the new bag on my shoulder and addressed Sam. "It'll be time for supper soon."

He had little reason to play as my ally, considering he'd known Corin for five thousand years and my "saving" of him was only one small thing, but for whatever reason, he did, and I could have hugged him for it. "You're right. It's been a long walk from the edge. Can we catch up another day, Corin? Ana and I still have to unpack."

The guard shook his head. "I'm afraid not. I mean, you can go, Sam"—he jerked his chin toward the open door at the end of the long room—"but Ana hasn't been cleared."

"What?" Sam's tone was suddenly less pleasant.

The extra bag dug painfully into my shoulder. "I thought you just had to write my name in a ledger or something. What do you mean cleared?"

"For entrance into the city. You aren't a citizen."

"I was born here." Surely everyone knew that. Li had told me how they'd all come by to ogle the nosoul, and that was one of the reasons she'd taken me away. Not just to hide her shame, but, she insisted, to protect me.

"You aren't documented as being a legal resident of Heart."

"But I was born here!"

"She'll stay as my guest." Sam edged closer to me, as if proximity would convince anyone. "We'll work out citizenship in the morning."

"I'm afraid there's nothing I can do." Corin crossed his arms. "You know I would if I could, but it's against the rules."

"What rules? There are no rules about who gets into Heart."

Corin swiped papers off the desk and thrust them at Sam. "The Council passed it a few years ago. Weren't you paying attention? In order to enter Heart, one must be a citizen, and in order to be a citizen, one must have owned a home in the city for the last hundred years."

Sam dropped his bags on the floor—I put mine down a little more carefully—and grabbed the papers, reading quickly. "This is ridiculous." He hurled the papers across the room. They fluttered and whispered against one another before settling on the smooth floor. "Call Meuric. Call the entire Council. Tell them to get here immediately."

"They're in session. Ana is free to stay in the guard station tonight; there's a more than adequate bunk that way." He pointed somewhere beyond me. "I doubt anyone will protest."

The last thing I wanted to do was stay in the guard station all night. I'd feel safer by the geyser. I'd feel safer at the bottom of Rangedge Lake. "Sam—"

He shook his head. "You're coming home with me, no matter what anyone says."

I could run for the door and try to get lost in the streets—probably not hard—but the million to two odds weren't good. Sam and I would get caught and put in prison, so my only good choice was to let him handle this. I hated that choice.

"Sam," Corin said, "calm down. It's not a big deal."

"Not a big deal, my foot!" Sam seized Corin's sleeve and hauled him across the room. They were just out of earshot if they spoke quietly, which they did. I hated that too, but I didn't want to make Sam look bad by stomping after them and demanding to be included in the conversation.

While Sam no doubt told Corin all about how I needed help and didn't trust anyone, I sat at the desk and unwound my bandages. My hands looked better. Pink, with sensitive skin, but we'd been careful about keeping them clean while we traveled, especially after the blisters burst. I felt like a fool for having believed Li's lie about sylph burns never healing. Soon, I'd be well enough to hurl rocks at her if I ever ran into her again.

Angry whispers sizzled across the guardroom, too obscured for me to understand. I sifted through the papers on Corin's desk, finding shift schedules and other mundanities. It looked like whoever lived closest to each of the guard stations was responsible for keeping an eye on it while they were in residence. They rotated days with a few others, but overall it didn't look like a difficult job, so long as you remembered the rule: anyone but Ana was allowed to come into the city.

"Alone in the woods? It's midwinter." Corin's surprised hiss made me stiffen, but I didn't look behind me. Sam didn't need to know I'd heard anything of his secret meeting.

The stack of papers at the back of the desk had lists of armories throughout Heart, and the contents. Now *that* was interesting. Old catapults and cannons, newer armored vehicles and air drones. Laser pistols. I had no idea what half these things were, but I flipped through the pages. Maybe Sam could tell me, or I could find something in the library— if I was ever allowed farther than the guard station.

"Okay." Corin stalked up behind me and ripped the papers from my hands. "Those aren't for you."

"Don't worry." I stood and glanced at Sam, who was digging his SED from his bag. "Li never taught me how to read."

Sam snorted and strode to the other side of the room to call the Council.

It took half an hour for people to start arriving. Corin had taken Shaggy and the travel supplies to the stable nearby, making Sam and me promise not to leave. And we didn't, because I knew Sam wouldn't go anywhere, and I didn't feel like wandering the city without him.

The first to arrive was a woman in her late eighties, perhaps. Since Li had kept me away from everyone, all I had to go on was pictures of people at various ages; guessing was tricky. This woman had gray hair pulled into a taut bun. Shallow wrinkles spiderwebbed across her face but made her look more dignified than old. She introduced herself as Sine and took a seat in one of the chairs along one side of the guard station.

Geyser-incident Sine. Huh.

Meuric came next. He looked younger than fifteen, but aside from emergencies, you had to be past your first quindec to hold a job because of physical size and hormones. At least that was what I'd heard.

Though Meuric was only my height and kind of pointy with that chin and those elbows, his deep-set eyes showed his true age. The way he looked at me, I'd never felt more insignificant. Sam had said Meuric was the leader of the Council, so he was the one I really had to impress.

Frase, who'd been the one to tell Li about Ciana, and Antha joined them.

Sam said, "Clearly this rule was made to keep Ana out of Heart. It's cruel and unfair to exclude her simply because she hasn't been alive for five thousand years."

Meuric scratched his chin and looked thoughtful. "If I recall, that was because no one was sure whether more new-souls would be born. What happens if Ana isn't the only one? Do we find housing for all of them? Can our community support them?"

Sam shot me a warning glance before I could open my mouth.

Them. I crossed my arms and stood by my bags. There wasn't a *them.* There was only *me.*

"This wasn't to segregate Ana, but to protect our city." Antha ran her fingers through her hair. "You remember how clumsy we were with Heart when we first arrived? We were so young, as Ana is now."

"I'm not going to break your city." I scowled, ignoring Sam's pleading look. "I don't want to change anything or disrupt your routines."

"You already have," said Frase. "Simply by existing."

"Blame Li and Menehem. I had nothing to do with that." I tried to make myself taller, but standing next to Sam, that was pointless. "It seems to me you're changing and disrupting your own lives because of my existence more than I have. I've been away for eighteen years, and you're making laws when I'm out of sight—"

"What I think Ana is trying to say," Sam interrupted, "is aside from being born, which she couldn't help, she hasn't disturbed anyone."

"Except Li," said Antha.

Sine nodded. "Li chose to face her responsibility, unlike Menehem. That was noble of her."

That was *not* the story I'd heard.

"If Li hadn't," Sam said, "someone else would have. Someone, maybe, who realized that in a few years Ana would grow up and become a member of our community. She has her own useful skills, but she can't contribute unless someone allows her."

90

"Would you have taken her in?" Meuric mused. "No, you were an infant then, too. That was quite a year, if I recall. You the first day, and Ana a few weeks later. Two births that year. I remember because I died three days after Ana arrived. Shock is bad for old hearts."

I glanced at Sam; he'd said we shared a birthday, hadn't he? Why would Meuric say something different?

Sam didn't seem to notice. "If I could have, I would have, but as you said, I was incapable of caring for anyone. I'm offering now."

"And the fact that the law prevents her from living in the city?" Meuric asked.

"How many other newsouls have been born in the last eighteen years?" Sam's voice was as hard as ice. "She's the only one. The law was made against her. It's inhospitable at best, and a death sentence at worst, especially since we don't know if she'll be reincarnated. And I believe there's another law about that."

I watched Sam, hoping for answers to a million questions—there was a law about my death?—but he didn't acknowledge my stare.

The Councilors glanced at one another. Sine shrugged first. "I wasn't for the law in the first place. If Sam wants to care for Ana, he should be allowed. She's not hurting anyone." She sent me a warm smile, but I couldn't bring myself to return it.

Meuric nodded. "I suppose it would be a chance for young Ana to have a bit more guidance. Li was no doubt a capable teacher, but perhaps Sam will be able to help Ana find who she is so she can, as he said, become a contributing member of the community."

"I don't need another parent," I started, but Sam interrupted me again.

"Then you'll rescind the law?" If he wasn't on my side, I'd hit him for talking over me all the time. How could I *be my own person* if I didn't have a voice about my own life?

"Frase? Antha?" Meuric glanced at the other two Councilors. "We need a unanimous vote, since the others aren't here."

"On the condition that she obey a curfew and submit to lessons and tests." Frase leveled his gaze on Sam. "To ensure that Ana has a quality education, of course. If she's reincarnated after she dies, then we'll have gained a valuable new voice. If she isn't, well, we all know how Sam enjoys taking on new projects. This should keep him busy for a lifetime, and should any more newsouls appear, he'll have the experience to aid them as well."

I squeezed my hands together behind my back. The sting of raw flesh was the only thing that kept me grounded. I wasn't a *project*. I wasn't an *experiment*. I wasn't a blasted *butterfly*.

"That sounds reasonable to me." Antha lifted her chin and

looked at me. "Will you abide by these conditions?"

My jaw hurt from clenching it, but I stopped myself from checking with Sam to see what he thought. I didn't need his *guidance.* "Sure."

"Then it's settled." Meuric used the arms of his chair to push himself up. "Ana will stay with Sam as his student. Progress reports will be expected and reviewed by the Council monthly. Why don't you both come by the Councilhouse in the morning. Tenth hour. We'll introduce everyone else and finish working out the details."

Not a question or invitation.

After a round of overly polite welcomes—welcome home and welcome to Heart—the Councilors left, Corin left, and Sam and I picked up our bags.

He met my eyes briefly before motioning me to the door, and I couldn't tell whether he was satisfied with the verdict or not until he said, "They planned that."

8
SONG

"WHAT DO YOU mean?" I stepped outside, into Heart, onto a wide avenue. Conifers and hints of white stone houses filled the left side of the road. Smaller streets wound between the trees, which gave an illusion of privacy, though I got the feeling the plots of land each house stood on were large.

Sam motioned to an odd assortment of buildings on the right, stretching to the far side of the city, visible only because the wall was so big. "This is the industrial quarter. Warehouses, mills, factories."

"Who does all those jobs?"

"Whoever wants whatever is necessary. Or, for example, if you want bolts of cloth, you can buy them during market day, since there are a few people who *like* working on those things, and produce more than they can use. It's their job, and how they earn enough credit to buy food."

"And those?" I pointed at a maze of huge pipes that ran between buildings. "You could fit a person in them."

"Used for conducting geothermal energy. This part of Range is on top of an enormous volcano; there's a lot of power just beneath the ground. We moved to solar energy almost a century ago, because it's less potentially destructive, but we keep the pipes in place for backup."

"I see." I gazed up at windmills that reached higher than the wall. Above everything, the temple pointed at the sky. I couldn't drop my head back far enough to see the top. Shivering, I turned my attention back to Sam. "Why do you need so much energy? It seems like there's a lot more coming in than even a million people can use."

"A lot of the power is used for automated city maintenance systems and mechanical drones that don't need people to control them. Like snowplows or sewage." He flashed a grin. "And when you get in trouble a lot, like Stef, you become very familiar with monitoring and cleaning those systems as punishment."

"What if no one does anything wrong?"

He snorted. "There's almost always someone. But on the rare occasion there's not, we have to take turns."

"Yuck." I decided to behave. I didn't want to spend my first—possibly only—lifetime scrubbing unspeakable things.

"I'm surprised no one's come to greet you," Sam muttered.

"Gawk. Not greet." I followed him down the cobblestone avenue, doing my best to avoid dropping my bags while still taking in my surroundings. My first time in Heart since I was born, and the place was dead. "What did you mean before when you said 'They planned that'?" He couldn't avoid my question forever.

"What it sounds like. While they were taking their time getting to the guard station, they were deciding what they would offer. They made it sound like they were doing you a favor."

I hmmed because I hadn't caught that, but when I considered the conversation again, I agreed. "They don't seem to respect you very much. Aside from insulting me, what did they mean by 'projects'?"

He gave a dry chuckle. "Just that I tend to try something new every lifetime. Lots of people learn new things, because it's simply easier to know how to do everything yourself than it is to realize your plumbing is broken and the only two people in Heart who could fix it are either away from the city or between lives."

"So you know how to fix your plumbing. That's not a crime."

"But if I make it a point to learn something new every life and try—and sometimes fail—to keep up with old projects from previous lives, it makes me appear directionless. They think I've taken on too many things and don't stick with enough of them."

"Very contradictory." I struggled to keep up with his long strides, especially now that I was carrying double what I had been. I didn't blame him for his haste now that we were this close, but the day was considerably warmer than the past few weeks. My head buzzed with strain.

"That's life."

Apparently. "What did you tell Corin to make him change his mind about calling Meuric?"

Sam didn't quite manage to shrug, thanks to the bags on his shoulders.

"About how useless I am? How I need help and would die if left on my own?" It was all probably true. I hadn't lasted a day after leaving Li's house.

"No, nothing like that." His focus was straight ahead.

After fifteen minutes of trotting after Sam in silence, I said, "I don't like Corin."

"He isn't a bad person. He's just stiff and follows too many rules. Don't blame him for what happened today."

We turned down a street wide enough for five people to walk shoulder to shoulder. Bushes and tall evergreens lined the way. Other streets and walkways broke off from this one, but everything was still so far apart. Half the city's population lived in this quarter, but I doubted they could hear one another if they hollered out their windows.

I caught sight of only a few houses, since most were guarded by trees and distance. They were all made from the same white stone as the city wall and temple, but their exteriors had been decorated differently. Some were plain, with merely serviceable shutters or glass in the stone openings. Others were more opulent.

"Are all the windows and doors in the same places on every house?" I huffed, trying to keep up with him as he walked even faster. Maybe if I got him talking he'd slow down.

"They are. Like I said, the city was waiting for us. The houses were already built, but they were shells with holes for doors and windows. The insides were hollow. We had to build interior walls, stairs, different floors—everything. You'll see."

I stopped walking. Jogging, rather. Trying to catch my breath, I knelt and let the heavy bag rest on the street. It had to weigh at least half what I did. My heart raced, and a cramp jabbed at my side.

"Ana?" Sam turned around and finally noticed I wasn't there. He came back for me and crouched. "Are you okay?"

"No." I scowled and pressed my palms on my face, damp with cold sweat. "No, I've been chased into a lake, burned, babied for weeks, then I walked half of Range to get here so a bunch of people who don't know me can direct my life, and now you're practically running away from me." I slapped my bag, wincing at the shocks up my wrists and forearms. Darkness tinged the edges of my vision, receding as I took deep breaths. "You have all this time. Can't you walk slower?"

A mask fell away from his expression as he dug a handkerchief from his pocket. He dabbed the cloth across my forehead and cheeks. "I'm sorry. I wasn't paying attention."

"You're preoccupied." I'd seen it before, a few times in the cabin when we talked about sylph or Li. Not that he ever admitted it.

"Excited to get home." He stuffed the handkerchief away.

Liar. Well, maybe not completely a liar, but I wasn't stupid. The mask had been there since we'd left the guard station. No, before. Sometime between standing up for—and interrupting—me, and the Council deciding what to do. Maybe in the same way I didn't want another parent, he didn't want a child. Though he'd said he'd take the responsibility . . .

But I wasn't a *child*.

I lurched to my feet, bag gouging my shoulder, and nodded for him to continue. His mask returned, but he kept a slower pace this time. We didn't speak as we turned down a few more streets and headed up a long walkway, and I caught my first glimpse of Sam's house.

Like all the others, it was tall and wide, with a white exterior and the same placement of doors and windows. Nothing like Purple Rose Cottage, which had been small and wooden, perpetually dusty.

Shutters were painted pine green, and below each one rested a thick bush. Roses, perhaps. I glanced at my hands, thinking of the scars the purple roses had left. They were gone now, burned off in the sylph fire.

The outside had a generous garden, a few bare fruit trees, and small outbuildings scattered on the sides and back. Chickens clucked nearby, and cavies made quiet wheeking and bubbling noises in another building.

Sam walked beside me as we approached the door, green like the shutters. "What do you think?"

"Pretty." But the stone walls and roof, the perfectly tended lawns . . . It all seemed cold. Ancient, and watching. When I glanced over my shoulder, the temple rose into the sky, even more sinister than before.

Sam didn't notice my lack of enthusiasm, just found his key—what did he do with it between lives?—and opened the door wide to let me in first.

The interior was cool and dim, only slivers of light leaking through cracks in the shades. Aside from the staircase and a second room at the back—a kitchen?—the parlor took up the entire first story. White sheets fluttered over huge pieces of furniture, much more than one parlor should possess.

I started to ask about it, but Sam flipped a switch, and light poured across the hardwood floor, making me blink and squint to adjust.

"Pull off the sheets and put them in a corner for now," he

said. "I'll make sure there's a room for you upstairs." He left the big bags by the doorway and headed up the spiral staircase with my backpack. An L-shaped balcony overlooked this quarter of the parlor, guarded by a thin rail carved from wood. He checked on me before disappearing beyond my line of sight.

Carefully, in case there was something fragile hidden beneath the sheets, I drew the lengths of synthetic silk aside to find bookcases and shelves, chairs and stands of some kind. The furniture was all hard, polished wood, and decorations carved from pieces of obsidian, marble, and quartz. Sam had told me about learning these crafts, and I hadn't been sure why he bothered. It seemed like a lot of work. But now that I saw the glossy curves of a stone shrike, the delicate etched feathers, I understood.

It was beautiful, and if I was going to live somewhere for five thousand years, I'd want to enjoy looking at it, too.

Then again, he'd said some people did these things as a job. He could buy them, if he wanted. So what was *his* job? I'd ask when he returned.

Once the edges of the room were uncovered, I turned to all the items in the middle, starting with a particularly strange lump.

The sheet rippled off a large plane of maple wood, over a length of keys, and slipped off a bench.

A piano. A real one.

My chest constricted, and I wanted to call up to Sam and ask why he hadn't told me, but I hadn't yet finished my task. There might be more treasures.

In a giddy daze, I moved through the parlor uncovering things I'd seen only as drawings in my favorite books. A large harp. An organ. A harpsichord. A stack of cases with various instruments engraved in the polished wood. I didn't recognize most of them by sight, but I could identify the violin, another—bigger—stringed instrument, and a long one with a reed and intricate metal keys. Clarinet?

This was too wonderful. Had he called ahead and had a friend bring these over, just because he knew I'd like them?

I couldn't imagine why, but it did seem like something Sam would do. He was so nice to me, always doing things just to make me happy.

I drifted back to the piano in the center of the room. Carved wood framed the instrument and its bench, and rows of ebony and yellowed ivory keys glimmered under the light. My fingers reached to touch them, but these weren't my things. I snatched my hand back at the last moment, pressed my palm against my racing heart.

A real piano. It was the most beautiful thing I'd ever seen.

"You don't like it?" Sam's voice, tinged with annoyance, came from the balcony. I jumped and stared up at him, struggling to control the questions crowding my mouth. "Does it feel wrong too?"

"Fingerprints." First thing that came to mind. "I didn't want to smudge anything."

His tone lightened as he headed downstairs, fingers trailing along the banister. "Play something." He'd washed his face and changed his shirt, but he was still flushed from the walk. Or maybe something else, because he hadn't been the one panting outside. "You won't hurt it." Maybe that hadn't been annoyance after all, but I didn't let down my guard.

I chose a key in the middle. A clear note resounded through the airy room. Sparks traveled up my spine, and I pressed another, and another. Each note was lower than the last as my fingers crept toward the left end of the piano. I tried one on the right, and the note was higher. It wasn't like a song at all, but hearing the sound bounce across the polished stone and furniture—my cheeks hurt from grinning.

Sam sat on the bench, dragged his fingertips across the keys without pressing any, then picked out my four notes. They came staccato. Tuneless.

But there was something about the way he sat there, something familiar. This wasn't a borrowed piano.

Lots of people probably had pianos.

The four notes sounded again, this time in a slow rhythm, and when he glanced at me, some indecipherable expression crossed his face.

I couldn't stop staring at his hands on the piano keys, the way they fit there so comfortably.

He played my notes again, but instead of stopping after, he played the most amazing thing my ears had ever heard. Like waves on a lakeshore, and wind through trees. There were lightning strikes, thunder, and pattering rain. Heat and anger, and honey sweetness.

I'd never heard this music before. There seemed no room to breathe around my swollen heart as the music grew, made me ache inside.

It went on forever, and not long enough. Then my four notes came again, slow like before. I struggled to breathe as the sound echoed against my thoughts. And quiet blanketed the parlor.

I couldn't remember sitting. Just as well. My legs didn't feel strong enough to hold me up.

"Sam, are you—" I swallowed the name. If I was wrong, I would be really embarrassed. But I was already on the floor, the music still thick inside me like the first time I'd stolen the player from the cottage library. A hundred times more, though.

This was here. Real. Now.

"Are you Dossam?"

His hands rested on the keys, at home there. I willed him to play again. "Ana," he said, and I met his gaze. "I wanted to tell you."

"Why didn't you?" If only I could stop thinking of my

drug-induced confession of infatuation. If there'd been a hole to crawl into, I would have.

He caressed the keys again, some strange expression crossing his face. "At first I didn't think it mattered. And after"—he shook his head—"you know. I didn't want you to feel different around me."

That was either really kind of him, or really moronic. "You told me your name was Sam. Everyone else called you Sam, too." I was really sure I'd have noticed people calling him Dossam, at any rate.

His face reddened. "It's shorter, and everyone's been using it forever now. Back at the lake, when I told you my name, I didn't know you wouldn't know. I should have clarified, but—"

"It's okay." I stood and tried to collect myself, but *Dossam* was *right there* and how could I ever look at him again, knowing he'd seen me at my worst? How could he ever be Sam again, now that he was Dossam?

This was what he'd tried to avoid by not telling me his true identity. If I didn't get myself together, he'd think horrible things about me.

I forced myself to look at him, still sitting at the piano, palms on his knees. He still looked like the Sam who'd pulled me from the lake, and the Sam who'd wrapped my hands after they'd been burned.

"What was that you played?" I edged closer. To the piano. To him.

Same wide-set eyes, same shaggy black hair. Same hesitant smile. "It's yours," he said. "It's called whatever you want."

I staggered back. So much for collecting myself. "Mine?"

He took my shoulder, stopping me from crashing into something. "Didn't you hear?" he asked, searching me. "I used the notes you picked, things that remind me of you."

My notes. Things that reminded him of me. Dossam thought of me, the nosoul.

He didn't think I was a nosoul.

Oblivious to my thoughts, he went on. "It isn't often I have the pleasure of performing for someone who hasn't heard me play a thousand times. I think Armande and Stef are bored of it."

"I can't imagine ever getting bored of that. I could listen forever." I bit my lip. Why couldn't I say anything halfway smart? But he smiled. "You made that up? Just now?"

"Some of it. Some I've been thinking of for a while. I'll have to start writing it down before I forget." He offered a hand, which I just stared at because a minute ago, that hand had been on the piano making a melody *for me*, and suddenly I wasn't no one anymore. I was Ana who Had Music.

I had the best music.

"Are you all right?" He held me by the elbows, as if I'd

been about to topple over from the weight of all my thoughts.

"Fine." Overwhelmed. Dizzy. But I didn't want him to realize I'd made more of his gift than he'd intended. I didn't even know how to thank him.

"It's late. Let's clean up and rest. Does that sound okay?"

Dumbly, I nodded and let him lead me up the stairs, down a corridor, and into a bedroom decorated in shades of blue.

Lace hung over the shuttered window, covered the bed, and hid a closet alcove with hanging clothes. The walls were little more than sheets with hand-cut shelves pressed against both sides. Some cubbies held folded blankets and things, while others held books or small instruments carved from antelope horns. One wall had been made into a desk. Only the outside wall was stone, but he'd covered that with paintings of erupting geysers, snowy forests, and ancient ruins.

"Help yourself to anything that fits. I'm sure there's something, even if it's outdated." He motioned at another door, made the same way as the walls. "There's a washroom. Everything you need should be in there."

"You have all this stuff in case a girl comes to stay awhile?"

Sam shifted his weight away from me. "Actually, it's mine."

I was imagining him in a dress before I remembered he'd been a girl in other lifetimes. He wasn't the strange one.

"Right. Sorry." It was a poor apology, but I couldn't make myself come up with anything better. I was tired and sore, and echoes of his song—my song!—stayed in my head. My chest felt tight with need. "Sam, will you play your piano more?"

His expression softened. "And anything else you'd like to hear."

Everything I'd felt downstairs, all my stupid childhood fantasies: they all returned, hitting me hard.

How could my insides be so taut and relaxed at once? After a lifetime of hoping to meet him, imagining what he might be like, he was not what I'd expected, mostly because he put up with me.

9
REPRISE

HE'D BEEN RIGHT about my needs being met.

In one of the cubbies, I found cozy shirts and trousers made of wool and synthetic silk. I laid them out for after I was clean. He had feminine underwear, too, but that was too weird; I left them.

After a quick shower to remove the worst of the road grime, I ran a hot bath to soak my poor muscles. When I turned the water off, strains of music floated upstairs. He was playing my song again. But just as I relaxed into it, the whole thing stopped in the middle of a phrase, then started again. He continued like that, sometimes only a few notes. Perhaps he was writing it down, like he said.

I closed my eyes and listened until the water grew cold, then dried and dressed and braided my hair.

When I peeked over the balcony, he hadn't washed yet, just sat at the piano with a stack of lined papers and a pencil. He hummed as he made circles and dots across the bars, and tested the notes again with the keys.

I tried to be quiet going down the stairs and to a wide chair, soft with pillows and a lace coverlet.

He didn't acknowledge me, too engrossed in his work. I let my gaze drift over the parlor with all its instruments and echoing music. No silk walls down here. Fabric absorbed sound. I'd read that in one of his books.

Shelves sectioned off the kitchen, though few actually held books. They were filled with bone flutes, something made of osprey feathers and pronghorn antlers, and wooden boxes of various shapes. It was hard to tell in the wan light, but I thought I detected etchings of animals in the wood, like at the cabin.

There were few doors in the house—nothing between the parlor and kitchen—which probably meant that only bed-rooms and washrooms were private. Sam probably never needed to worry about strangers wandering through his house.

Light had faded. I'd fallen asleep, and a heavier blanket was tucked up under my chin.

Sam wasn't at his piano; the silence must have awakened

me. Water gurgled through pipes, stopped. New silence, deeper like snow silence. In the dim parlor, I listened for his footfalls, creaks in the ceiling, but either this house was much sturdier than Purple Rose Cottage—that was very likely—or he wasn't moving around upstairs. Perhaps he'd decided on a bath, as I had.

I blinked away imaginings of him reclining in the tub, long limbs stretched out, and water in his hair.

No, no, no. I pushed myself off the chair, muscles groaning, and tapped a lamp by the piano. Pearlescent light illuminated the ivory and ebony, and the thick paper with music written as dots and dashes and other indecipherable things. I settled on the bench, blanket tight around my shoulders, and studied the pages.

"Figure it out?" Apparently Sam wasn't happy if he wasn't sneaking up on me. How unfulfilling his hundred previous lives must have been.

"Maybe." I scooted over to give him space, then pointed at the first sheet. "So far I've been thinking about the dots here."

He nodded. "That's a good start."

"They're the thing that seems consistent throughout, like the notes in the music. They go up and down like the music, too, so I was guessing they tell you which key to press."

"And how long to hold it." He laughed and shook his head, like he couldn't believe I might be smarter than a squirrel who'd learned how to steal food without setting off the trap. "If I'd left you down here for an hour, you'd have been playing it yourself."

I clenched my jaw and slid off the bench. Just when I'd thought we were getting along.

"What?" He had the nerve to sound confused.

"You keep patronizing me." I faced away from him and crossed my arms. "You keep saying things like that, acting like I should appreciate your praise because you're so much better than me. After all, you're not new and trying to catch up to everyone else—"

"Ana." His voice was so soft I almost didn't hear. "That isn't it. Not at all."

"Then what?" My jaw hurt, along with my chest and head, and I was tired from the long trek, and tired from trying to guard myself.

"I wasn't patronizing you. I meant everything I said."

"You laughed at me."

"At myself, for not realizing how serious you'd been when you said you taught yourself to read. Because you were on the verge of reading music a moment ago, and you'd only been at it, what, five minutes?"

I couldn't speak around the knot in my throat.

"Ana," he whispered. "I'll never lie to you."

And how was I supposed to know he wasn't lying now? About that? Maybe watching me was like watching a newborn kitten, blind and mewing for help, food, and love. Cute, but helpless. Little victories like finding its mother's milk got praises. Little victories like figuring out which markings were musical notes got praises.

"A long time ago, before the Council, before we realized we were going to keep being reborn no matter what happened, there was a war. We fought each other, thousands against thousands." Suddenly he sounded old, as if the millennia weighed down his words. "I didn't have much of a stake in the war, and I didn't want to fight. I stayed away most of the time, but I had friends on the battlefield. While I was experimenting with different sounds one day, I realized that a string stretched on a curved stick made a pleasant twang, and different lengths made different notes. If you used a bunch of them together, it would make music. I rushed to show my friends what I'd discovered, thinking they could use a respite from the war."

Wordlessly, I sat on the corner of the bench again, but still couldn't bring myself to look at him.

"They were so pleased, and since archery had just been discovered, there were a lot of strings on curved sticks to go around. But when they thought I was out of earshot, I heard everyone start laughing and plucking the strings on their bows in a tune. They'd been practicing it for weeks already."

I let my hands fall to my lap. "It's not the same thing." My words didn't come out as fierce as I'd intended.

"Certainly not in this case, because I truly am impressed. But I imagine growing up was like that. Discovering how to read, only for someone to laugh because they'd known how to do it for thousands of years. Realizing more efficient ways to do chores, only to discover someone else had always done it the easy way and decided not to tell you."

"Assuming something has gone horribly wrong, even when it's normal and no one had told me. And—" I shook my head. Past lives or no, I didn't want to talk to *him* about my first menstruation, or pimple, or anything.

"Being laughed at." He played a few notes on the piano and hmmed. "Did you have friends?"

"I've read about them, but I don't believe they exist."

"Your cynicism is amazing."

"Even if other children had visited Purple Rose Cottage, children aren't like me. They wouldn't have wanted to do the things I did. They were waiting until they were big enough to survive on their own to get back to their lives. Not explore the forest and collect shiny rocks, or read books about great discoveries and accomplishments. They were *there*. We'd have had nothing in common."

"I think you and I are friends."

"Nosouls don't get friends. Neither do butterflies. Don't you know?"

"So all our time together in the cabin was nothing to you?"

I remembered listening to him read aloud, telling him

about the roses I'd brought back to life, and falling asleep leaning against his shoulder. "It was everything," I whispered, half hoping he didn't hear.

Four notes sounded on the piano. "I saw how you looked at this earlier, and just a while ago you got up to study the pages. On your own. Because you like it."

I shrugged. "That doesn't mean we're friends."

"It gives us somewhere to start." Four notes filled the silence again. "In my experience, friendship happens naturally. By talking, doing things together, learning." He didn't give me time to ask what he could possibly learn from me. "I like your company, which is fortunate since you're living here now. Friendship isn't reserved for people who've been reincarnated over and over. Even a newsoul is allowed happiness."

There were still so many questions, like why should he bother with a nosoul and why was this so important to him, but I just bowed my head. "If you think it's worth it, we can try."

Sam touched my shoulder, ran his hand down to my elbow. "Let's go to bed. Tomorrow will be busy."

I shivered with the memory of waking up after nearly drowning, his body behind mine, his hand over my heart. That probably wasn't what he meant by 'go to bed.' And good thing, too. Good thing.

"Play for me again, first." Something was wrong with me,

with the way my insides squeezed up when he was near. I turned straight on the bench, next to him, and rested my hand over the keys. "Please."

"Of course." He adjusted the pages on the shelf above the keyboard; there were several still empty. "Pay attention, though. You're going to learn music. I hope you're okay with that."

It was probably the light, or weariness, but even though his voice was as level as ever, from the corner of my eye, he looked nervous. My retort died before it left my tongue. "Please," I said again, and before he could tilt his face away, I saw his relief.

As the music came, I tried to match the sounds to the dots and bars on the paper, but it went by too quickly for me to keep up. Over the music, he said, "Second page," and then after a while, "Third page," and I heard the music match what I saw for a moment before the dots were just dots again.

Music overwhelmed me, soaked into my skin like water. I didn't have words for the squiggles and dashes across the pages, or the way his fingers stretched across the keys to make my heart race. If I could hear only one thing for the rest of my life, this was what I wanted.

He let his hands rest on the keys as the music faded from the room.

"You changed it. It's not the same as before." I caught his raised eyebrow and fought for the right words. I *did* need lessons, if I wanted to sound even halfway knowledgeable. Or at least describe what he'd done to the music. "It's softer. Not as angry at the end."

"Is it all right?"

I laid my hand across his.

10
IMPULSE

SAM WALKED ME back upstairs as sleepiness threatened to engulf me.

The exterior wall made me uneasy, so he dragged the bed across the room until it rested in the corner of two interior walls. Then I climbed up while Sam tried—unsuccessfully—to hide dust on the floor where the bed had been.

"The first thing I want you to learn about music is that you have to hear everything." He sat in a chair at the desk, while I perched on the corner of my bed. "This is something I started doing every lifetime to retrain myself. Close your eyes and listen to all the sounds at once, especially those that are hard to hear."

Like I was going to do that in front of him. I just nodded.

"You can hear the cavies and chickens, the noises they make. You can hear the wind in the trees, and everything in the house. Pay attention to each sound all at once, and one at a time."

"That *sounds* like a lot of work."

He grinned. "Well, it is. But having a good ear is an important part of music, and it's easiest to train yourself while you're young." He crossed the room toward me. "I've always enjoyed how everything is slightly different in every life. Raspier or deeper, warmer or kinder. Some bodies were harder to train. Some had better hearing."

I hoped I got to experience that.

"Once, I wasn't able to hear at all."

But I didn't want that. I almost asked how he'd coped—a lifetime without music—but he yawned, reminding me he was probably tired, too. I slipped under the covers.

"Good night," he murmured as my eyes fell closed. He leaned toward me, so near I could feel the warmth of his breath on my skin, and I waited for whatever came next.

Nothing did.

He sighed and left the room, and I lay there, suddenly too awake to sleep. There was no reason for me to imagine him kissing my forehead, or remember the way he'd touched my arm by the piano. He was Sam.

That was it. He was *Dossam.* Of course I was going to think about stupid things now.

I lay in bed and listened to him move about the house, and after a while, he paused outside my bedroom. His silhouette darkened the silk wall for a moment before he padded down the stairs, almost silently, and the front door shut. Locked.

I sat up and glanced toward my window, but it faced the wrong direction. We'd been walking all day. *I* sure didn't want to go anywhere, though I was awfully tempted to sneak after him. I'd need a flashlight; he'd spot me and be angry.

It was after midnight when he returned, muttering something—I strained my ears—about wasting time with genealogies. I didn't know much about those because Cris's old books weren't explicit, and Li hadn't bothered answering my questions. I did know that genealogies were the best-kept books in the library, because they needed to be referenced so often. The Council was careful about approving who could have children—something about genetic defects and constant danger of inbreeding. Bleh. Not something I cared to learn about.

None of that explained why Sam had gone to the library in the middle of the night. If that was where he'd gone. Maybe he'd forgotten who his parents were this life, and just needed to look it up. I couldn't imagine trying to keep track.

Swimming in thoughts, I drifted into unrestful sleep, though it was my first night in a real bed in a week—and my first night ever in a bed that had been repaired in the last hundred years. I should have tried to enjoy it, but I could only think about all the strange things that had happened since arriving in Heart—and about Sam.

In the morning, getting dressed took some work. Sam must have been taller than me as a woman, and bustier. A dress that probably fallen knee-length on him came to mid-calf on me. Using a small sewing kit in the desk, I adjusted the shoulders and took in places to account for my smaller endowments.

Clean clothes and a bath had done wonders. Nevertheless, my bones felt as if they creaked when I tiptoed downstairs and started a pot of coffee.

Sam's kitchen was big—well, small compared to the parlor—with spacious stone counters along one side, and a rosewood table on the other. Though everything still had a delicate appearance, it was probably hundreds of years old, and very sturdy.

The back door revealed several outbuildings for cavies and chickens, a small greenhouse, and storage sheds. Sunrise here was . . . different. The sky lit up first, along with the treetops, and it seemed forever before the rays slanted over the wall. More watery, less honey golden. Another something-not-quite-right about Heart.

If Sam hadn't gasped, I wouldn't have heard him in the kitchen doorway behind me. I spun to see him staring, like he hadn't expected to find me still here. Or— It was hard to tell. I still couldn't interpret his expressions well.

"What?" I pretended I'd assumed something different entirely. "Surprised I know how to make coffee? I watched you do it enough."

That seemed to snap him out of the stupor. "Not at all." He shuffled toward the coffeepot, rubbing his cheek. His skin was smooth now, newly shaven, and it made him appear younger. "The light caught your hair. It looked red, like flame."

That was a weird thing for him to say, and not necessarily good or bad. Why couldn't he just speak in ways I'd understand?

I shut the door and leaned against it while he poured coffee for both of us, adding generous spoonfuls of honey. Then he handed a mug to me as if we did this every morning.

But in reality, all our mornings—until we began the walk to Heart—had been him feeding me and helping me wash.

I'd told him about my infatuation with Dossam. With him.

I gulped down coffee, hoping if he noticed my cheeks were red, he'd assume it was my drink. All the times he helped me clean up, take care of embarrassing things—and there I'd been hoping he would kiss my forehead last night.

I thudded onto the nearest chair. Sam followed, only the length of the table between us. He kept his face down, but I could half see him watching me through dark strands of hair. When he noticed that I wasn't fooled, he turned his gaze out the window so light poured across his skin.

I wanted to ask where he'd gone last night. Instead, my words came out, "You look pensive," like my mouth was saving me at the last second. If he'd been sneaking, I wasn't supposed to know.

His scowl deepened. "How can you tell?"

"You get a wrinkle. Right here." I dragged my forefinger between my eyes. "If you keep at it, your face will stick that way." I pressed my hands over my mouth, a traitor after all. "Guess wrinkles don't matter to you."

He sipped his coffee.

"And now you're thinking too hard about how to respond to my stupidity. Have to be polite, don't you?"

"You're really aggressive this morning. Coffee makes you mean." He leaned back in his chair, wood creaking as his weight shifted. "Or did I do something offensive?"

"No, I'm just annoyed." I stood and crossed my arms. "I said something stupid, and you didn't even react. You don't care. You're too calm, even when you should be mad or happy."

Sam lifted an eyebrow. "Too calm?"

"Yes!" I stalked around the kitchen, looking everywhere but at him; he'd only make it worse. "When something happens, you sit back and ponder it. You don't act."

"Eventually I do." His tone shifted, lightened like he enjoyed taunting me. "So you don't think you're just impulsive?"

I halted, glared. "Impulsive?"

"You know the word, don't you?"

"Yes." He really thought I was stupid, didn't he?

"It's just," he went on as if I hadn't spoken, "you're so young and sometimes I forget what you do and don't know."

My chest hurt, like he'd hit me square against the heart.

I spun and marched toward the back door. Sam lurched to his feet and caught my wrist, my waist, and even though his grip was gentle, I didn't have the energy to wrestle away.

"See? Impulsive." He smiled and didn't loosen his hold. "But I didn't mean to push so hard."

I bit my lip, trying to catch up. Always trying to catch up. "So you didn't mean that?"

"Oh, I absolutely did. But not," he added as I drew back, "the part about you knowing words. I only meant the impulsive part."

"I'm a passionate person, that's all."

His mouth turned up in a sly smile.

"If I only get one life, I don't want to waste it by hesitating." I stepped away from him, and his hands slid off my hips. "After all, Sam, when was the last time you gave in to your passions?"

"Every time I play music or write a new melody."

"What about the last time you did something that scared you?" I shook my head. "I mean, not rescuing drowning girls or saving them from sylph. Something else. Something actually scary."

He wore the thinking line again, long enough to make me wonder about all the secrets he wouldn't tell me. The secrets were his real fears, and whatever he said next would be to humor me.

"Last night," he whispered. "When you saw everything in the parlor and I played for you."

As if someone like him got nervous about playing music for a nosoul. "You already knew how I felt about music. What about something you didn't know you were perfect at, or how it would be received?" I stepped close to him, so close my neck hurt from keeping his gaze, and so close I could feel heat from his body. "When was the last time you were impulsive, Sam?"

I willed him to know what I wanted, focused so hard on it that for a moment I believed he was already kissing me. I didn't care where he'd been last night, or that he'd pulled back from kissing my forehead. If he kissed me now . . . He hadn't told me he was Dossam until he could show me properly. This could be like that, if he felt anything for me. His expression was something I imagined mirrored mine.

For that moment, standing so close I could practically hear his heartbeat, I wanted nothing as much as I wanted him to kiss me.

The light shifted, and so did something in his eyes. Decision. One that made him lean away from me, and lower his gaze.

"Sam?" I turned away as my vision blurred. "You think too much."

"I know."

11
DANCE

WE STOOD IN the middle of the kitchen without speaking for what seemed like eons. The stinging in my eyes kept me staring at the coffee cups on the table, steam rising, and he probably knew it. If he'd had any decency, he'd excuse himself to use the washroom or something, give me a chance to beat my embarrassment into submission.

I'd thought— Well, with the way he'd touched my arm last night, I'd thought this was my chance to find out whether he saw me as more than a butterfly.

Maybe I already had.

The front door opened and closed, and footsteps sounded through the parlor. Quickly, I chafed my fingertips under my eyes. Stupid tears. Stupid Sam. I could still feel echoes of his hands on my hips.

"Dossam?" A melodic, feminine voice came from the parlor, and she stopped in the doorway. Tall, slim, with perfect blond hair that framed her suntanned face. An ankle-length dress clung to her curves, making me extra aware of how my dress didn't fit me right in the bust and waist. "I'd heard you came back early, and with a friend." Her smile glanced off me and hit Sam as she sauntered into the kitchen, synthetic silk swishing around her legs.

He hugged her and kissed her cheek like nothing had just happened. Almost happened. No, actually, nothing had happened. "Stef, this is Ana."

She was older than us, with a delicate web of lines around her eyes and mouth from years of smiling. My cheeks burned from thinking about kissing him earlier, and the easy way he stood beside her now. They made a gorgeous pair.

"Hello," I managed. "I've heard a lot about you." Sam's best friend, creator of the SED and other electronics, and well-beloved troublemaker who spent a fair amount of time picking prison locks after the latest hijinks gone wrong. It might be wrong to hate Stef because she was a woman this time around, but seeing Sam embrace her like he wouldn't me—

I didn't care.

Before I could stop her, she'd wrapped her arms around

me and kissed my cheek, too. "Is something wrong, dear? You're a little red around the eyes."

"No, nothing. Just a long night." I retreated toward my coffee. The kitchen had suddenly shrunk. Stef's presence filled the room, leaving no space for anyone else.

"I bet I know." Stef glided toward the cupboard and coffeepot to help herself. "Did Sam step on your foot?"

"What?"

She winked at me. "I have *stories* to tell you, Ana. All the times he stepped on my feet? You'll either get used to Sam's gracelessness, or give up dancing altogether."

Sam echoed my question. "What are you talking about?"

"You *were* teaching her how to dance, weren't you? Isn't that why you were both standing in the middle of the kitchen while your coffee gets cold?" She took a sip from her mug, eyebrows raised. "I assumed this had something to do with Tera and Ash's rededication coming up."

"Oh, that. Right." Sam slid back into his chair with his coffee. Dark hair half covered his eyes, and he had to shake his head to clear his vision. "Just a few weeks."

Stef gave a dramatic roll of her eyes. "Yes. Which is why you were teaching Ana to dance. But clearly you were doing a terrible job. Look at her!"

They both looked at me.

I avoided Sam's eyes. "It's not his fault." It was definitely his fault, but I had to lie because I didn't actually know what kind of dancer he was. "I couldn't do it right. My feet and head aren't connected."

Stef laughed and set her coffee on the counter again. "Of course they are. You just need the right teacher. Now, what was he trying to teach you?"

As if I had the smallest clue.

"Ah, I can see Sam didn't even bother to tell you." She winked again and turned to him. "Darling, go play some music. We'll figure it out."

He took one last drink of his coffee before abandoning it. "Be careful with her hands. They're still healing."

She took my wrist so quickly I didn't have time to back away; her hands were smooth and cool, unlike mine, which felt sweaty. "So they are. Don't worry, Dossam, I'll be careful with her." And then, when Sam left the room, she leaned close and murmured, "Don't let him break your heart, sweetie. He never settles."

Before I could get more than a word out—"What?"—Sam began playing, and Stef swept me across the kitchen. For someone so lithe, she was *strong*.

"First thing," Stef said over the piano, "is to relax. You're doing this to have fun, not hurt yourself."

The song was one I'd heard a recording of in Sam's cabin, so when Stef said to step on the beat, I knew which one she meant. When she said twirl here, and demonstrated, I mimicked that too. Music filled the house, and the lightning-fast notes made me *want* to dance. I did everything Stef did, and when I did it incorrectly, she took my arms and placed them where they should be, or nudged my foot with hers.

When the first piece ended, Sam went right into the next. It was fast, too, but the beats came at different times from the first.

"Count," Stef said. "One, two, three. No four. Not on this one."

Connections snapped in my head, and when I tried to mimic her movements, my body obeyed. Hips, arms, legs. Step here, here, and here. Giddiness surged through me as we finished the dance and she called for him to do that one again.

"Do you remember it?" She grinned as the music began. "You can do this dance for any song with this beat. Simply adjust to the tempo. Ready?" She didn't wait for me to answer, just started dancing, every motion fluid but precise. Hair whipped around as I followed her, flashes of blond and red in the corners of my vision. My body remembered what to do, how to move to this song. Our dresses flared as we spun and circled each other. It was hard to be angry or jealous like this. Maybe she wasn't so bad.

When the music ended, I was sweaty and breathing hard, but smiling. Stef looked smug.

"Now what?" Sam peered in from the other room, his expression carefully blank as he watched us. "Another one?"

131

Stef glanced at me as she smoothed back her hair; she wasn't even sweating. "I think that's enough for today. I'll come back tomorrow, so clear space in the parlor, because the kitchen is no place to dance. We'll try a different one. Slower maybe. It's a dedication of souls, you know. It won't be all spinning around until you can't stand up. Ana might find someone nice to dance with."

"Hmm." Sam returned to the kitchen, still not looking at me.

I took several deep breaths before sitting again, letting the dance-induced euphoria leak out. "What's a dedication of souls?"

"Ah, leave it to Sam to forget to explain." She kept up the charade, though I was certain we all knew she getting revenge for something. For what she'd walked in on earlier? "Some people believe souls were made as matching pairs. It can take time for them to realize or grow into their roles as lovers, but eventually the matches find each other. They dedicate their souls to each other for every life. And because everyone likes a party, they rededicate every time they're reborn."

"That's really sweet." I took a drink of my cold coffee, trying to imagine loving someone so much I'd want to spend thousands of years with them.

"Yes, some people think so." She slid into the chair between Sam and me. "But the real fun of the rededication is the masquerade. See, the idea is that when you passionately love someone and feel like your souls are a matched pair, you should be able to find that soul, and love them, no matter what body they're in. We all get told who's who when they're born, of course, so when it comes time for the rededication, everyone dresses up in costume."

I nodded slowly. "Because you should be able to find your match when you can't tell who you're looking at."

"Exactly."

"You're not supposed to tell anyone what you're going as," Sam said, "especially if you're the ones dedicating. But people usually do. It's embarrassing if you end up dancing with the wrong person by the end."

"I'm sure."

"At least you don't have to wait through all the speeches if they get it wrong." Stef grinned.

"Guess what Stef's favorite part is," Sam muttered. "But there's more than just dancing and the two hunting around for their match. There's—"

"Don't spoil it for her, Dossam." Stef waved his words into nothingness. "Everyone is invited. Let her see when she gets there."

Well, I hadn't been invited into the city. The Council could say no masquerade for me, and I'd be stuck inside while everyone else went to have fun. I bit my lip. "Have either of you had a ceremony of your own?"

"No," they both said, and Stef continued, "It's very rare, and most people aren't even sure matching souls are real. But they like the party. There's always lots of food and drinks, and it's a wonderful excuse to dress up."

"You both usually go?"

"Stef dances. I play music."

I tried not to smile at the thought of Sam playing music. Like last night. "Were you going to come back from your cabin to play?"

"Depending on how much work I finished." He shrugged, speaking mostly to the window. "There are lots of recordings they could have used. But since I'm here, maybe I'll bring the big piano from the warehouse, or see if I can get Sarit, Whit, and some of the others to play with me. I know you won't." He nodded at Stef.

"Let them use the recordings." Stef drank the last of her coffee. "Dress up and dance. You might have fun."

"I don't know. Maybe. I don't like the idea of asking people to prove their eternal love for everyone else."

"Do it for Ana. Don't you want her to have fun?" There was a tone about her voice, not the same flirty teasing as before, that made me think she wasn't really asking on my behalf.

If Sam noticed, he didn't react. He studied me, and I studied my coffee cup, and after a minute he said again, "Maybe."

"Well, Ana's going to dance." Stef beamed at me. "Story

has it that when you meet your match, it's usually at a dedication, because you're not seeing what body someone is in. You're drawn to their soul. Maybe someone's been waiting for her."

"Unlikely." I forced a smile, trying to keep my tone pleasant. "It sounds like fun, but . . . just fun."

Stef pouted, and Sam chuckled and said, "Ana is the most cynical person I've ever met." Then, for an instant, things were right between us.

"But you'll go?" she asked me, and I nodded. "Do you know how to sew? Everyone's responsible for their own costumes, and you're not supposed to tell anyone what it is, but if you need help, you let me know."

"I know how to sew." I'd spent enough time altering Li's old clothes to fit me.

"Excellent. Well then, I'd better go. I'm sure you have a lot to do today. I heard about the incident in the guard station yesterday."

"Yes," Sam said, checking the time, "we need to take care of a few things at the Councilhouse."

I stood, happy to have an excuse to go away. "I'd better change into something less sweaty." After we'd said goodbyes, and Stef promised—or threatened—to see me tomorrow for another dance lesson, I headed upstairs and stopped on the balcony when I heard Sam's low voice.

"You don't even know what happened."

135

"I don't have to know the details when I recognize that look. I've seen it enough times."

"That's unfair." His shoulders were slumped when I stretched to peer over the balcony rail, and I almost felt bad for him. Stef had to be the most formidable person I'd ever met, besides Li. "They made me her guardian. Neither of us wanted that, but there's so much going on—"

"Figure it out, Dossam. I don't want to see her like that again." She squeezed his arm and left.

12
FRIENDS

SAM WAS QUIET when we left the house, probably still smarting from Stef's jabs. There had to be something I could say to make him smile again. Not that I wanted to pretend nothing had happened in the kitchen, but aside from a tentative alliance with Stef, Sam was my only friend. I needed him.

The day was beginning to warm, but I was grateful for the sweater I'd found in my room; I pulled the sleeves over my hands to keep them from becoming chilled.

"Cold?" At least he wasn't running this time.

"Not anymore." We turned off the walkway and onto the street.

The city was a mess of roads and intersections, all wide

and friendly, except there were no signs, no way for a stranger to tell where she was.

"There should be a faster way to get around," I muttered. "I know there are vehicles somewhere. I saw them on one of Corin's lists in the guard station."

"We used to drive, but the reek of exhaust was unbelievable, and they tore up the roads. Maintenance was too expensive and annoying, and some people"—he coughed—"gained an unsightly amount of weight."

I couldn't imagine Sam anything other than tall and slender and young. "Vehicles couldn't have been the only reason."

"No, but they didn't help. Eventually the Council decided to put them in storage. People too old or ill to walk can use them. People with children too young to make long trips were also allowed."

Which meant Li had taken one when she fled the city in shame. "And there I was thinking I had never been in one."

"May you never have to again. May you always be strong and healthy." He took us down more streets, pausing to explain who lived where and how far from the Councilhouse we were. "Of course," he said, motioning upward, "if you're ever lost, you can find your way to the temple by cutting through yards. I don't advise that if you can avoid it. There are few fences, but people appreciate privacy."

138

I stopped in the middle of the street and tilted my head back, fists still balled in the sweater sleeves. The temple disappeared into the fluffy morning clouds. "What could be in there that takes up so much space?"

"Nothing. It's empty."

I jerked my head down and searched his eyes. "You've been in there? I thought there wasn't a door."

"There isn't." The line formed between his eyes again, and two around his mouth joined it. "I just know it's empty. No one's been inside, though."

"That's weird." Like the way the white walls had heartbeats, and just looking at the temple made my stomach churn. "Don't you think there's something wrong with that?"

"I never thought about it before." He glanced upward and scowled. "Not in five thousand years."

I hated when he did that, reminded me how old he was.

We turned onto the avenue from yesterday, and Sam pointed out the different mills and factories in the industrial quarter. "The city is a circle, temple and Councilhouse in the center. Four avenues go in the cardinal directions to divide it into quarters. Southwest and northeast are residential, southeast is industrial, and northwest is agricultural. You can see the fish ponds from the market field, and the orchards beyond that, but I doubt you'd have fun exploring the grain fields."

"I might." I definitely wouldn't, but I had to keep him guessing. "If I were looking for hints about who made Heart, that's where I'd start."

"Historians did start there, and found a few skeletons and artifacts, but no one has been able to tell where they came from." He gave that funny half smile he did when I said things he didn't expect. "Why do you think about the past so much?"

I shrugged. "Because I wasn't there."

He shook his head and chuckled, then hastened to explain. "Not laughing at you. I just— I think you're amazing."

Sarcasm escaped before I could contain it. "Earlier you thought I was impulsive." That wasn't wise. He should have added reckless and stupid to the list.

He stopped walking. "Ana."

I wanted to ignore him, but his strained tone didn't bode well for future friendship. "Sam." I kept my voice low so it wouldn't carry; there were people nearby, looking at us. "I shouldn't have said that."

Thinking too much again. He wore a distant look while I held my breath, then came back. "You have every right to be upset. What happened earlier—"

"Nothing happened," I said quickly. Before it could become awkward. Before he apologized for not feeling whatever it was I thought I felt.

There was no need to apologize for the absence of those

feelings, and I knew he liked me enough. He'd taken care of me when I couldn't do it; he'd taken me into his home when I didn't have one. He wrote a song for me. Dossam, the one person I'd always wanted to meet. Of course I felt— Well, of course I thought I felt something for my hero who turned out to be a good man, too. I shouldn't have expected anything else.

"Nothing happened," I whispered again. Saying it, deciding it, made the pain less.

His lips parted, and he looked unsure. It seemed he might argue, but instead he gave a small nod. "Okay. That's probably best."

I exhaled and adjusted my hands in my sleeves. "So do you think they'll let me use the library?" We started walking again. The tension between us hadn't quite dissipated, but it was easier.

"By their own order, they have to let you. How else are you going to learn everything they require?"

"What about all the things I want to learn that they won't approve of?" Like what happened to Ciana, where did I come from, and, if there were more unborn souls out there, why *me*? How did I get to be born? Luck? Or was I supposed to have been born five thousand years ago with everyone else, and just got stuck along the way? That sounded like something that would happen to me. "In order to find out what happened, I'm going to have to figure out why everyone is reincarnated. I doubt they'll like me looking into that."

"Trust me. You'll have access to everything you need. Even if they move things from the library, I'll find them for you. Somehow. Everything was digitally archived two or three generations ago. Convenience, they said." He rolled his eyes. "I might be able to remember how to fetch the information, but Whit or Orrin definitely can. They're the library archivists."

My hand floated over his for a moment while we walked, but I withdrew it before he—or anyone else—noticed. "I'm glad you were the one to find me, Sam," I said instead. "I could have done a lot worse."

"I'm glad, too." The look he gave me was—fondness?

It was too confusing, trying to figure out what he really thought of me. Maybe when we were done here, he'd play the piano for me again. I knew how to handle that, at least.

"What's going on up there?" I motioned toward the crowd of people around the temple and another large building beneath it. People milled around, chatted with one another, drank from paper cups, though I couldn't tell where they'd gotten them. The perfume of fresh bread and coffee drifted toward us.

"This is the market field," Sam said as we approached a cobblestone expanse that surrounded the temple. "Once a month there's a market where you can buy most anything you need."

I'd never seen so many people in my life; they were so noisy, all shouting and laughing. "And it's happening now?"

Sam edged closer to me, like I needed his protection. "No, this is just the morning crowd. It's the best social spot, and if you're too lazy to cook your own breakfast, Armande almost always has a stall open."

I paused as a pair of children raced by, heedless of anyone they might crash into. "Are you sure this isn't the market?"

He led me around a cluster of tables and benches, away from a handful of people staring at me like I had four heads. "This is only a fraction of the population. Market day will be packed."

"All my life it's been just Li and me." And the occasional visitor, but they'd only come to see Li. "I guess I didn't realize— There are so many people." And so *loud*. All the laughing, singing, gossiping.

Sam pressed his hand on the small of my back, guiding me toward a collapsible stall that held glass-covered trays of food. "Let me know if it's too overwhelming."

"I'm fine." My words felt stiff, though. Every time we walked past a group of people, they looked at me. News about the nosoul's arrival had spread quickly.

"Who's next, do you think?" a woman not-quite-muttered to the man sitting next to her. "First Ciana. Anyone could be replaced next."

I reminded myself I'd had nothing to do with my birth. I'd

had nothing to do with Ciana's disappearance. That didn't stop the guilt.

"Someone said the temple went dark when Ciana died," said the man. "Meuric and Deborl told everyone it was Janan punishing us, or maybe Ciana . . ."

When I glanced up to see if Sam had heard the discussion, he wore a dark glare aimed at the couple. "Ignore them, Ana," he said.

At this rate, I would have to ignore everyone in the world. All the million souls of Heart. "Everybody hates me."

"They won't." He smiled at me, that warmth again. Fondness. *He* didn't hate me, though I had no clue why. "Just try to smile a lot. Look pleasant."

"Hmph."

"Here, I know what will help." He checked his SED. "We have a little time before they're expecting us."

We approached the baker's stall, and Sam bought cups of hot apple cider to warm our cold hands, and a pastry for us to share. I did smile then.

"This is Armande," he said, introducing the baker. "He's my father this time around. He's also the best baker in Heart."

While Armande told me about his kitchen, how early he woke to get muffins and pies ready for the day, I studied his features. He had the same wide-set eyes and black hair as Sam. Same build. Interesting. I didn't look much like Li. Maybe I looked like Menehem.

144

Sitting on a bench near the pastry stall, I tore off a piece of flaky bread with honey drizzled on top. It melted on my tongue, and I shivered. "I've never eaten anything this good in my entire life."

Armande grinned and hugged me, and didn't seem to notice when I stiffened and nearly spilled my cider. Sam reached over as if to steady my cup while Armande disengaged himself. "I didn't mean to startle you," said the baker.

"We're just very careful with her hands." Sam drew back, meeting my eyes briefly. "She burned them trapping a sylph that had me cornered. If I'm going to get her on the piano, she'll need those fingers."

Armande's eyebrows rose, and he gave us a muffin. "Then I owe you. I'd been intending to take singing lessons soon, and I can't get them from Sam if he's dead. Do you bake, Ana?"

"Maybe?"

He filled my cider cup again. "Come by and I'll show you a few things. I tried to teach Sam, but he just eats the batter."

Sam gave an exaggerated sigh. "I was five and storing up for a growth spurt. You were practically starving me by making me wait for things to bake."

Armande grinned widely.

When we'd finished breakfast and dropped our cups in the bin for recycling, Sam and I headed around the temple to an enormous white building set beneath it. A half-moon stair led up to a wide landing and a series of double doors, which were guarded by columns, crumbling statues, and iron trellises threaded with thorny vines. Roses, perhaps.

"Is that the Councilhouse?"

Sam nodded. "Most of the exterior is like houses or the city wall. It was here when we arrived. But other things, like the columns and relief along the top"—he pointed upward—"we built."

When I'd touched the wall the day before, the stone had been frictionless. I doubted anyone could hammer a nail through it. "How did you get the extra rock to stay up there?" In the morning light, I could just see the seam where the Councilhouse shell met marble.

"Oh, by we, I mean people with better engineering skills than myself. If you really want to know, we can find out."

"Yes, please." I wanted to know how to do *everything*. As we rounded a crowd standing around a pair playing some kind of game, I edged closer to Sam. No telling if they hated me, too. Armande had been nice, though. "By the way, are you going to tell everyone that horribly inaccurate story about the sylph?"

"It isn't inaccurate, and people need to know *something* about you. So far they'll only have heard whatever Li says, and anything Corin and the Councilors you met yesterday reported."

"Not good things, I'm sure." I sighed.

"Perhaps, but that's exactly why they need to hear this very accurate story. And why you need to get back to smiling. I can't imagine what you're feeling, meeting everyone who already knows who you are, but you need to make a good impression."

Overwhelmed ought to cover it. "I understand."

"After this, we'll go home, unpack, and relax."

"I've never had a home before." That must have been all the sweets talking; I'd never have told him otherwise. "I mean, staying with Li, I never felt like I belonged. That's all."

Sam touched my wrist, making me shiver. "You always have a home with me."

Before I could respond, a group of people stopped us on the stairs, and Sam introduced me.

Things like, "Ana is my student," were uttered, along with, "We'd like to visit the rice fields when it's time for planting." We also made dates to visit the apiary, pottery and woodworkers' buildings, and textile factories.

A black-haired girl, maybe a couple years older than me, wrapped her arms around my shoulders and squeezed. "I'm so glad you've decided to come to Heart at last," she said. "Let me know if you need anything at all. I'm only a ten-minute walk from Sam's, and I promise the bees won't bother you."

I barely had time to thank her before Sam insisted we

were running out of time. When we were out of earshot, I said, "That was Sarit, right? The hugging girl with bees?"

"Yep. Every time you add honey to your coffee, you have Sarit to thank."

"I like her better than most of the other people we've run into."

Sam flashed a grin at me. "I thought you would."

"Honestly, though, I'm a little nervous about meeting anyone else." I followed him around one of the immense columns guarding the landing at the top of the staircase. "We could end up scooping manure from horse stalls."

"And pig runs."

"At least you'll have to suffer with me."

"You'll actually be suffering by yourself. Since I've already paid my dues on that, I'll supervise. From afar, and with some kind of nose and mouth protection when I must endure your presence afterward. But the rest of it, sure. We'll do it together. You might even find something you enjoy." He looked . . . wistful.

"Dossam!" A girl who looked like she was barely out of her first quindec launched herself at Sam, and they embraced. "You're back, just in time for the rededication. Will you be playing after all?"

Sam glanced at me. "I haven't decided yet. Stef is bullying me into dancing. Ana and I have lessons with her every morning now."

The girl finally noticed my presence. "You're Ana?" She didn't give me time to nod. "I hope you're planning on dancing at my rededication. Maybe you can convince Sam not to hide behind his piano the entire time, too. We can use recordings."

I smiled, per Sam's advice, and the girl seemed pleased.

"Well, I have to run. I was just confirming the ceremony details, but I need to get back to Tera now. She's not feeling well."

"I hope she recovers," I called, but the girl—Ash, presumably—was already halfway down the great staircase. She waved and vanished into the crowd.

At last, Sam hauled open a door for me, and I ducked under his arm. The entrance hall was cool and quiet, save the echoes of footfalls and voices beyond heavy doors. I resisted the urge to drop from exhaustion right there. The number of people— Well, maybe I'd get used to it.

"You were great." Sam motioned me down the hall. "Now they'll remember that they like you—"

"Or they like you and you don't seem to mind me."

"—and they'll tell everyone great things about you. Especially Armande. I think he'd do anything for you."

"You just introduced me to people you knew would feel that way. Did you take lessons from all of them, too?" Maybe I'd get to hear embarrassing-for-Sam stories to help restore my dignity. *Surely* Armande would have some.

Sam's mouth turned up in the corner, always the same one. Soon, he'd have a line there to match the one between his eyes. "I can't sneak anything past you."

Not for lack of trying.

I couldn't forget him creeping from the house last night.

13

FACES

"ALL THIS SPACE for the Council?" I asked, trying to keep up with Sam's long strides.

"Oh, no." He slowed his pace. "The library is here, as well as the prison and hospital. Grand reception rooms, a concert hall—which you must see later—and entire chambers devoted to preserving artifacts the Council and archivists deem important enough to keep on display."

"I wish I could look at everything now." Oil paintings of faraway places lined the walls. Lush jungles with flowers of every color, rivers with otters playing, and deserts with enormous cacti and forever-stretches of sand. "And I wish I could see all this for real."

"There's no reason you can't." He motioned me around a

statue-guarded corner. "After you've completed your training, we can go anywhere you want."

I liked that he said *we*. I couldn't imagine exploring by myself. While I'd seen maps of Range, I didn't even know where oceans were. I didn't know anything about what was beyond, except that it was dangerous. People had been exploring for thousands of years; sometimes they died, but they could tell everyone about it when they were reborn.

"Have you been everywhere?"

He shook his head and stopped in front of wide double doors with intricate carvings—maps of Heart, it looked like. "The Council is in here," he said, voice low. He reached as though to touch my face, but hesitated. "You've got a strand of hair." His hand dropped to his side without doing anything.

Cheeks hot, I gathered my hair into a ponytail—out of my face—and combed a tangle out. "How's that?" I smoothed my dress.

"Beautiful."

Not "better" or "needs more work," like I'd expected. Before I could summon a response, he pulled open one of the doors and ushered me inside a tall chamber as big as the first floor of his house. Statues stood against the walls like guards—and some like guardians—and fraying tapestries hung behind them. Fading images of animals and geothermal features surrounded us.

152

All ten Councilors were present. They sat on one side of a long table carved of a dozen kinds of wood, with precious metals inlaid in elaborate, flowing patterns. In addition to the Councilors, a man at a desk sat in one corner of the room, tapping on something that might have been a bigger version of an SED.

Meuric rose from the center of the line of Councilors and said, "Dossam. Ana. Welcome." The others nodded their greetings, and Sine smiled warmly at me. "Please sit, both of you."

Sam pulled out a chair and motioned for me to sit first. I kept my hands in my lap where the Councilors couldn't see me fidget. They appeared to be of various ages, but they all had that air about them, the same depth in their eyes that Sam had no matter how *eighteen* he looked.

"We're here to discuss the terms of Ana's stay in Heart, and the requirements she must fulfill in order to remain Dossam's student and guest. In the event neither Dossam nor Ana wish to comply with the Council's requests, other suitable arrangements will be made." Something in the way Meuric said that made me think the arrangements wouldn't be suitable to me. "This is a closed session for now, but the records will be public within the month."

The announcement hung on the air like a warning. The terms of my stay. Other arrangements. Ugh. I liked Meuric least of all the Councilors, but he was the Speaker. The leader. If he didn't like me, the others might not either.

From what Sam had explained, Councilors queued up to serve when there was an opening—which only happened when one died—and served the rest of that life. Meuric signed up every lifetime. His constant association with the Council probably made him the most powerful person in Heart.

Sam had also said Meuric believed in Janan. Why would anyone believe in something so fiercely, without any proof?

"So, Ana." Meuric's tone shifted. Kinder, maybe, but I still didn't trust him, or anyone on the Council. They'd voted to keep me out of Heart. "What do you think of Heart so far?"

"It's lovely." My throat itched from nerves, and I wished we'd brought water. But then I'd probably drink it all at once and have to pee for the rest of the meeting. "Very big."

Sam took the chair beside me and nudged my leg. I couldn't interpret what he wanted, so I ignored it. He probably didn't want me to mention the thing with the walls and temple. Not that I'd been about to.

"We haven't had much time to look around yet," Sam said, leaning toward the table, "but we're already planning piano lessons, and Stef has offered her services as well."

Oh, right. I tried to appear pleasant, like he'd suggested. "This morning we made appointments with a bunch of people. Armande is going to teach me how to bake next week."

"That's wonderful. You should come visit me, too. If

you're studying music with Sam, you might enjoy poetry also." Sine spread her hands on the table. Wrinkles and veins crisscrossed her flesh; she looked so old and fragile.

My eyes were liars. In truth, Sine and Sam were the same age.

That thought made my head hurt, but I managed to nod when Sam tapped my foot with his. "Sounds great," I gasped. "Thank you."

I couldn't imagine Sam any way other than how he was now, no matter how hard I tried. None of the books I'd seen had sketches or photos of him, and the video I'd seen had mostly been his back. And blurry, besides. Would I recognize him if I saw a clear photograph?

Stef's description of the dedication ceremony made me shiver again. How could anyone continue like that, risking not recognizing the person they loved? How could they look in the mirror and recognize themselves? I looked like me. Sam looked like Sam.

I was wearing a dress Sam had worn in another life. And his sweater.

Someone across the table leaned over and muttered to her neighbor. Both eyed me like they thought I might vomit.

"Ana, are you okay?" Sam touched my shoulder.

I blinked. Nodded. He was counting on me. "Sorry."

"This has been a big transition for her," he explained to the Council. "We've been here less than a day and already people are gossiping about her."

"Of course." Sine smiled, like she had any clue what I was going through, but the other Councilors all looked at me queerly.

One by one, they introduced themselves; I'd heard of most of them before, and remembered Antha and Frase from yesterday. Deborl's name was familiar, but I didn't know much about him. Like Meuric, he looked younger than me.

I tried to focus while Sam outlined our arrangements with teachers, but I felt as though walls inside me were crumbling. Confined to Purple Rose Cottage and the surrounding forest my whole life, it had been easy to *know* that Heart was filled with people so old I couldn't comprehend. But I'd never been faced with the evidence so clearly until now. Their lives and histories were so much bigger than me.

Before meeting Sam, when he was a name in a book, I'd thought it wouldn't matter what he—she?—looked like, that I'd feel the same way no matter what. And maybe I would. But also, there was so much that was *physical* about him— hands, hair, eyes, voice, scent—that made him attractive. I'd felt something before, perhaps merely a reaction to his music or the way he wrote about it, and that was still inside me. But I craved his physical presence. *This* Sam. These hands, hair, eyes, voice, and scent. Another incarnation of Sam wouldn't be the same.

That was probably the point of the souls ceremony. Maybe the physical shouldn't matter.

I wished I could stop thinking about having seen the grave of Sam's first body. There was probably nothing in there by now. It was probably dust.

I shuddered out of my thoughts as the subject changed.

"I'd like to discuss Ana's library privileges." Sam rested his hands on the table. He didn't look ancient or decayed. When his shoe bumped mine, he felt real and alive. "If she's to have a complete education, she needs unrestricted access to the library."

"There are books someone so young shouldn't have access to," said Meuric. "I'm sure Ana is very responsible, but knowing how to build a catapult isn't a necessary skill for her."

"Learning how to build weapons isn't one of my goals."

"What is your goal, then?" Deborl asked.

I glanced at Sam, who gave a minute shrug. "I was hoping to find out where I came from." I worried I wouldn't be reborn, but I didn't want these strangers to know my secret fear. "I realize wiser minds have most likely already looked, and I doubt I'll discover anything new, but actively searching for an answer would bring a lot of comfort."

Sine nodded. "I imagine it's very lonely being the only newsoul in the entire world."

Especially when she put it like that, but I appreciated that she didn't call me a nosoul. "It is." I pretended not to notice

Sam's foot against mine. "I'd like to know what happened, to see if there's a chance it could happen again." Maybe the existence of another newsoul would make me feel less like a mistake, less alone.

Antha crossed her arms and leaned back. "The last time, we lost Ciana. I can't say I'm eager for it to happen again."

I swallowed hard. "I don't want to lose anyone, either."

"As long as it doesn't take away from her studies," Frase said, "I don't see how looking into her origins could hurt. However, I do think someone should be there to supervise her time in the library. Dossam, or someone else we can all agree on. As Meuric said, there's simply too much in the library that could be dangerous, not just to Ana, but to everyone if she isn't careful."

"I'll be careful."

"I'll accompany her as often as possible," Sam said. "She's my student."

Sine raised a hand. "When Sam can't, I will join Ana. After all, Sam has other work."

"Orrin and Whit spend half their lives in the library," said another Councilor, whose name I'd forgotten. "I think it's safe to assume there will always be someone to supervise Ana's studies."

"Does this sound reasonable to everyone?" Meuric checked everyone's faces, then gave a quick nod. "Very well. We'll also assign an SED to Ana so she can call someone if

158

one of her appointed companions isn't there. Ana, I trust we can count on you to do that."

"Of course." Probably. I trusted exactly one person not to rat on me if I did something the Council wouldn't like: myself. As wonderful as Sam had been, with everything he'd done for me, he was still one of them. He'd known them for almost a hundred lifetimes, and me less than a month. I couldn't expect his loyalties to shift that quickly.

"All right." Meuric shuffled a stack of papers. "Next on the list is a curfew."

I raised my eyebrows.

"Twenty-first hour, every night, you're expected to be at Sam's. You'll be subject to random checks. If you're not there, or late, you'll have to face the consequences."

"Which will be?" Now they were interested in making sure I was safe inside at night? Now, after I'd been eighteen years with Li, who didn't care if I slept in the forest and got eaten by wolves?

"The severity of your punishment will reflect the severity of your crime."

Being late to bed was a crime? I opened my mouth to ask, but Sam interrupted.

"Surely exceptions will be made for lessons that require Ana to be available at nighttime." Sam gave Meuric a pointed look. "Such as astronomy or observing nocturnal animals."

"Neither of those were on your list." Meuric scowled at

his papers. "But yes, if the need arises, exceptions can be made. Make sure to put in a request first. I'd hate for Ana to get in trouble needlessly."

"Monthly progress reports." Frase slid a sheet of paper across the table to Sam. "We've made a list of skills Ana should learn, in addition to those you've already scheduled. Don't feel the need to plow through everything immediately, but keep in mind we will be requiring an examination of her progress this time next year. We've also included a list of potential tutors for these subjects."

Sam glanced at the list; his arm blocked my view. "She already knows how to read."

"I figured it out several years ago," I added.

Frase made a face that might have been a smile, but all I saw was teeth. "Then she won't have a problem in this area. The Council still requires study and examination."

"Half the people on this list have been vocal about their"— Sam eyed me—"distaste for the idea of newsouls. It's unfair to make Ana study under them."

"We don't always get to work with our friends," Antha said. "Perhaps getting to know Ana will change people's minds about newsouls."

That seemed unlikely.

"It's all right, Sam." I fought to keep my voice steady. "I'll make it work."

His jaw muscles jumped, but he nodded. "Very well."

"I think that should cover everything for now." Meuric turned to me. "Do you agree to these terms?"

Afraid to ask what would happen if I didn't, I nodded.

"Then we're finished." He stood and offered me his hand to shake. When everyone had a turn—some more gentle than others with my still-healing skin—Sam and I started to leave the Council chamber.

"A word, Sam," Meuric called.

Sam nodded for me to wait outside. As soon as the door shut behind me, people began speaking in low, angry voices. The heavy wood muffled their words, but every so often Sam's deep voice came through, and he wasn't happy.

I leaned against the wall and dreaded finding out what they were talking about.

After fifteen minutes, I couldn't take listening to them anymore. I pushed off the wall and headed back the way we'd come in. Just as I was about to turn the corner, the door clicked open.

Sam scanned the hallway, and his glare stopped on me. His jaw was set, and his shoulders were tense. The line was more a crevice between his eyes as he strode toward me and loomed over my face. "Try not to wander off."

I resisted the urge to step back. "I was going to look for the library."

161

"You could have waited five minutes."

"It was more like fifteen, and you'd have known where I went."

"That's not the point." He started to walk around me, but I didn't move. "Come on."

"Why are you mad?"

He faced me, looking at me like I was the stupidest person in the world. "Were you in the same meeting I was?"

"Yes." I crossed my arms.

"No," he growled, "you weren't. You completely left us for a while. People said your name five times before you finally joined us again, and even then, you were barely there. What were you thinking? You knew how important it was to make a good impression. Next time you want to doze off, do it somewhere the Council isn't deciding whether or not you can stay in Heart."

I staggered back, and my spine hit the wall as I stared up. His face was flushed with anger and disappointment, and I couldn't think of a good defense, aside from the truth.

"You don't know what it's like." Anything louder than a whisper and my voice would shake. "You have no idea what it's like to be surrounded by people more than two hundred times your age, all judging and deciding whether or not you're *worthy* enough to live in the city they just found lying around one day. None of you can understand. I'm *alone*, Sam."

His anger cracked; pity showed through, and I almost stomped off, but he said, "You really will be alone if you're not careful, Ana." In spite of the harsh words, his tone was gentle. I wondered which was the lie.

"Threatening to give up on me already? I didn't ask you to take me in." My eyes hurt, swollen with memory of this morning, and anger and betrayal now. "I didn't ask you to do anything for me."

His throat jumped when he swallowed. "They threatened to take you away. From me."

The wall at my back blocked further retreat. "They can't."

"Li has returned to Heart."

I couldn't breathe.

"It's common knowledge that she doesn't want you, so the Council won't do anything yet. But if I can't control you—Meuric's words—they will take you away from me. If you're lucky, you'll go back with Li and continue the training we had planned. We wouldn't be allowed to see each other."

I felt faint. "And if I'm not lucky?"

"You'll be exiled, not just from Heart, but from Range." He took a long, shaking breath. "This isn't going to be easy. I never said it would. All the same, you need to try harder. I don't want to lose you."

If the wall hadn't been holding me up, I might have fallen. "I don't want to be alone."

"No one does." He closed his eyes, and the line deepened.

"I don't want you to feel alone, either. I know there isn't much I can do. I know I'm one of everyone else—"

"It's okay." I wanted to hug him, or apologize for yelling. *Something.* It wouldn't help, though, and after realizing he had more in common with Sine than me, I just— I couldn't right now. I hugged myself.

"I don't want to lose you," he whispered again.

And I didn't want to be lost, or put back with Li, or exiled where sylph and other creatures roamed. "I'll try harder."

14
RECOGNITION

THE LIBRARY HAD its own wing of the Councilhouse. If not for the conversation with Sam, I'd have been giddy when he heaved open the mahogany doors and we entered the enormous chamber.

The walls were bookcases, and every shelf was full.

There were no separate rooms for different sections, like I'd imagined, but high bookcases gave the illusion of privacy in corners or on balconies over the main floor. Solid mahogany tables dotted the empty spaces, along with delicate lamps with stained-glass shades. Tiny sparrows and squirrels glowed.

Soft rugs covered the aisles; hardwood floors peeked from

beneath the edges. I stepped over diamonds and snowflakes, inhaling the scent of leather and ink and dust.

"Maybe," I said, turning to find Sam watching me explore, "we could just move in here." The heavy air blanketed my words, even though the chamber was a dozen stories tall. "We could move the bookcases in the middle of the floor for the piano."

He made a noise that was not quite a laugh and let the door close behind him. "The acoustics are terrible, though. And where would we sleep?"

I swept my hands through the air, toward the giant cushiony chairs and sofas, blankets draped across their arms and backs. Subdued, velvety colors matched the wood all around. Everything was so cozy and sleepy; I couldn't imagine why people weren't fighting to stay here forever.

"But the acoustics," he protested.

"We'd rearrange things to help." I dropped my head back and relaxed. "Where's the section on music history? I'm sleeping there."

He gave me a look I couldn't decipher.

I cringed and turned away to hide the heat on my face. "I guess we do have that at your house, huh?"

"Let's have a tour. I'll show you where everything is so you don't get lost." He offered an arm, but I didn't take it and he let his hand drop as if he'd never tried.

"I might need a map and emergency flare." I brushed my

166

palms across a smooth leather chair, which hissed under my skin. The polished wood squeaked when I touched the desk Sam was opening.

He pulled out a pad of paper and a pen and handed them to me. "You can fold paper into a glider. Don't know anyone will see it to rescue you, though. You'll have to make your own map."

Of course.

With exaggerated pride, he motioned toward the far side of the library. "Everything on the north wall and nearby bookcases is personal diaries. On all floors. Professional diaries are kept in sections related to their studies."

I glanced up again. Twelve stories packed with nearly five thousand years of diaries for a million people. My brain hurt just thinking about it.

"Feel free to look at any of them you want. That's why people bring them here—for others to learn from." He reached for the nearest bookcase and hooked a finger on the top of a book's spine, tipping it out of its resting place. "In the beginning of every new life, people usually go back and write an end for their previous lifetime. Usually they mention how they died so others can avoid that fate." He grinned and winked, but it didn't sound funny to me. "Genealogies are on this floor—"

"Can we look at something first?" I'd rather have tried on my own, but someone had to tell me if I was right. If anyone was going to see me make an idiot of myself, it might as well be Sam.

He waited, of course saying nothing about the rude way I'd interrupted him. Li would have hit me for that.

I let the dusty peace of the library soothe me before I forced out the words. "Are there photos or videos of you? From before?"

Silence for a stuttering heartbeat, then he nodded. "Some."

My head swam. "I need to see them."

He bit his lip—first time I'd seen him do that, and I wondered if he'd picked it up from me—and gazed upward. "Will it change anything? Between us?"

I wanted to remind him there was nothing to change. *Nothing had happened* this morning. Still, it wasn't exactly true, and after all my thoughts in the Council chamber, things had already changed. It was just a matter of discovering how. "I don't know."

Sam bowed his head, then led me upstairs and around a maze of bookcases packed with stuffed photo albums and videos from various ages of technology.

We entered a secluded area where the full shelves would muffle sound. He motioned at one of the big chairs and bade me sit while he searched for memory chips and photos on the shelves. At a button click, a panel slid aside to reveal a large, blank screen. He pressed the chips into appropriate slots, and while they loaded, he placed a photo album on the desk between our chairs. An egret lamp made cheery light over the glossy cover.

He flipped through album pages and indicated a color photo of two men in their early forties, arms around each other's shoulders. They grinned at the viewer, one wider and with a hand on the brim of his hat. The other had a slier smile that turned up one corner of his mouth more than the other. He wasn't attractive; he had bad skin and limp hair, but that smile and the energy he radiated— "That's you." I pointed.

Sam—the young, handsome one—eyed me askance. "Are you sure?"

"Absolutely."

He gave a single nod. "The other is Stef. He died in an accident a week after this was taken."

As hard as it was to believe the Sam in the photograph was the same Sam sitting next to me, it was even more difficult to believe the woman I'd met this morning was also the fellow in this picture.

Sam flipped to a photo of two men and a woman playing music. A man sat at the piano, and my first instinct was to say that was Sam, but it didn't seem right. I studied them more closely, searching for something familiar.

I glanced at Sam for a hint, but he just leaned his elbow on the desk and stared at the photograph, expressionless. I wished I could tell what he was thinking.

The man at the piano definitely wasn't Sam. Something about the way he sat over it. I'd only seen Sam play a few times now, but he never possessed it. He caressed it. The other man had a flute; he wasn't playing, so his expression was easy to read. It wasn't a Sam-I-knew expression. Too . . . someone else. I turned to the woman with the violin.

She was tall, soft, and curved, wearing a wistful expression as she cradled her violin. Something about her relaxed posture and the way she looked at the piano or its player. I couldn't tell which. I touched her face. "Found you."

"Did you recognize the dress?"

I looked again. Sure enough, she was wearing the dress I'd worn this morning. She—he—filled it out better, too, and I tried not to be envious. "No, I hadn't noticed it."

The videos had long since loaded, and the screen glowed brightly, waiting for instructions. Sam obliged, and we watched a group of people chatting in the market field. The images were low quality, but the faces were clear enough. "This was shortly after we learned how to record videos. *Someone*, I won't name names, went around recording everything he could. We have years' worth of videos like this. No one watches, but no one will recycle them, either."

I might watch. But I didn't say so out loud.

It seemed we sat there for hours, watching old videos and looking through photo albums. I found him in crowds in the market field—Heart hadn't changed at all in the last three hundred years—in groups of musicians, or giving rude gestures to whoever was recording while he mucked horse stalls. I found him holding someone in a rainstorm, or being held, and leaning toward a stranger with a smile. Twice I spotted him kissing a man or woman, and my throat closed up so I just nodded that I'd seen him, and he believed me.

The screen went dark, and the stained-glass lamp was the only light in our alcove. I'd heard him sing, seen him shuffle away when someone approached with a video recorder—his friends usually grabbed his arms and made him stay—and watched him laugh until his face was red. I'd seen him old and young, skinny and fat, male and female, ugly and beautiful. None of those Sams looked like my Sam. I just knew they were him.

"Are you okay?" he whispered. Other than my thudding heart, the silence was complete.

I couldn't figure out how I was supposed to feel about this. It was like drowning, the cold and the aching lungs and heavy limbs, with things bumping you, and not being able to tell which way was up. I pulled my hands into my sleeves. His sleeves.

"No," I said, "but it doesn't matter. We have work to do." I stood up and pretended to be brave.

15
MARKET

WE MANAGED TO finish the library tour, and he showed me how to escape the wing without needing to trek through endless halls of the Councilhouse. Then, awkwardly, we made our way through everyone in the market field and went back to his house. I clutched my crude library map—and crude street map—against my chest as we walked. I went upstairs.

Everything in me hurt. For over an hour, I didn't leave my room, just sat on the soft bed and tried to sort through feelings.

Mostly, it was seeing a dozen different Sams that confused me. "He's still Sam," I told myself, the bedcovers and lace and walls. Anything that would listen and not talk back. "He is who he's always been." I'd always known he was old, had previous lives, and probably had a thousand different lovers.

It didn't matter. It couldn't.

I needed to focus on the Council threatening to take me from him. No matter what didn't matter, I couldn't let them put me back with Li. I couldn't risk being exiled.

Which meant I needed to take everything seriously, do better than they expected. Awkward or not, I needed Sam. I could take my time sorting out everything else.

I washed my face and went downstairs to find Sam on the sofa, writing in a notebook. Not words. Music? He lifted his eyes as I sat at the piano, tugging on a pair of fingerless mittens.

The keys were cool and smooth, and when I pressed down on one, a clear note resonated through the house. I closed my eyes and smiled. No wonder Sam loved this so much. Maybe this was something we could share without awkwardness.

I played a few more notes, went seeking patterns and familiar things. A series of notes almost like what Sam had played earlier sounded under my fingers, but I was doing something wrong. I played it twice again, discovering the correct rhythm as I went, but not the right note. I tried the keys around the one I knew was wrong. Nope.

"Black key." Sam's eyes were on his book, but I could feel his attention. "Then you've got it."

I wasn't surprised when it worked, only that *my hands* did

it. Stabbed by rose thorns, frozen, burned—and yet they still made music. "Will you show me the rest?"

He laid his pencil and notebook aside so quickly I wondered if he'd even been working to start with. "Nothing would make me happier."

Market day brought freezing weather, but I bundled up in one of Sam's old coats, found a hat and scarf and mittens to match, and waited for him by the door, bouncing on the balls of my feet. "Hurry!"

At last he came downstairs, dressed warmly, but without so many layers. "You look ready for a blizzard." He offered a canvas bag, which I looped over my elbow. "Everyone is going to be there. You might get hot."

"I'll remove things as necessary. Besides, this way if someone knocks me over, I have lots of padding to land on."

"You plan for that?" Cold air zipped inside as he opened the door. The sky was blue and clear beyond the skeletal trees and, except for the chill, it was the perfect day for my first market.

"I do now." I hadn't forgotten the way people had glared at me my first morning in the city, and their muttered opinions that I shouldn't be allowed to stay in Heart. I *couldn't* forget, because it happened every time we left the house.

We headed down the walkway and road, chatting about this week's song. Étude. I was supposed to remember there were different forms of music. He corrected my use of the word "song" when I used it to describe everything. Songs had words, he insisted.

As we neared South Avenue, voices, clopping hooves, and whistles drifted on a breeze. I hopped, holding my hat steady. "I can hear it!"

He laughed and waited for me to finish bouncing. "I don't think I've ever seen you this excited."

"I've been wearing someone else's clothes my whole life. Li's, whatever Cris left behind, and now yours. Having something that's my own will make it seem like—" Like I was a real person, not just the nosoul. But I didn't want him to feel bad for not magically conjuring new clothes for me.

"Race you to the avenue?" It was only a hundred feet away, and no contest if he was serious, but he was trying to keep the mood light, so I didn't wait to agree, just sprinted as fast as I could. He caught up easily but let me win.

The market came into view, shadowed under the temple and Councilhouse. Hundreds of colorful tents filled the area, cheery as a garden. The voices of thousands of people became a dull roar that grew louder as we neared. They milled around in bright colors, some with shopping bags, some with arms full of pottery, wooden whatevers, and clothes. A hundred scents assaulted my nose: cooking chicken, fresh bread, and spicier things I couldn't name.

Sam pulled out his SED. Light flashed, and I blinked away

stars. "So I can keep you like this forever." He showed me the screen, which held an image of me grinning like an idiot.

"I look dumb."

"You look adorable."

I rolled my eyes as he put the SED back in his pocket. "Later, when you're not expecting it, I'm going to take a photo of you."

"That's mean. I hate having my picture taken."

I let my tone go mocking. "I'm sure you'll look adorable."

Strains of music floated along the breeze. I twirled and performed one of the steps Stef had taught us that morning, and Sam clapped. "Nicely done."

"I like dance lessons."

"They're endurable." He smiled, and I imagined he secretly enjoyed our morning routine as much as I did. Dance, chores, and music. Always music.

"Your lessons are still my favorite," I said, earning one of his rare true smiles. After my turn on the piano, though, when he took his personal practice and I was supposed to be studying, it was really hard to focus on mathematics.

In the two weeks since we'd faced the Council—then each other in the hallway—we'd managed to find a place where our relationship was friendly and comfortable. Not like before we'd come to Heart, but we'd never be like that again. The Council's rules made sure of that.

176

Still, happiness had been foreign to me before now. I never wanted this to end.

"Sam!" Stef waved us over as we approached the outskirts of the market. She peered at me. "The clothes are walking, so I assume Ana is in there. Somewhere."

I stuck my tongue out at her as we waded into the fray. People held jewelry and clothes, jars of fruit preserves and baskets. We stopped to look at everything; Sam and Stef must have been bored silly, even when Sarit and Whit joined us, but they endured my ogling for two hours. In addition to serviceable trousers and tops, I finally chose a soft wool sweater in cream, and a deep blue skirt that went down to my ankles. I also ended up with a pair of shoes and boots, since Li's castoffs were too big. Sam's, from when he'd been a teenage girl, fit better, but they were old.

With all that and handfuls of underclothes, I felt . . . real. Special. Like when Sam first played my song. Waltz, he'd corrected.

"Where next?" Whit sipped from his bottle of water while we took a break on the northern edge of the market mayhem. The temple rose above, bright white against sapphire. I angled away from it, trying to spot the orchards in the agricultural quarter of Heart.

"Cheese. Oh, and fruit preserves. I saw some on the south end. Sam doesn't have any. He wants both of us to get scurvy."

177

I winked at him and began rolling up my scarf; as he'd warned, so many people, all young and old and in between, made the market field hot. I'd never seen such a crowd, but it was less intimidating with Sam and his friends around.

"We had a lesson with Armande last week. Ana is convinced she can bake anything."

"I can. I'm going to make tarts and you're going to like them."

Stef grinned. "If you need help putting out fires, I'm next door."

While I shot mock glares Stef's way, Sam produced his SED and embarrassed me by taking more photos. After pairing me with each of his friends for a picture, he stopped someone and asked him to take a photo of the five of us.

"I've never seen *you* take photos before." Sarit wrestled the SED from him and browsed through images. She giggled at one. "Decide it was important after all?"

My hat was suddenly fascinating while I pretended not to see Sam's glance. "For now," he said.

"You don't have one of just you and Ana." She smirked and motioned the others away from us. "Hold still, both of you. Ana, what are you doing with your hat?"

I held it against my chest with one hand and tried to work out tangles in my hair with the other. "I thought we were finished."

"Here, let me." Sam used his fingers as a comb, but before

he was done, the flash went off several times and light boxes floated in the corner of my vision. "Maybe this was a mistake." He angled his face away from Sarit as he eased my hat back over my ears. "Better?"

"Yeah." The heat and attention had probably made my cheeks bright red. Maybe there was a way to get rid of the photos before anyone saw them. Even as I thought it, Sarit took half a dozen more.

An hour later, we had coffee beans, cheese, and supplies for tarts. The crowd and noise were becoming too much, but there were a few more things I needed. Now that we'd made a full circuit of the market, I knew where to find them.

"Can we meet somewhere in half an hour?" I couldn't imagine needing more time than that. "I want to find things for my costume."

"Sure. Ask them to write a bill and we'll take care of payment later." He gave a shy smile. "I've got a few things to get, too."

"You're going to dress up?" I hated how excited I sounded, but he didn't seem to notice.

"Maybe. I should have stuff just in case." Again, he looked shy, but I didn't mention it and we decided on a meeting place with everyone else. "Call me if you need anything."

I patted the Council-issued SED in my pocket.

"Want company?" Stef asked as we started on our separate ways.

"Nope. I don't trust you not to tell Sam what I'm getting. He'll have to wait and find out when people start demanding payment."

She grinned and waved me on. "See you later, then."

I wove my way through the crowd with only my new clothes and shoes to weigh me down; Sam had taken the rest of our purchases.

Now, walking through the busy market alone, I missed his presence. It wasn't as if we spent every minute together—there were plenty of times we were on completely opposite sides of the library, him researching whatever a five-thousand-year-old teenager needed to research, while I focused on the Council's demands—but I'd gotten used to having him nearby.

I didn't like being so reliant on him. I'd have to do more things on my own, now that I knew my way around the city a little better. Well, at least I knew how to get to the Councilhouse and back.

My first stop was the jeweler's stall, where I searched the coils of wire, overwhelmed with choice.

"What are you looking for?" the seller asked.

"I need something sturdy, but soft enough that I can bend it with my hands." After imagining the finished product for a moment, I held out my arms. "About triple this much."

He rifled around and produced several options. "I

recommend this"—he jiggled one—"because it's not expensive, and you need a lot."

"That sounds perfect." Thankful he'd made the choice easy, I gazed around at the other options. Silver, gold, things I couldn't identify. "Where do you get all the metal, anyway?"

The seller began writing my bill. "Most of it washes down from the mountains, but there are a couple of drone-mined caverns around." His pencil halted over the paper, and he squinted at me. "What did you say your name was?"

I tried to make myself taller. "Ana. But make the bill to Dossam, please."

His eyes narrowed, and I resisted the urge to retreat as he finished writing. "Don't come around here again, nosoul." He shoved the paper and coil of wire at me. "Dear Janan, why are we being tested this way?"

A high voice piped up from behind me. "Sure would be a shame if people knew how rude you were to customers, Marika." A young girl, perhaps nine years old, smiled widely at me. "Have a good afternoon, Ana."

I grabbed my things and hurried away. Everyone knew me. People who hated me, people who didn't seem to care one way or another, and even people who liked me for inexplicable reasons. Like Sarit, or the girl in the jeweler's stall.

The masquerade was coming up. No one would know me then.

It didn't take me long to find Larkin, who sold dyed cloth. I mimed how much synthetic silk I wanted, and we discussed colors and prices before settling. Only then did he ask my name, but he fell into the category of people who didn't care. That was a relief.

While he folded my things and wrote a bill for Sam, I scanned the market. The crowd hadn't thinned at all. People still haggled over trinkets and shared bites of food. Children marched between stalls, behaving just like adults. I even saw an infant like that, quiet and mature as he directed his current parents to things he wanted. I must have been such a shock to the world, unable to communicate except by mindless screaming.

Armande spotted me and waved, as did a few others I had lessons with. I waved back, half wondering if Sam had sent them to keep an eye on me.

A tall figure appeared in the corner of my eye. She touched my shoulder.

"Stef, I said I—" I turned and stuttered, staggered back. "Li." She looked just as she had on my birthday, fierce and ever-annoyed by my existence. My body turned wooden.

Larkin returned from packaging my items. "Here you go, Ana." Then he was quiet, too.

"So." Li plucked the bill from Larkin's hand. "You found someone else to take care of you. Dossam has always been a fool."

182

My throat was broken. So was my tongue. I wanted to snap back and say no one *took care* of me, but didn't he?

"Nothing to say?" Li sneered and shoved the paper back at Larkin. "I suppose I should be impressed you made it here, what with your sense of direction."

"You gave me a bad compass." Part of me wished someone would step in to help. Most of me wished I could stand up to her on my own. "You nearly got me killed."

"You know to check your equipment."

"Go away." My voice was surely lost beneath the crowd's cacophony and the pounding of my heart. "You're not part of my life anymore. Leave me alone."

She pinched my chin and turned my face up. "On the contrary, I've asked the Council to return you to my care. You're my daughter, and there's so much I should teach you."

I shook my head. "You can't." I hated this, feeling pitiful, feeling unable to fight back. After everything Sam and I had talked about, and as many times as I'd called him rude names when I actually *liked* him, why couldn't I face Li? "He won't let you."

"He won't have a choice."

"The Council won't let you."

"Do you think people would coddle you as much if they realized what you really are? The beginning of more nosouls. The end of us. I doubt Sam would treat you so nicely if you'd replaced Stef. You've already replaced Ciana, though she might have been a phase for him. Like you are." She smiled and sailed off.

No telling how long I stared after her, paralyzed, but Larkin said, "Ana, your things," and I tried to thank him before I fled to the place I was supposed to meet my friends.

Friends? Earlier they'd felt like friends, but if Li was right, if the Council was right, Sam was my guardian and the others were doing him favors. I *knew* he cared about me, but still.

I dug the heels of my palms against my temples, struggling to compose myself before anyone found me.

"Ana?" Hands closed over my shoulders and I leapt backward. Sine released me, alarm on her face. "What's wrong?"

"Nothing." I hugged my bags to my chest and started south, toward Sam's house. He could meet me there. I didn't want to see anyone.

Sine kept up easily. "You looked scared out of your mind. What happened?" She was on the Council. Maybe she could help.

"It's Li." I led her away from the crowds and checked the area for Sam or the others. No one. "Please don't make me go back with her. I can't do that again." My throat ached from holding back sobs. "Please."

"Why would I make you go back?" Sine shook her head. "Tell me everything that happened. Trust me, we have no

184

plans to remove you from Sam's care. Everyone says you're doing fine."

Shivering, I told her what had happened by Larkin's stall, but even as I did, I felt stupid. Li hadn't done anything. She'd barely touched me. She'd just been herself. "I'm sorry." My head throbbed. "I shouldn't go on about it. She just rattled me." I should have kept my mouth shut.

Sine ignored my attempts to wave it off. "Li can be intimidating," she started.

Beyond her, Sam and Whit arrived at the meeting spot. Sam glanced around. Just as he saw me, raised his hand, and noticed my distress, thunder shook the sky.

The market went silent as everyone looked up. All at once. They seemed to be holding their breath.

That was weird. The sky was as clear as it had been this morning, only geyser and hot spring steam misting over the wall. The thunder came again.

"Get inside." Sine shoved me toward the southwest residential quarter. "Meuric's house is the first one on the corner. Hide in there. You'll be safe."

"What?" Before I realized, everyone was moving, shouting. Most sounded like they were giving orders, but they grew louder and more panicked with each second. People surged toward the Councilhouse, toward the residential quarters. I looked to where Sam had been, but he was already hidden behind the wall of chaos. "What's happening?"

"Go to Meuric's house." She pushed me again. "We don't know what will happen if you die. Go now."

I looked up again, but there was nothing in the sky. Everyone was panicking about thunder, but—

"Dragons," she hissed, and even she looked terrified. "Dragons are about to attack Heart."

16
ACID

THE FALSE THUNDER punctuated the din of panicked people fleeing every which way. I feigned retreat to Meuric's house while shoving my shopping bag inside my coat. But when Sine was out of sight, I zipped up and darted into the mass of people. I wouldn't have been surprised to find out all million citizens of Heart were here, not with the way I had to elbow people aside.

"Sam!" I scanned the crowd for his face, tried to remember what he'd been wearing earlier. My mind was blank, so I kept shouting his name.

The thunder grew louder, more distinct. It didn't sound like thunder anymore, but growling and whapping of leathery wings.

North, just over the city wall, I saw a deep black shape that separated into three as they drew closer. They had long, serpentine bodies with wings that stretched wide. Sunlight glittered off scales. They were sinuous and elegant, deadlier than sylph. I stared, stupidly enraptured.

People slammed into me—"Move, girl!"—and jolted me back into reality. When I ducked and tried to push against the flow of people heading toward the residential area, my breast pocket chirped. I fumbled for the SED.

"Ana!" I could barely hear Sam over the double cacophony. "Go home."

"Where are you?" I had to shout, and my throat was already raw with cold. "I can't find you."

"Go home." The connection dropped. Of course he wouldn't tell me where he was; he knew I'd go after him.

I stuffed the device away and kept going. Surely he realized I wouldn't leave him in this chaos, no matter his orders.

The market tents were bright bruises against the Councilhouse and temple, cloth mazes that made every turn a wrong one. People scrambled about, some with purpose, most with panic. Still no Sam.

A high-pitched wail rippled through the city, emanating first from the Councilhouse, then shrieking through other buildings before silencing. The alarm was just an attention-getter, as if anyone could be unaware of the attack. Surely even the deaf could hear the dragon thunder.

Three incredible bangs came from the north wall. I strained to see, but the Councilhouse blocked my view. I pressed my palms over my ears, but it didn't muffle the noise. "Sam!" My voice was lost among everyone's, and I couldn't see over hundreds of people taller than me.

I jammed my coat-cushioned elbow against someone—who didn't seem to notice—and wiggled between two others. There, on the Councilhouse steps. A head of dark hair in need of cutting. Sam? I pushed through and forced my way up the stairs, but he was gone.

The throng finally thinned as everyone either reached safety or—I could halfway see from atop the stairs—reached weapons. At the top of the northern guard station, which was as tall as the city wall itself, a line of cannons had been raised, aimed toward the dragons, now mere yards from Heart.

Another series of thundering bangs, and metal and fire shot from the cannons. One hit the lead dragon, who buckled and tumbled through the air, but the other two flew sideways and dodged easily, in spite of their wingspan.

Cannons swiveled on their mounts as the two dragons flew over the walls, but they didn't shoot, not toward the city. Blue targeting lights shot up from the ground, followed by invisible laser blasts, but the damage was minimal. The dragons' hide was stronger than iron.

While one dragon headed straight for the center of Heart,

the other spat globs of green something—not mucus, but something that sizzled through the North Avenue cobblestones. Acid. It spread in huge, slimy puddles toward houses and farms.

When a laser finally got more than a glancing hit, it seared through a giant wing. The reek of cooking flesh ripped through the city, and the dragon spiraled toward North Avenue, flinging acid as it went. Hurrah, but by then, the dragon that had been hit by the cannon recovered enough to follow its fellows into the city.

"Ana! For the love of Janan, what are you doing out here?" Stef emerged from the Councilhouse, carrying a laser pistol. "Get inside. Now." Without checking to make sure I obeyed, she hurtled off the stairs and shot a beam of blue light at the nearest dragon, which had reached the temple.

I couldn't move. The dragon was right over the Councilhouse, and the other followed close behind, taking laser blasts as though to protect the first. Globs of acid rained on the market field, burning through tents and tables. People converged on the fallen dragon, firing weapons as it thrashed and spit. Humans and dragons all screamed.

The one above began wrapping itself around the temple, shrieking wildly as it bit at the building. Acid drooled downward, but neither it nor the knife-sharp teeth harmed the stone. I covered my ears at the scraping and keening. All these people with weapons, and it went after the temple?

Futilely? Its protector wouldn't last long, even with the rain of acid.

Lights shot upward, fast and blinding. More people, who only minutes before had been selling pastries, surged from inside the Councilhouse with weapons. They bounded down the steps, careful of the seeping puddles of acid that glowed green.

Sam caught my shoulder as he came outside, also armed. "Go inside." Fear and alarm contorted his face, and there was a darkness in his eyes I'd never seen before. "Please," he rasped. "Be safe."

Dumbly, I shook my head and pointed at the dragon guarding the one around the temple. Laser beams finally pierced the wide wings and armored hide, and the beast crashed downward, slinging a globule of acid toward the Councilhouse steps—toward us.

I yanked Sam behind a column just as the acid splashed onto the stone and began eating through. Spatters hissed against the back of my coat.

Shouting for Sam to do the same, I unzipped my coat and slipped my arms free. My bag of clothes and costume supplies dropped to my feet, safe. Dozens of holes appeared on our coats; the acrid stench of burning wool made my nose scrunch.

Holding my breath, I ran my hands along Sam's back, but he was clean. He did the same for me, then drew me into a tight hug as the third dragon hit the ground and everything shook. I shook, too, with cold and fear of what had almost happened.

The acid ate through the steps quickly and neutralized. Sam stared at it as dumbly as I had at the dragons, that darkness in his eyes. That must have been how I'd looked the night he saved me from drowning, when I'd run from his tent and found myself staring at the lake with nowhere to go.

The darkness was memory. He'd probably died in dragon acid before, maybe within the last few lifetimes. I didn't have to ask to know, so I wouldn't. Instead, I touched his chin and drew his gaze away from the hole in the stairs. "It's over." They hadn't even had time to launch the air drones, things specially made to defend against dragons.

I had no experience with dragons other than what I'd just witnessed. I'd only read about them: failed attempts to hunt the population into extinction, diseases and poisons introduced into their food supply, and experiments done on captured dragons. But still they attacked, as angry as they'd been five thousand years ago when humans first came to Range.

The people of Heart had endured these attacks for millenia. I couldn't begin to imagine overcoming that kind of terror every time.

More people swarmed from the Councilhouse, parting

around us as they wielded small hoses that sprayed chemical mist on everything the acid had touched. It smelled sweet, like crushed grass. The cleanup had begun and we should help, but I needed Sam to be okay first.

He lowered his eyes and kept his voice soft. "I wanted to be brave."

I held my hand over his, which still gripped the pistol hilt. His knuckles were pale, and veins showed sharp and blue. "Why didn't you stay in the Councilhouse?"

"I knew you wouldn't go home. I had to find you."

My chest tightened. "You *are* brave, Sam. You're the bravest man I know."

After we helped clean our share, we fetched our belongings and went back to his house. I read to him for an hour before he fell asleep, leaning against my shoulder. I put the book aside and adjusted myself on the sofa.

He shivered closer to me, one hand tight around mine. It was strange, being in this position of having to comfort someone when I'd only recently learned to be comforted. But I remembered how Sam held me in the cabin after the sylph, and that his presence had helped. I could do the same for him.

Breathing in the scent of his hair, I realized I'd needed him my whole life, before we even met. First, his music and the way he taught me through books and recordings. Then, he saved my life and refused to abandon me no matter how much I deserved it.

But as I pulled a blanket over both of us and combed my fingers through his hair, my perspective shifted.

There was no music in this quiet, and none of the tension of two weeks ago in the kitchen. Even with his body against mine, I didn't have knots or yearning, just desire for him to be himself again, unhaunted by past lives and deaths.

He held on to me like I was a rock, the only thing keeping him from drifting out with the tide of dark memories.

It was the first time I realized he needed me, too.

17
FOOTSTEPS

"NO SAM TONIGHT?" Sine asked from across the library table. It had only taken her an hour to bring it up. She'd made it sound casual, but I didn't have to be five thousand years old to know she'd been waiting for an opening. Apparently silence was as good an opening as any.

I gave a one-shouldered shrug and turned the page of my book. Philosophy. Lots of guessing why people were reborn. Why some took a year to return, while others took up to ten. No one agreed on anything, but because these were where my questions began, this was what I had to read. "We don't do *everything* together."

"Don't you? I don't think I've seen you apart since the market."

I'd been under the impression people in Heart valued their privacy. My alternate theory—that people already knew everything about one another, so they didn't bother prying—sounded more likely now. I was the exception, of course. If I was involved even remotely, people asked questions. The afternoon I'd dragged Sam outside the city so he could show me all the nearby geysers and hot springs, gossip had spread like wildfire. I still couldn't figure out what made fumaroles so scandalous, but maybe people were desperate.

"I'm just surprised he's not with you, that's all. You two have been spending as much time here as Whit, always off in your own corners, studying."

I flashed a smile. "He said he wasn't sleeping well and wanted to rest this evening. Everything should be back to normal soon." Maybe. He hadn't actually said anything. I'd *made* him stay in.

"Oh, good. I hope he feels more rested soon." She ducked over her book again, pen scraping against the paper grain.

"I hope so, too."

We worked in silence for a few minutes more, time dripping by like water from a leaky tap. But I couldn't focus on the philosophy book in front of me. The author seemed conflicted on his views about Janan, whether he was real and responsible for reincarnation, or whether humans were doing it on their own, by virtue of being human.

"Sine?"

She glanced up, eyebrow raised.

"Do you believe in Janan? Do you think he created everyone and reincarnates them every lifetime?"

She lowered her pen and sat back. "Sometimes I think I don't, simply because it annoys Meuric and Deborl. But honestly, I want to believe we humans aren't at this alone, perpetually reincarnated in a world where dragons, centaurs, griffins, and rocs are always trying to kill us." She shrugged and found my gaze. "Like you, I want to believe there is a beginning to all this. Life."

My beginning was so much more recent, yet no one could tell me what had happened. People who'd been there.

"What about the walls? Do they feel strange to you?"

"The heartbeat?" She shook her head. "Everyone can feel it, certainly, but it's comforting, and part of what makes me want to believe in Janan and his promise to return."

Or maybe he'd never left.

The heartbeat certainly didn't feel comforting to me. Sam seemed to think it was funny or cute how I tried to avoid touching the white stone, but it gave me the sensation of worms crawling beneath my skin.

"Thanks," I said, turning back to the book with a sigh. I really wanted to find someone else who didn't like the walls and see if they had any thoughts on it, but there seemed a definite connection between my newness and the creepy feeling.

"Perhaps philosophy and guesswork aren't where you should be looking." Sine eyed my book. "I never thought Deborl's views were all that astute, anyway."

I checked the cover of the book. Sure enough, Deborl, a Councilor who looked younger than me, had written it over sixty quindecs ago. Astute or not, these views were almost a thousand years old. I closed the book and slid it toward the middle of the table. "Maybe you're right. I thought the answers were in the distant past, but I could be wrong."

She slipped a marker into her book and nodded for me to continue.

Thoughts collated as I gazed around the dim library. "I know Li reasonably well." Better than I wanted. "She's a warrior. When I misbehaved as a child, she told me about the times she killed dragons. Before lasers and air drones were invented." Having seen dragons recently, I could finally appreciate what a feat that was.

"Li has always been formidable."

No doubt. "What about Menehem?"

"Not quite as formidable." She stood, using the table to brace herself. "A brilliant chemist. I didn't know him well, partially because we could never comprehend a word the other said." She chuckled. I couldn't tell if she was serious or not.

I followed her around a maze of shelves on the main floor.

Mahogany and glass shimmered in the lamplight, and the room smelled of wood polish and pronghorn leather. "A warrior and a scientist. I don't understand how you get me out of that."

"Because you love music?"

I opted not to argue about a nosoul's capacity for love. This time.

"Some things are inherited, certainly. Physical features. You look a lot like Menehem when I saw him last, actually, with the auburn hair and freckles. You show your mother's fierceness and your father's intelligence, but some things, like music and poetry, are passions of the soul."

I liked that. Sam had been born to farmers and woodworkers and glassblowers. Armande, his current father, was a baker. While Sam had learned hundreds of things out of curiosity and desire to help the community, he always came back to music.

Perhaps, if I was going to be reincarnated at the end of this life, I'd find myself similarly drawn, because there was music in my head, which sang me to sleep at night. It wasn't Sam's music or anyone else's. That probably made it mine. What a frightening thought.

"We're looking for Menehem's diaries?" I asked as we came to that area of the library.

Sine swept her hand across the nook created by bookcases.

"Since I cannot tell you about him, we might as well read Menehem's words. It's unfortunate he left Range so shortly after you were born."

Yeah, unfortunate he was so ashamed he couldn't even stay to help Li, who didn't want to care for me either.

I touched a lamp, illuminating the alcove. Two thousand books waited in their shelves while I searched the spines for the name of the parent who'd abandoned me.

While there were a few older volumes still in place, the newer ones, the ones I'd have needed, were missing. His diaries had abandoned me, too.

I swore, drawing a look from Sine. "Sorry," I said. "Would he have taken his books when he left?"

She scowled at the empty shelves. "It's very unlikely. Books are heavy, and he had a lot of them."

"And there are other copies." Sam had shown me how to find digital copies. Well, he'd asked Whit to show me. "Will you do me a favor while I check the digital archives?"

Sine nodded.

"Look for Li's diaries. I don't need to read any—not right now, anyway—but I'm wondering if they're still there."

She gave me a queer look, but nodded again and headed deeper into the diaries section while I made my way out. If she hadn't guessed my suspicions already, it wouldn't take long.

I didn't mind her knowing, either, but it felt weird to tell a Councilor I thought someone—maybe one of her friends—was trying to keep me from investigating my origins by removing the books I needed. Other than Sam, the only people who knew about my quest were on the Council.

The digital archives could be accessed in consoles upstairs, toward the alcove where Sam and I had watched videos. On my way up, I tapped on lamps and made a mental list of who might have taken Menehem's diaries.

Well, anyone could have taken them, but it was the Council I didn't trust. Most of them were against me. Antha, Frase, and Deborl didn't seem to despise me, but I doubted they cared whether I lived or died.

Sine was on my side. I'd liked her even before I found out she'd been Sam's mother in their previous lives. She'd died during childbirth, and was reincarnated when he was three. As a result, he'd spent his teenage years being mothered by a girl younger than him. Then she'd outlived him, and when he was reborn into this body, she was old enough to be his grandmother. I found it endlessly amusing and confusing.

As for Meuric, I couldn't tell. He was always pleasant, but he made me uncomfortable. He watched me all the time, and always waited to hear what others thought or wanted before deciding what to do with me, like his own ideas wouldn't be approved.

That left half the Council I didn't know well enough, and therefore couldn't trust. Any of them might be the one sabotaging my efforts—if there was any sabotaging after all.

I sat at the first data console and pressed the power button. When it gave a soft whir and a cursor blinked at me, I typed "Menehem."

Hundreds of diaries appeared, most marked as lab notes and other scientific things. Perhaps, during some of all that free time Sam had scheduled for me, I'd have a peek at those. For now, I narrowed the search to more personal things.

I half expected the console to refuse access, but it offered diaries up until a few years before I was born, which had been the 330th Year of Songs. That put his latest in the 329th Year of Stars. He'd probably finished it and left it for archiving, and taken his current diary with him.

Still, this could be useful.

I read until the stairs creaked and Sine sat next to me. "Find anything?"

"Nothing quite like reading about how your parents barely cared whether the other existed." I forced a smile. "The Council gave them permission to have a child, so they started planning it. Apparently Menehem calculated everything, because this was years before I was born."

Sine snorted. "Yes, that sounds like him."

"Anyway, he seemed more interested in a project for work, but there aren't any details. I may have to look into his science journals." I shrugged and tried to pretend I hadn't expected anything more. "What about you?"

202

"Many of Li's personal journals are gone, but if you found Menehem's on the console, you'll probably find hers as well."

I sat back in my chair, arms crossed. If someone had been trying to keep me from looking into my origins, they'd have been more thorough. But if someone wasn't trying to stop me, they were researching me.

That was an unsettling thought. Everyone else already knew more about me than I did.

"Goodness, it's late." Sine slyly checked the time. "I'd better head out."

I managed something resembling a laugh. "Sam could use some lessons in subtlety from you."

"Oh, I know. Don't you think I've tried? Unfortunately, I think I'm too subtle about it." She winked and grinned. "We can resume this research tomorrow, if you like. It's a new direction from endless philosophy."

"I agree. Thanks." I switched off the electronics as we headed downstairs. Before I lost my nerve, I said, "Let's say I have a friend who hasn't been sleeping well."

Sine hmmed. "I'll pretend I don't know you're talking about Sam. Go on."

"I'm worried about him. The only times he seems like himself are during music lessons and practice. He groans in his sleep half the night." Once I'd gotten up to check on him, but as soon as I stopped by his door, the light flicked on and he shuffled into the washroom. I'd waited, but he didn't emerge.

At least he'd stopped sneaking out every night, but I suspected it had more to do with how wretched he felt, and not . . . why he'd been sneaking to begin with.

Sine cocked her head as we stepped outside to the library. "And you want to know how to fix it?"

"I want to"—I wrapped my scarf around my neck and frowned into the darkness—"do something. Help him. He helped me."

Her smile turned wistful. "He'll sort it out eventually. Focus on your studies. He wouldn't want you so distracted, especially with your first progress report coming up next week."

Progress reports were the last thing I wanted to worry about. "What happened to him? Something with dragons?"

"Ana, if you don't want to ask him, check his diaries. See how they end." Her tone stayed flat, as much of a warning as I'd get from her. She always tried to be nice, but I'd upset her now.

I twisted my flashlight until a beam shot out, illuminating cobblestones as the library door shut. "I'm going to help him. Somehow. Anyone who thinks a progress report is more important can lick the bottom of my shoe. *After* my turn cleaning the pig runs."

Sine made a face. "You're learning that from Stef, aren't you?"

"I've gone along with the Council's demands." My breath misted on the chill air. "I like learning things. I probably would have asked, regardless of the Council's instructions. But I'm just one nosoul. The only one. What does it matter to you if I know the best time for growing rice? What is the Council so afraid I'll do if you don't keep me busy?"

She just stared at me, wrapped in the armor of her coat and hood. "Curfew. Better hurry."

Blinking away tears of frustration, which threatened to freeze on my eyelashes, I spun toward South Avenue and walked as quickly as I could. There was a shorter way Sam sometimes took us, but it involved more turns on unfamiliar roads, by unfamiliar houses.

Maybe I shouldn't have been so harsh to Sine, but now that I considered my own words, it *was* a good question. Were they afraid of me?

I tried to imagine what Sam would say, were he in a mood to talk. The people of Heart had been . . . how they were . . . for five thousand years. They knew one another, and could more or less predict what everyone would do in certain situations. But I was a new thing. Unknown. I'd been tucked away for eighteen years, and they hadn't had to think about me, but now I was back, filled up with my own thoughts and opinions.

What *would* I do?

Right now, I just wanted to help Sam. And, come masquerade day, I wanted to be invisible. Just a few hours of no one knowing me, judging me, and waiting to see if I would destroy everything.

I counted roads until I found the one that led to Sam's. The flashlight illuminated nothing unusual, just my breath on the air and a few flakes of snow swirling on the breeze. I shivered as trees rustled, as though preparing themselves for blankets.

My new shoes tapped on the cobblestones in a steady one-two. A three-four came from behind me, muffled with attempts at stealth, but with the whole city hushed and waiting for snow, every sound mattered.

Perhaps it was nothing, just someone else going home late, but when I glanced over my shoulder, I couldn't see anything, not even a shadow. Darkness thickened, as complete as the should-be silence. If I turned my flashlight behind me, they'd know I was aware I wasn't alone.

I almost did it, ready to yell for whoever to stop sneaking behind me, but then I remembered Li at the market, and dread crept inside me with the cold. Choosing the cowardly route, I walked faster, bringing my scarf over my face so the chill didn't dry my throat.

The footsteps followed me all the way to Sam's road, and by then my heart had raced ahead of me, taking my weakness with it. I spun and swung my flashlight beam across the street, but the thin glow met only a dusty veil of snowflakes and darkness. Brush hissed along the side of the road, but I was too slow to see if it was anything more than a deer.

No, I'd definitely heard footsteps. I stared toward where

the pine needles still whispered in someone's wake, but nothing happened. For a few minutes, I stood in the middle of the road, trying to decide if it would be worth going after my pursuer.

Visions of someone leaping out at me made me stay where I was. Going after someone unknown in the dark and cold and almost-snow—that wasn't brave. That was exceedingly stupid.

After straining my ears a minute longer, stretching to hear *something* other than my own breath and heartbeat, I ran the rest of the way down the road as fast as I could, repeating to myself that facing anyone would have been stupid. Running away was smart.

Fleeing like a mouse with a cat on its heels was smart, but definitely not brave. I hated letting someone get to me like that.

When I finally reached the walk up to Sam's house, I slowed to breathe. The last thing Sam needed now was to hear me stagger in, afraid of footsteps in the dark. Footsteps that hadn't even done anything.

Straining all my senses for the unfamiliar, I crept up the snow-dusted walkway and into the house. The parlor was dark as I closed the door behind me, careful not to let it click too loudly. I turned off my flashlight and rested it on the table, closing my eyes to let them adjust before I moved farther into the room.

If anyone had been following me, they weren't anymore. And I was safe with Sam—though maybe not right now.

He was sprawled on the sofa, book fallen from one hand while the other rested on his chest, which rose and fell with long, steady breaths. I didn't fight my relief as I crossed the room and knelt beside him. When he tilted his face toward me and smiled, then mumbled, "I waited up for you," I dared to think he'd be okay again.

"Come on," I whispered, putting his book on the table so he didn't trip. "Let's get you to bed."

He mm-hmmed and let me drag him to his feet. We stumbled upstairs and into his room, crowded with dark shapes. Wardrobe, shelves, harp, and bed. Books waited like traps across the floor, surprising, given how tidy he usually was. He must have been feeling more awful than I'd realized. I nudged them out of the way with my toe before guiding Sam to the near side of his bed.

He sat with a sleepy grunt and sway, and I steadied him with my hands on his shoulders. "Are you sure you want to sleep in your clothes?" Not that I knew where he kept his nightclothes.

"Yeah." He dropped to his side and tugged blankets over his waist. "Thank you, Ana. Glad you're home." He squeezed my wrist and was asleep again without waiting for a response.

"Sleep well." Before I lost my nerve, I leaned over, kissed his cheek, and breathed in his scent. Herbs, like what he'd given me the night he saved me from Rangedge Lake. "Tomorrow will be better. You'll see." I tiptoed through the gauntlet of books on his floor, glanced at his sleeping figure one more time, and sighed.

On the way to my bedroom, I paused by the stairs, on the balcony overlooking the parlor, and tiptoed to the front door. Sam didn't usually, because everyone knew and trusted one another—sort of—but tonight, thinking about someone following me through the streets of Heart, I locked the door.

18
PAST

DANCE LESSONS WITH Stef. Chores. Even with last night's footsteps haunting my dreams, our morning progressed as usual.

After a quick shower, I headed downstairs to the piano. Sam always gave me a few minutes of practice before joining me, and while I still made plenty of mistakes, he never said anything unless I did the same thing during our lesson proper.

He'd explained about rhythm and dynamics, showed me their markings on the sheet music, and helped me find the best way to reach keys with my smaller-than-average hands. When I made mistakes, I practiced that section until I could do it correctly ten times in a row; for whatever reason, this made him proud. I just wanted to be good.

I played through a short étude, trying to focus on the notes rather than the way Sam and I had danced this morning. But it was difficult.

Stef usually taught me, but sometimes she took a turn on the piano and made Sam get up and dance. He always obliged, but his posture was all reluctance: his shoulders curled forward, he didn't meet my gaze, and he moved stiffly. Until about halfway through whatever piece Stef was making us practice. Then, he'd be *in* the dance as surely as anyone who'd known it for a thousand years. During the slow dances, like we'd practiced this morning, he held me as if I were the most precious thing in the world. As if I were someone else.

I blinked and tried to find where I was in the music. My hands had worked without me, but now that I was paying attention again, I couldn't remember where I was. I glanced at the end—the coda—just as I played the last chord. Hopefully I hadn't messed it up too badly. Just because he didn't say anything didn't mean he wasn't listening to every note.

A prelude was next on the stack of music. It was one of his recent compositions, merely a hundred years old. It was also my favorite so far, because it had a quirky melody all the way through, even the serious parts. Like a private joke.

He should have been down by the time I reached the end of the prelude—I managed to hit a note I usually missed—but when I let my mitt-clad hands fall to my knees, he wasn't there. It was a challenging prelude; my success with it should have lured him downstairs. I'd try one more thing, then go up to drag him to the piano bench.

Music was the only time he seemed normal. Forget what Sine had said about Sam sorting it out on his own. I wanted to help him, so if music was the only thing that made him happy now, I'd try something new.

There was music in my head, melodies that made me shiver into sleep. Not Sam's, and not anyone else's. Mine. I hadn't told anyone about the music stirring inside of me, but it seemed right that Sam should be the first to know.

I'd only ever hummed the tune, and only when I was alone. And when no one was looking, I'd played a mute and invisible piano on my lap, or a table, or my desk in my room.

Here at the real piano, yellowed ivory keys firm beneath my fingertips, there was more pressure for it to sound as perfect as it did in my head.

Low notes came long and round, deep and mysterious. High notes sang like sylph. If I was honest, it was music of my fears. Shadows made of fire, drowning in a lake, and death without reincarnation. Giving those fears up to music—that helped.

"Please let it help Sam," I whispered beneath an arpeggio. "Please let him like it."

I played as carefully as I could, focused on each note and the way it resounded across the parlor. Hearing it outside my head made it real. Solid. Was this how Sam felt every time he wrote something new?

The last note fell. Still no Sam.

Maybe he hated it.

I slipped off my fingerless mittens and left them on the bench. Upstairs, the house was quiet. No water gurgling through pipes, no clothes swishing around as if he couldn't find something he wanted to wear. And when I knocked on his door, no answer. Nor the second or third try. I let myself in.

Sam sat on the floor, staring blankly at the wall, not moving, hardly breathing. Sweat wormed down his face; it must have itched, but he didn't brush it away.

I rushed inside, thumping my knee on the floor as I knelt in front of him. "Sam."

Nothing.

"Sam!" I shook his shoulders, said his name again and again, but he seemed trapped somewhere else. Some*when* else, like when the sylph outside his graveyard had made a dragon head.

Dragons. That was *his* fear.

"Sam, it's okay." I cupped my palms over his cheeks, leaned close until the scent of him filled me. "Please. You're safe."

He blinked, and his eyes focused on me. Confusion for a moment, then recognition. "Ana," he rasped. "What happened?"

As if I had any clue. "You were just staring when I came in." I smoothed hair from his face and whispered, "I thought you were gone."

He closed his eyes and leaned into my touch, and his expression betrayed emotions I had no names for. "Ana." My name slipped out like he hadn't meant to say it.

"You're safe." I didn't know what to do. I wanted to draw out his fears and hide them far away, but it seemed impossible. "Please don't go away again."

Sam hugged me, too tight, shaking like he'd run a thousand leagues. When he loosened enough for me to breathe, I sat sideways on his legs. His heart thudded by my ear as I dragged my hand along the cords of muscle in his arm. Tensed, untensed.

We sat like that for a while, his face buried in my hair. I didn't know how else to reassure him, so I continued petting his arm while the quiet lingered, and he seemed to be collecting his thoughts.

His heartbeat steadied. "I was remembering dragons and all the times—" He sounded like he'd swallowed glass. "I couldn't stop remembering."

I spoke softly so as not to shatter the moment of his confession. "All the times?"

"All the times dragons killed me." The words came thick with dread and grief.

"How many?" I'd assumed it had been only once, which was stupid, and *only* once would have been enough to give me nightmares forever.

"Thirty." He glanced toward the window, though I couldn't see anything but trees and the tip of the city wall. "If you hadn't saved me last week, it would have been thirty-one."

Thirty dragon deaths. I believed him, but it was so impossible sounding. I just couldn't grasp it. "I want to know what happened earlier, but I don't want to ask." I couldn't bear to see him like that again.

He squeezed me. "Most people have triggers, things that send them spiraling into horrible memories. No one goes through any life unscathed. Smell is most subtle, but sound has always done it to me. Never quite like this, though. Sometimes I think you can—"

I could what? If sound was his trigger and I'd been playing the piano, this was my fault. I'd wanted to help him, but had done the exact opposite. "I'm so sorry." Now I felt like the one who'd swallowed glass. I leaned away, tried to stand up, but his fingers tangled in my hair and he looked wretched.

"Don't go." His jaw clenched. "It wasn't you."

It didn't happen all on its own. But when he put his arms around me, like that helped, I let him. This felt nice, the way we curled together. And strange, because I'd wanted to be this close to him—but not like this. Not because he needed someone, and I was handy.

Then he kissed the top of my head—I tensed all over again—and he acted like there was nothing unusual. This whole thing, it was too much. I wished he would just talk to me. I couldn't stand the silence anymore.

"Sam." His skin warmed beneath mine. "I can listen. I *want* to listen."

He turned his hand over to hold mine, silent acknowledgment.

"Please. For both of us."

"It was your music," he said at last, and his words became a flood. "But not only that. The attack at the market, the way everyone reacted or didn't. It's been so long. Everything happened so quickly, and then your music made me feel like I was reliving all those times at once.

"My first memory is of singing. We'd come to what would be called Range, and everything was perfect. Pure. Hot springs, geysers, mud pits of every color. There were birds—every kind you can imagine—and I remember walking behind a group of people. I was trying to mimic the birds' whistles.

"The dragons came from the north. They looked like giant

flying snakes with short legs, and talons like eagles. Their wings were as wide as their bodies were long. They were beautiful, but we'd already fought our way through shadow creatures that burned, horse people who used human skin as clothing, and giant humanoids who destroyed everything they saw. We were cautious."

Sylph. Centaurs. Trolls. I'd be cautious after that, too.

"Stef and I watched them coming. The way they moved through the sky was hypnotic, and we'd never seen something so large that could fly. But then one darted toward us, and I was the slowest to run away." His voice snagged on memory. "There was green slime everywhere around me, and on me. Acid. It burned and itched, and then I saw bone."

I shuddered. That was the first time a dragon had killed him.

"When I was reborn, it was in Heart. It seemed like the dragons had been guarding it from us, or trying to destroy it." He still had that faraway expression, like he was seeing five thousand years past. "They attacked in the same way every time, one always straight for the temple as if to rip it from the ground. They were always unsuccessful, but it never stopped them.

"Fifteen more times in my early lives. Acid, teeth, or just getting knocked off a wall." He sighed. "No one else had luck so terrible. I thought they were after me in particular."

I twisted and touched his cheek, drawing patterns across his skin. It was dry now, sweat all evaporated.

"I'm *old*, Ana." He said it like that would change anything. I already knew this was only one incarnation of the musician I'd always admired. He closed his fingers around my wrist, gently. "I've died so many times. It always hurts."

I paused with my fingers resting on the tip of his chin. "Always?"

"Some worse than others. The easy ones are when you die of poison or illness. Sometimes you get to go from old age."

The room turned into winter. "What does it feel like?"

"Dear Janan. You shouldn't ask that." He shook his head. "I shouldn't be willing to tell you."

Someday I would die too. I might as well be prepared.

"It feels like being ripped out of yourself. Like being caught in giant talons or fire or jaws. It's suffocating. And then there's nothing for what seems like eons, but when you come back just as painfully, it's only been years. Any time you're killed—sylph, dragon, giant, anything violent—the pain lasts even after your soul is out. Something incorporeal shouldn't be able to hurt so much." He hesitated, and his voice turned gentle. "I've been burned by a sylph too. It never feels quite right again. Sometimes, even generations later, I can still feel the fire."

I held my fists to my chest.

218

"That's why everyone focuses on the present and future. The past is too painful when you remember how lives end. Often abruptly." He shook his head. "In a dragon attack four generations ago, Stef had to save my hat for me to bury. It had been thrown aside, and was the only thing left."

I couldn't imagine living, or dying, like that. For millennia. And then I'd come along, always asking about things that had happened before me. I hadn't meant my curiosity to cause so much pain.

Before I could find an apology good enough, he said, "I think last week wouldn't have been so dramatic if I hadn't already been killed by dragons not twenty years ago."

That was before I'd been born, but it probably felt recent to him. "What happened?"

He stilled, arms loosening around me. "I went north because I was lonely. I felt empty, and I needed inspiration. Stef, who'd just reached her first quindec, told me not to go because I was too old, but I didn't have a reason to wait. Ciana had died a few years prior."

I nodded; Li had said Sam and Ciana had been close.

"After traveling for weeks," he murmured, sounding far away now, "I came upon a white wall that must have gone up a mile . . ." He trailed off.

"Was it like Heart's?"

He blinked. "What?"

"The wall. Did it have a pulse like the one around Heart?"

"I—" He looked as confused as the day I'd asked how he knew the doorless temple was empty. "Dragons came from all around. Before I could do anything, they'd killed me."

"What about the wall?"

"What wall?" He inhaled deeply, shook back into himself, and kissed my temple. "You're trying to distract me. Good job."

My skin tingled where his mouth had touched. "But— Never mind." Maybe the wall was a question for later. I could look it up in the library.

"I think we should see how much time is left for your lessons."

"Are you sure you're up for it?" I scrambled off his lap and onto my feet. As much as I'd liked being that close, it wasn't fair that he could keep kissing my head when I wasn't sure if that was something we were doing now. Library time, lunch, head kissing. Today was probably a trauma exception, but still.

He took my hands when I offered to help him up, but he didn't let me hold any of his weight. "Music lessons would restore some much-needed normalcy, and I'd like to hear what you were playing."

I shifted and shrugged. "I don't want you to . . . you know." My insides flip-flopped. It had been easier to play when he wasn't there.

"I'll be fine." He brushed his knuckles across my cheek.

I ignored his touch and headed for the door, forcing my tone light. "Okay, then. But no laughing. I don't have a million years of practice composing in my head."

He scoffed. "I'm not *that* old."

"And the piano wasn't even invented yet. Yeah, I know. Sing another tune, Sam." I strained a smile. He wanted normalcy? Fine.

He feigned shock as he followed me into the hall. There he reclaimed my hand and stopped, spinning me toward him as though we were dancing. "I just thought of a name for your waltz."

I waited.

"If you like it, that is. We can always change it." His voice shook, probably because it had been such an awful morning, but I imagined he wanted my approval. "'Ana Incarnate.'"

My heart felt too big for my ribs to cage.

For all the unfair head kissing, the way we *hadn't* kissed in the kitchen, and his grudging agreement to dance with me every morning—it suddenly seemed he knew me better than anyone in the world. Better than anyone ever would.

He'd seen my deepest need, buried so far I'd hardly been aware of it.

There was no telling if I'd be reborn when I died, but the waltz began and ended with my four notes. He'd built the music around things that reminded him of me. And now this name. *My* name.

A hundred or a thousand years after I died, someone could play my waltz, even Li, who'd always resented my presence, and they would remember me.

Thanks to Sam, I was immortal.

19

KNIFE

TRUE TO HIS threat of having the rest of today be normal, we made our way downstairs, no time for me to bask in the revelation of my immortality. Still, I felt I glowed a little as I approached the piano.

Maybe the worst was over. Maybe we really could get back to normal, which meant I needed to tell him about the footsteps, but I squashed that impulse for now. He did need to know someone had followed me, but I could tell him later, when we hadn't just discussed his many deaths, and when he hadn't just immortalized me through his music.

I took my place at the piano, not entirely comfortable with the way he looked over my shoulder.

"Warm up again."

I knew better than to argue, just donned my fingerless mitts. Scales and arpeggios flew from under my fingers while Sam perched on a stool nearby, looking thoughtful. "What?" I asked.

He shook his head, as if knocked from a trance, and reached for a notebook and pencil. "Play what you wrote."

"Are you sure?"

"If anything happens, you're right here to rescue me." He flashed a smile, and for the next two hours I played and struggled to translate it to paper while he took notes and hmmed at me.

"This is much harder than I thought it would be," I said when we took a break for lunch. "It's not even a complicated song."

"I think you'll find that the simple things are often the most challenging. Everything shows in them. Everything matters." He slid his notebook across the table and raised his eyebrows. "Another hour of practice before we head to the library?"

That was a good sign. All last week, he'd practically ripped me from the piano so he could get back to his research, though he never said what he wanted to know so badly. As anxious as I was to find out what else Menehem had written in his diaries, I was happier Sam was behaving more like himself. Learning about my father had waited eighteen years. It could wait another hour.

"That sounds perfect." I leaned over to see what his

notebook held. Scribbles and musical notes stared up at me. "What's this?"

"Some things we might discuss about your music."

I slumped. "It was awful, wasn't it?" He'd let me work on it for hours before telling me? I couldn't decide whether to be angry or devastated.

I wanted to run upstairs and hide my shame, but that wouldn't help me improve. Instead, I grabbed the notebook and started toward the parlor. Might as well get it over with.

"Actually, I thought it was pretty." He touched my elbow. "Did you even read what I wrote? Or did you just assume?"

"What do you think?" I pressed the notebook against his chest. "You didn't say anything about it, and I just started. I knew it wouldn't be perfect, but this page is filled. I think the next one is too."

He gave me an exhausted look as his hands closed over the notebook. "Nothing is perfect, not even when you've been playing for several lifetimes." Without waiting for me, he marched back into the parlor and set the notebook on his stool. "I know you think either you're amazing the first time, or you're a failure, but that's not how this is. *Nothing* is like that. Yes, there's room to improve this piece, but that doesn't mean it's bad. Remember? You just started. And you didn't bother to notice I wrote things like, 'This is lovely.'"

I searched for an insult strong enough to hurt him, but gentle enough so he wouldn't decide he didn't like me anymore. Nothing. I hated this, not being good enough, being lifetimes behind everyone else. My jaw hurt from clenching it.

"Fine." I sat on the piano bench again, determined to do better. Even my scales sounded angry.

Sam slipped onto the bench next to me, interrupting a major scale. His hands covered mine.

"Music is the only thing that ever mattered to me," I whispered to the ringing silence. "Every time I hurt, I had one place to turn. I need to be good at it."

"You are. I don't, and probably won't, tell you enough. Can't have my students getting cocky." He smiled; I didn't. "But you are good at this. I've never enjoyed teaching someone as much." He curled his fingers with mine and leaned toward me. Our thighs pressed together and his voice deepened. "I want to tell you something."

"Okay." All this touching today. It was disorienting and distracting, because he'd mostly been so careful to keep his distance. What if he did the same thing he had in the kitchen our first day here?

I couldn't let him hurt me—even unintentionally—because he'd had a tough morning. I had, too.

"Wait," I said when he started to speak. "Not right now. It's just too much. I'm sorry."

He drew back a fraction, released my hands. "You're probably right. We still have a lot to do today."

I exhaled relief. "Okay, so this music. First tell me all the things you like to help my ego recover. Then you can tear it down again."

We didn't make it to the library until after dinner, and it was mostly my fault. I kept asking questions, trying to understand the things I'd done right without knowing, and the things that didn't work. My harmonies, he said, didn't coordinate properly with the melody, and we discussed ways to fix that without changing the heart of the piece.

He swore it took practice to find the right balance, but I was determined to write a masterpiece next.

At the end of the day, we were both exhausted, but I was happier. We took care of chores and ate a small dinner before heading to the library; I pestered him with more questions the whole way, clutching my flashlight in mittened hands.

Though the snow hadn't lasted, the cold had. With any luck, the weather would warm in the next couple of days; the masquerade was coming up, and I hadn't been smart enough to plan for freezing temperatures.

Sam hauled open the library door, letting me duck inside first. Heat made my cold skin prickle as I escaped the temple's glow.

"There you are!" Whit pushed up from the desk he'd been hunched over. "We thought you two had given up on us."

"Unlike some people I know," I said, removing my mittens and scarf, "we don't live here."

"She says that now." Sam followed me toward Whit's and Orrin's desks, where they worked over flat electronic screens. "But the first thing she said when I showed her the library was that we should move in."

Orrin lifted an eyebrow, oddly delicate for someone so large. "The acoustics would be terrible."

"Exactly what I said." Sam laughed—it was really nice to hear him laugh again—and took my coat and cold-weather accessories to stash away, like he usually did. Well, like he did until the market attack. This cheered me, too; he hadn't run straight to his mysterious research, and he remembered my existence for more than two minutes.

"We could still rearrange things." I sniffed, feigning offense. When I caught his eye, his grin stretched wide, and there was something about it that made me blush, something I didn't have a word for but would have liked—in private. Face still hot, I peered over Whit's shoulder. "What are you two doing anyway?"

"Well," he said, shifting to give me a better look, "we had a thrilling morning scanning genealogies into the digital archives. Now we're reviewing logs to see where books have been going. A large number of diaries have—" He shifted and covered the screen. "Huh."

Ominous. "I was actually looking for some diaries last night. Sine was with me. She thought I might have better luck if I researched Menehem and Li, but the diaries weren't here. Still in the digital archives, though."

"There are no rules about taking books from the library, as long as they're returned." Orrin smiled from behind his desk. "Did the console give you any trouble?"

"No, it was fine." I glanced at Sam, who was no longer smiling. Last night, there'd been a death trap of books on his floor. More worried for Sam's health, I'd barely noticed they were gone this morning. "So did you find out who took them?"

"Sorry," said Whit. "Who takes what is privileged information for archivists and Councilors. But you're welcome to continue using the consoles."

"Oh, all right." Torn between annoyance and suspicion, I headed upstairs. Surely if Sam had been the one to take the diaries, he'd have told me. He didn't need to research my parents, and the books on his floor might have been music books.

"The reason we were late," Sam said, "is because Ana started composing a minuet."

"And you made her work on it until her hands were blue?" Orrin chuckled.

"You should both ask her to play it for you next time you're over. It's very nice."

Beaming at his praise, I found the console I wanted and called up Menehem's diaries. Reading like this hurt my eyes, but I made it through every page, searching for a hint of Menehem's research goals and where he might have gone after abandoning Li and me.

He seemed like the curious type, which fit with his being a scientist. There were entire diaries dedicated to the geothermal features around the caldera, especially the gases a few gave off. He questioned the Council's decisions, Heart and its glowing temple, even the reasons for everyone's existence when there were a dozen other dominant species in the world: dragons, centaurs, phoenixes, unicorns, and giants. Not to mention everyone's nemesis, the sylph. He hated Meuric's insistence that Janan was responsible for humanity's existence even more than Deborl's idea that we were here because we were superior to other creatures, and eventually we'd claim the rest of the world.

Both thoughts seemed foolish to me. I hadn't settled on an opinion about Janan yet—he *might* be real, though I doubted he was benevolent—but I definitely didn't agree with Deborl's idea. As far as I knew, no one had ever *tried* claiming the rest of the world, and if that was his goal, he should have started before "eventually." Besides, you couldn't kill sylph.

By the time I finished reading Menehem's latest diary, I got the feeling he wasn't well liked in Heart. He was defensive and cynical, and often accused society of having become stagnant, complacent with the world as it was. I didn't agree about the stagnant state—people were still coming up with lots of interesting things—but I appreciated that he didn't accept simple answers to hard questions, and thought people should challenge themselves.

I'd always hated him because he'd abandoned me to Li, but getting to know him through his journals, there were some things to admire.

Before I ran out of time, I peeked at his professional journals. He'd been studying sylph before he disappeared, trying to use chemicals to influence or incapacitate them. There was no indication whether he'd succeeded, though.

If someone could control sylph . . .

I was staring at my hands, remembering Li's sarcastic, "Safe journey," before I'd left Purple Rose Cottage, when Sam appeared on the stairwell. "Time to go home."

After switching off the console, I followed him down and tapped lamps dark. Whit and Orrin had already gone.

"Is everything okay?" Sam offered my coat.

I glanced at the desks where the archivists had been working, knowing who had those diaries and not telling me. Maybe Sam had the books. Maybe he didn't. Regardless, I didn't think he would do anything to hurt me.

"Last night, there were books all over your floor. What were they?"

Shadows darkened his expression. "I'm not sure this is a good time for this conversation."

I snatched my coat, shoved my arms through the sleeves,

and pulled up my hood. "Fine." Wrapped up in my scarf, I heaved open the door and strode outside.

"Ana." Sam stood near me, but not touching. Only temple-light lit his face; I was still fumbling with my flashlight. "I was doing research on dragons."

I spun, my light finally working, and almost blinded him with the white beam.

He blinked out of the way. "I wanted to see if I could learn anything." His face shone pale in the glare of my flashlight. "It's happened so many times, I keep thinking they're coming after *me*, and it's not just horrible luck. So yes, I had those books in my room. I also had books about sylph, because I was equally concerned about you. Two attacks in two days."

My throat closed up, and I hugged him tight. "Oh, Sam." I pressed my face into the soft wool of his coat, inhaling his warm scent. "I'm sorry. Don't worry about me. If you want to research dragons, let me help."

"I don't want to burden you. Everyone has their own worries and fears they're reborn with. Eventually— Eventually it sorts itself out, and we're all right again."

That sounded like what Sine had said. Maybe she hadn't been so insensitive on purpose. It was just all she knew.

I reached up, touched Sam's face. Stubble caught in the wool of my mittens. "Burden me."

"You have more important things to worry about. The first progress report—"

232

"Next week. I know." With a sigh, I peeled away from him and gave my flashlight a few more twists. Nice everyone was so eager for me to do well, but *my* biggest incentive was not being exiled from Range or, worse, dumped with Li. "It's difficult to focus on my studies when my best friend is struggling just to get through the hour."

He hesitated. "So I'm your best friend now?"

My cheeks heated, and I shrugged. "It was between you and Sarit, and you have the piano. She just has honey."

Sam laughed, and his knuckles brushed the back of my mitten, as if he'd been about to take my hand, but changed his mind. "Even though I'm pretty sure you chose the piano, not me—"

I bumped my shoulder to his arm, making him laugh again. Now that I was getting used to the idea that he wasn't laughing *at* me, I enjoyed the sound more and more.

We continued down South Avenue, but our easy silence thickened as I remembered the previous night's events. The footsteps.

Cold air stirred around my hood, rustling my hair. I shivered with the temperature and memory, vainly peering at the houses we passed. How could I figure out who had followed me? My thoughts kept turning back to Li, her threats from the market day, and whether she might have learned how to control sylph.

Sam touched my arm.

I startled, almost dropping my flashlight. Wool slipped on metal, but I scooped the tube against my chest and pinned it there.

"You seem uncomfortable." His expression was impossible to read in the dark. Only starlight and the eerie temple glow brightened the city. The moon hadn't risen yet; some nights its light reflected off the walls, giving Heart numinous radiance. But not tonight. It was just dark. "Ana?"

I shifted toward him and started walking again, quickening my pace. "I'm fine." Really, I just wanted to get inside.

He kept up easily. "I hesitate to call you a liar, but I can tell when you're not being honest. Did something happen?"

"Last night." I kept my voice low, smothered it with my scarf. "When I was coming back to your house, I heard someone following me. There were footsteps. They vanished when I turned around."

He didn't ask me if I was sure like I thought he would, just put his arm around my shoulders and gave me a gentle squeeze. "I have something for you at home."

Inside the dim parlor, Sam motioned for me to sit, and headed to one of the bookcases. Old hinges squeaked as he opened a box.

He crouched in front of me and laid a small, sheathed blade on my knees.

I tried to draw away, but it was already touching me.

"What is this?" Carefully, I nudged it toward him, off my knees, and into his waiting hands.

"A knife." He slipped off the leather covering to reveal a tiny blade, as thin and long as my index finger. "You need to promise me something."

I didn't take my eyes off the steel. "I don't want that."

"Please, Ana. I wouldn't ask if I didn't think it was necessary. I believe someone followed you last night. If their motives were benign, why didn't they announce themselves?"

"You think someone might try to hurt me."

Something flashed in his eyes, but I was too slow to fully see it. I had a hard time looking away from the knife. It was such a little thing, much too tiny for his grip. Perhaps if I thought of it as an oversize needle, it wouldn't seem so terrible.

"When you were born, the Council passed a law forbidding anyone to do you harm. Because you might die."

Suddenly, I remembered the first meeting with the Council in the guard station, and Sam saying there was a law about my death. I shivered, trying not to wonder what other laws the Council had made about me.

"The rest of us, we'd come back, but there's no way to tell about you. The Council wouldn't allow anyone to steal your life."

For a moment, I felt bad about the assumptions I'd made

about the Councilors, but Sam pressed the knife handle against my palm and held it there until I relented. It fit my hand perfectly.

"Just because there's a law doesn't mean everyone's going to obey. It's unlikely that anything will ever happen, but there's no harm in your carrying a knife, even if it simply makes you feel better when walking home." He hazarded a smile. "I'll never let you get hurt if I can help it, but you don't want me following you around everywhere, do you?"

Maybe. Yes. "Absolutely not. The masquerade is coming up, and I don't care if everyone else cheats. No one is supposed to know who you are, right? I won't let you see what I'm wearing, and I don't want to know how you're dressing up."

"I know. But you'll be carrying that." He nodded toward the knife still in my hand.

It wasn't heavy. The rosewood handle was smooth but not slick, and smelled sweet, while the delicate blade had been recently cleaned. No doubt it was sharp, but I didn't touch it to see. Other than prettiness and whether I could carry it, I had no idea what to look for in a weapon, but I imagined this was a good one. Sam didn't keep things he didn't feel were worthwhile.

"Do you promise to keep the knife with you?" He looked earnest, and I really didn't want to rely on him.

Carrying a weapon seemed extreme when someone had only been following me, especially if there was a law protecting me. But, as he'd said, not everyone observed laws. I wouldn't care about curfew if the punishment wasn't Li or banishment. What was the punishment for trying to kill me?

Again, I thought of what Menehem had been working on before he'd left Heart.

I slipped the sheath over the blade and set the knife on a nearby table. "Only because you asked so nicely."

"Excellent." He smiled, but a shadow lingered behind his eyes. He wasn't telling me something, but I hadn't told him everything, either. Not about Li in the market.

I let it go; my heart couldn't take any more today.

"How about some music before bed?" he asked.

"My fingers are all played out."

"I was going to play for you. If you wanted, that is." His smile was genuine when I nodded. "I thought about starting you on another instrument sometime. Is there anything that interests you?"

"Everything." For the moment, I didn't care how eager I sounded. He understood what music meant to me.

He laughed, taking three long strides to the stack of instrument cases. A long one waited on top, and he chose that. "Sometimes I think you sound like I must. We make quite the pair, Ana. Now"—he turned, holding a slender silver instrument—"how do you feel about the flute?"

When he played, I melted.

20
SILK

STEF HAD CANCELED dance practice the morning of the masquerade because I'd warned her how late I'd have to stay up to finish my costume. She'd looked absolutely gleeful and said something to Sam about having to fight to get a turn dancing with me.

I hadn't slept as late as I'd anticipated, which was probably the only reason I overheard Sam on his SED. His voice was low, like he didn't want to wake me. Or didn't want me to hear.

"So you'll meet me at the gazebo on North Avenue?"

Grit stung my eyes as I sat up in bed, glanced out the window. The false dawn of the walled city bathed the back-yard in cobalt and shadows; the city wall made sunrise even later than usual, though it was well after midwinter.

"I think she's in danger, and tonight is the best opportunity for something to go wrong."

What? I peered at the silk walls, though of course I couldn't see him through the shelves and all the instruments and books he kept in the rooms between ours.

"She's my best guess. I can't think of anyone else with better reason to hurt—" He paused. "I don't think she's working alone, either. I haven't been able to find *anything* useful."

Too many feminine pronouns. Was he talking about me?

"Thanks, Stef. Will you call Whit, Sarit, and Orrin too?" He chuckled, but the fact that someone was clearly in trouble—maybe me—kept it from sounding genuine. "Yeah, only took five thousand years to find a use for them."

Even though he was joking about his friends, I shivered, glad he hadn't said that about me.

"Of course I still need your help. Don't be ridiculous. No one could replace you." He sounded—irritated? Insulted? It was hard to tell. "Okay. I'll see you in an hour."

While he moved around the house, his footsteps quiet down the stairs, I washed my face and dressed. Just simple trousers and a sweater for now. It was chilly; hopefully it'd warm up before this evening.

The scent of coffee lured me downstairs, along with the hiss of something in a frying pan. A mug waited for me on the table, probably because Sam had heard me getting out of bed, but he was standing over the stove, frowning at eggs.

I took a gulp of coffee for courage and leaned on the counter near him. He acknowledged me with a half smile. "Sleep okay?" His voice was rough, as if he hadn't slept at all.

One more long drink of coffee. I didn't want him mad at me, especially not today. "I overheard part of your conversation with Stef. What's going on?"

He glared. "Private discussion."

"The walls are silk. Next time you talk with her, I'll just go deaf, okay?" I carried my mug back to the table. "And you're burning the eggs."

Swearing, he used a spatula to prod at the pan, and a few minutes later we had runny-in-the-middle-crispy-on-the-outside fried eggs. He was usually a better cook than this, and though I considered skipping what he referred to as "breakfast" and I considered "gross," I didn't want to insult him further. I ate the parts that looked like eggs should, and cut the rest into bits. With luck, he wouldn't be able to tell how much I hadn't eaten.

"I need to go out for a few hours." He sat back. His plate looked like mine.

"All right." I scraped my eggs into the compost bin. "You don't have to tell me everything. Some things can be private."

He sighed and pushed off his chair. "Ana . . ."

I put my plate in the sink and faced him. "Look, you asked

240

me to live here. Your walls are not exactly soundproof. I'm going to overhear things. I don't snoop around or bother your belongings, but if you're talking in the house, I'm probably going to hear it." I dragged in a heavy breath. "I don't want to go, but if you don't want me to live here anymore, all you have to do is say."

Sam crossed the kitchen in four long strides and stood as close as we had the day he hadn't kissed me. His mouth opened and shut, whatever he'd been about to say trapped inside. "Don't leave."

There were a thousand things I could have said, mostly rude, but he actually looked worried—as well as a dozen other emotions flickering across his face too quickly to read. Too complex. "Then I won't leave." I kept his gaze. "I wish you'd tell me what's going on."

He closed his eyes and again, I wasn't fast enough to comprehend his expressions. "I promise I'll tell you, just not right now. I really have to go."

"If you're not telling me so I'll still have fun tonight, you're stupid. Now I'm going to worry about everything." I balled my fists in my sleeves. "I mean, you gave me a *knife*. How am I supposed to feel after that?"

"I'm sorry, Ana. There's just too much to explain right now."

"When you get back, then." I didn't lower my gaze, even though he towered over me and my neck pinched from holding my head at this angle. "If it involves me, I have a right to know."

"Very well. As soon as I return." His smile was forced. "Please don't leave."

"You'd have to be a lot meaner than ruining breakfast to drive me away. After all, it took me eighteen years to leave Li, and you know how awful she was." My equally forced smile dropped when we both realized how those last words could have sounded, like I could really compare Sam to Li. My tone hollowed. "I'll be here."

He nodded, brushed hair off my face, and headed from the kitchen. "I hate being a teenager."

"Why?"

"Hormones." With a sad half smile, he left.

Since he was out for the morning and I had no engagements—the library was closed for masquerade preparation, and no lessons had been scheduled for today—I took the opportunity to try on my costume to make sure I liked the way everything fit. It made me look like not-me, and took ages to put on right, but I was satisfied with the results.

Carefully, I removed everything and returned it to its hiding spot.

I went outside to take care of chores. Animals didn't feed themselves. Just as I finished everything, I heard Sam and Stef over the murmur of cavies and clucking of chickens. I dropped the old work gloves on a shelf and started around the house to tell them I was outside and could hear their very private discussion.

"It explains a lot about Ana, doesn't it?" Stef asked.

I stopped by the walkway. They were just beyond the trees by the street, close enough that their voices carried clearly. With the rustle of pine boughs, they might not know I was here. I didn't want to eavesdrop, since I'd *just* told Sam I didn't sneak, but if their *private discussion* was about me, it wasn't fair that I was excluded.

Sam said, "When we were warming up by the lake, she kept waiting for me to toss her back into the cold. I think she was afraid I'd take her food, too." His tone was all disbelief. How ridiculous I must have been. "She was convinced that everything I did was somehow a joke against her."

"She doesn't act like that now." Stef's voice came from the same place as before. They weren't moving. Probably so they wouldn't carry their conversation into the house where I could hear.

"She doesn't, but it's taken a lot of convincing, and I'm not sure her first reaction isn't still defensiveness. Eighteen years of Li doesn't seem like a long time to us, but that's her whole life."

Stef hmmed. "It's a shame our first newsoul had to grow up like that." In the pause, I imagined her pushing back her long hair, or doing something else thoughtlessly graceful.

"Do you think what Li said about Ciana could be true? It's been, what, at least twenty-three years since she died. She isn't coming back."

I didn't want to hear this. Not about Ciana. But my feet were too heavy to lift, as if the hot sunshine had melted them to the grass.

"I don't know," Sam said, and I couldn't breathe. "Ana had nothing to do with it, just as we have nothing to do with being reincarnated." At those words, I started breathing again. "For a while, I thought there was a finite number of times we could be reborn, but you've died a lot more times than Ciana."

"Weaving isn't usually explosive."

He ignored her sarcasm. "Ciana and I became close after you cleverly crushed yourself in the compactor—"

This time it seemed my heart stopped. He'd said as much before, but now I wondered. How close? Lovers? And I'd taken her away forever. How could he stand to look at me?

"A laser went off and I fell," Stef insisted. "It hurt a lot, just so you know."

"You didn't spend the next three weeks cleaning you out of there. I have just as much right to complain as you." Sam gave a tired laugh. "Anyway, after you died, Ciana and I became close. I guess I felt like we hadn't done much together in a long while, so it was time to catch up. I'm glad we did."

I squeezed my eyes shut, hugging myself so tight my ribs

hurt. Save the occasional mention, he'd never talked to me about Ciana. Of course he wouldn't.

"We all expected her to come back," Stef said gently. "It's good she wasn't alone at the end."

"Li would have had her, and Ana wouldn't exist." Sam's tone was impossible to read. Sad, melancholy. But that didn't tell me if he wished I were Ciana.

I wished I were Ciana.

"That's if Li is right about"—Stef's voice hitched— "replacements."

Sam heaved a sigh. "Even if we had a say in the matter, how could we choose between them? Ciana had a hundred lives, and Ana might not have had any. What if there are more like Ana, not yet born? They could be waiting for someone to not come back. And how could anyone choose between someone they've known five thousand years, and someone . . . like Ana?"

I had to make them stop. One foot in front of the other. I forced myself onto the walkway.

Stef sounded just as melancholy. "Wish I could tell you. I think you're right, though, that we don't have anything to do with it. Maybe it's Janan. Maybe it's something else."

"Janan isn't real."

"Don't say that around Meuric. He's worse than ever about it, since Ana joined us. He's getting others convinced, too. They think we're being punished."

"For *what*?"

"Not believing in Janan? Not worshiping enough? I don't know, but ask anyone. They think Ana's just the beginning." A flash of bright blue became visible through the pine boughs as I walked. Stef's dress. "All I was getting at is, it's not up to us. Good thing, too, because I'd never be able to choose."

"Me neither," Sam whispered.

I stepped onto the street to find the two of them facing each other, expressions drawn and shoulders hunched. When they both looked at me, I said, "I came to tell you I was outside and could hear you."

"Ana—" Sam reached for me, but I stepped back, turned around, and raced for the house.

My legs got me to the door, but I couldn't make my hands work right on the knob. My fingers were too stiff and my arm shook, so when Sam appeared next to me, I was still biting my lip and staring at the door. I focused on the wood, the pine green paint and how it soaked into the grains. I didn't want to look at him.

"Ana." His hand moved toward mine, but I sidestepped out of the way.

"Will you open the door, please?"

He did, like it was the hardest thing in the world. But he hadn't just overheard friends contemplating whether he'd replaced people they loved, or talking about him like he was a feral puppy hesitant to accept scraps.

246

I really was a butterfly.

The floor thumped hollowly beneath my shoes as I dashed through the parlor with all its instruments, piano in the center. I wondered if Sam had written Ciana a song, too.

Up the stairs, as fast as I could. When I reached the balcony overlooking the parlor, I faced him, resting my hands on the railing.

He paused midway up the stairs, looking haggard, ripped open, and all his centuries exposed. I imagined I could see his first life, ended abruptly by dragon acid. His life before this, ended when Ciana had died and he'd gone north; there'd been nothing to keep him in Heart, so he'd given himself to dragons.

My hands prickled with memories of rose thorns and sylph burns. I'd never died, but not for lack of the world's trying.

We stared at each other until he said my name, and I said, "I didn't know you were in love with her."

I stayed in my bedroom the rest of the afternoon, pillow over my head to muffle his piano practice. It was all old sonatas and melodies I didn't know. Maybe he hoped the new-to-me music would lure me downstairs. I was just glad he didn't play the one he'd named "Ana Incarnate." It would have driven me to madness.

Sunlight lengthened beyond the lace curtains, and Sam knocked on my door. "It's only an hour until dusk. That's when the masquerade begins. If you wanted to get ready."

My throat felt scratchy when I spoke. "Go without me."

There was a long pause, and his silhouette shifted beyond the silk walls. "You don't want to go?"

"Identities are supposed to be secret." I desperately wanted to be someone else for a while, and for no one to know who I was. What I was. Nosoul.

"Oh, okay." His footsteps receded, and when I heard sounds from his bedroom, I went into my washroom and began dressing.

I wore wings, silk stretched across a wire frame. They attached to a synthetic silk dress, layers of deep ocean green and blue that draped from my shoulders to knees.

My hair went up in a wreath of flowers and ribbons, with the back hanging long and loose between the wings. I smoothed kohl across my eyelids so when I donned my mask, the black matched the whorls.

Purple, blue, and green silk swirled across my face. Butterfly wings.

I found the tiny knife Sam had given me and threaded it in with my hair, among the crown of flowers and ribbons. Even that slight weight might burden me, but I hadn't forgotten the footsteps the other night.

"I'm going," Sam said from the hall.

Light doused so he couldn't see my shadow—my wings would give me away—I said, "I'll see you there."

"How will you know who I am?"

Sometimes I wanted to hit him. "I didn't look at your costume. You don't have to assume the worst about me all the time. I really was going to tell you I could hear you outside. It's not my fault you both talk so loud." Or talked about me when I wasn't around.

"That wasn't my question." His voice cracked. "Neither of those was ever a question. Dear Janan, you're the most defensive person I've ever met."

My lip was going to have permanent indentions where I bit it so much. I bit the top one instead this time.

"Be careful on your way to the market field." Footsteps sounded toward the stairs.

"Sam." I felt like I was choking. Or drowning. Maybe some of both. He stopped walking, at any rate. "You asked how I'd know who you were."

Silence.

"I'll always know."

A minute later, the front door closed and I was alone in the washroom, only the reflection of a stranger in my mirror. When I thought he'd had enough time to get to South Avenue, I checked that my mask and knife were secure, then slipped sideways through doorways because my wings wouldn't let me pass through head-on.

As I left the house and darkness closed in, I tried to imagine myself having fun tonight. I tried to imagine myself smiling and laughing and maybe ending up in someone's arms by the last dance, like the magic of the masquerade was real and could help you find the match to your soul.

I couldn't imagine myself doing any of that, but that was okay.

Tonight, I wasn't Ana.

21
MASQUERADE

COOL AIR SLITHERED around my dress, ruffling the edges around my calves. The breeze pushed on my wings, so every step took a smidge more force than usual. It was unsettling, but by the time I reached the market field, I'd mostly compensated. If only I'd had the foresight to work that issue into dance practice.

The market field was gloriously lit with silver-tinged lights from the Councilhouse, and poles scattered over the field. The temple glowed; I carefully ignored that, as well as the accompanying twist in my gut.

People in costume drifted in as evening encroached. Hawks, bears, pronghorns. Someone had dressed as a troll—such bad taste—while an osprey flirted with everyone.

The market field filled with bright fish and ferrets. A sparrow chased a lizard, and they embraced. Hundreds of people swarmed across the field like herds of gemstones.

I glanced toward the landing atop the Councilhouse steps, where Tera and Ash would be dedicated later. Only a robin and house cat prowled there now, fussing with controls to something

The robin stepped up to a microphone and cleared his throat. Meuric's voice carried from the speakers fastened to the light poles. "Tonight, we celebrate the rededication of two souls."

Costumed guests turned as one entity to face him. I was trapped in the back and couldn't see around most of the crowd; I wondered what people on the other side of the temple did, where they were looking. The party stretched all across the market field.

"Every generation, our souls are reborn into new and unfamiliar bodies, as are the souls of those we love. Rarely does romantic love transcend incarnations. Rarely. Some souls, however, were created as matching pairs. Those Janan-blessed partnerships have continued over centuries. Millennia. Every generation, these souls are drawn together, regardless of their physical forms. Their love is pure and true.

"Tonight's festivities celebrate the commitment between

Tera and Ash. As they search for each other in this sea of unfamiliar faces, let us all remember that Janan created us with a purpose: to value one another, and to love."

He stepped away as the opening chords of a pavane came through the speakers, and lights flooded the market field with a dreamy glow. Interesting that Meuric didn't make his announcement before he changed clothes. It lent credit to my theory that I was the only one who cared about being anonymous tonight.

At least I knew how Meuric was dressed, so I'd be able to avoid him.

With the music playing, people began taking partners to dance. This pavane wasn't one of Sam's compositions, but it was pretty, different from what I was used to listening to. A chorus of strings and woodwinds sang across the evening.

I kept to the edges of the mass of dancers, though bodies still bumped against my wings. A few muttered apologies, while most either shot annoyed looks beneath their masks, or didn't notice, and I felt like a jerk for wearing something so cumbersome.

Self-consciously, I walked a complete circle around the market field, followed by the sensation of being watched.

So much for anonymity.

Perhaps this was like my birth. Everyone already knew one another. They'd cheated, revealing identities beneath disguises, and I was the only one they didn't know. The only new person.

A peacock tracked my progress from a light pole, but didn't approach. Familiarity surrounded an owl and praying mantis who kept up with me, but I couldn't peg who they were.

Sam had probably asked his friends to watch me. The thought had irritated me at the market, but after seeing Li again, I was sort of glad. Maybe I should have come with him. I shouldn't have let my feelings get so bruised earlier. It wasn't like I'd expected him to say he'd have chosen me over Ciana, even before I knew they'd been lovers.

A gray and white shrike turned away as I sensed a gaze from that direction, toward the Councilhouse. Ahead, a hunting hound stared.

I angled toward the southwestern edge of the field. Everything was beautiful, and the thousands of dancing people—that was wonderful. I was alone, though, with just a few of Sam's friends staring from afar.

Or maybe Li. No telling if she was here or what she might be wearing. Suddenly, every tall, slender figure was suspect.

A ferret touched my arm. "Dance?"

I jumped, but I knew that voice. Armande.

He grinned beneath the whiskers and a mask of a mask, then drew me into the dance, allowing me to use the steps

Stef had taught me. We went through the end of a galliard before he escorted me to a buffet I hadn't seen before, filled with tiny sandwiches and pastries, upside-down paper cups next to urns of coffee and hot cider. Lace covered the table, along with dozens of portraits of a couple I assumed was Tera and Ash, though they wore different faces in each image.

"They must really love each other," I breathed, before remembering I was in costume. I glanced at Armande to see if he noticed, but he just smiled.

"Your secret is safe with me. But you're pretty identifiable, even in disguise." He gave a one-shouldered shrug.

"Oh." I blushed beneath my mask and took the coffee he offered. "How many lifetimes?"

"Fifty," he said, and sipped his own drink. "Almost since the beginning. We don't get many parties like this, but Tera and Ash are always good for one. Every generation."

If they lived to be about seventy-five every life, that was 3,500 years together. I couldn't imagine that kind of love.

"For the first few generations, they couldn't stand being different ages or the same gender, so they used to kill each other in order to be reborn about the same time. No one could talk them out of it."

I thought loving someone shouldn't involve so much death. Not that I had any experience with that. "They're both women now."

He nodded. "They decided that dying all the time was too painful, and if they loved each other, it shouldn't matter. Still"—he leaned closer—"when one dies now, the other does, too. I imagine it's hard to be physically very old while your greatest love is learning to walk again."

"I bet." I finished my coffee and dropped the cup in a recycle bin.

Armande and I had a few more dances before he released me to a crow, all shiny black feathers on his mask and clothes. I didn't know him, but he said something nice about my costume before passing me to a woman dressed as an elk.

I recognized some of my partners—Stef and Whit made appearances as a jewel-toned dragonfly and a lion—but plenty were strangers, as far as I could tell. We had fun. I found myself laughing and asking other people to dance with me, rather than wait to be acknowledged.

Maybe anonymity didn't matter as much as I'd thought.

I found Sarit, a crest of gray feathers protruding from her black hair, and a bright mask covering the top half of her face. Sharp orange cheeks stood against the yellow silk. Long folds of gray cloth draped across her arms made wings—much better than mine.

"What are you?" I hadn't seen that kind of bird in Range.

"Cockatiel." She grinned beneath the wide, hooked beak. "They're from the other side of the planet."

Even just southern Range felt far away. I'd have to remember to ask her about the birds, but for now, she took my hand and dragged me toward the Councilhouse steps, where a series of archways had been placed, though not in a straight line. They were everywhere, random. "What's this?"

"The arch march!" She giggled. "No, don't actually call it that in front of anyone who does the rededication. They get mad because it sounds silly."

"I bet you started it."

"Ma-a-aybe." She drew the word out into several syllables. "The idea is really sweet, though. They start at the first arch at the base of the stairs, then find their way through the others until they reach the top. The whole time, they're blindfolded."

"Blindfolded? The arches aren't even in a line. They're all over!" I stared at her. "You're making this up."

"Nope. It's to symbolize the uncertainty of the future. They get to hold hands and offer each other suggestions which way to go. They'll have seen the layout while they're dancing, anyway."

It still sounded crazy to me.

"Each arch symbolizes something important. The obsidian one is night, the flowers—since it's winter, they're silk—are happiness, the pine is health. You get the idea."

"What happens if they don't make it through all the arches?" I asked as we drifted toward the buffet.

"They always do." She leaned toward me. "Except that once, they skipped the pine boughs. It was probably a coincidence, but a lot of people got sick that year. . . ."

I shuddered, guessing from her tone that Ash and Tera didn't live long after that. Still, it was romantic the way they kept coming back to each other.

Revelers danced all around. Sarit pulled me into the nearest circle for a fast eight-person dance, which involved so much clapping my palms stung by the end. We moved on to another group after that, then another, sometimes finding new partners, but always keeping each other in sight so we'd have someone to dance with, just in case.

For two hours, I was a butterfly going from flower to flower, swirling about the masquerade in a flurry of silken wings. I'd never felt pretty before, but so many people complimented me I almost believed them.

The sensation of being watched never eased. If anything, I felt it more strongly as the evening wore on. I still hadn't found Sam, but he'd probably gotten bored and gone back to his house. He hadn't wanted to come to begin with.

Regretting having drunk so much coffee, I excused myself from Sarit and slipped inside the Councilhouse to use the washroom. I needed the break, anyway. My legs were tired and my cheeks numb from grinning.

I hadn't known what exactly to expect of this ceremony, but it *was* fun, as Stef had promised. Plus, I liked how this was important to people. Maybe they didn't bother to hide identities, but the fact they put so much work into making a special evening for Tera and Ash . . .

This was something I could appreciate.

I felt better when I came out again, surveying the crowd from the stairs. Masks glittered, but the night held dark pockets. I saw the shrike again, as well as the peacock, both pretending not to watch as I descended.

A fast song played, making people prance and skip around. Someone caught me and spun me, grabbed me again. Rough hands squeezed mine, dragged me through the press. Fingers dug into my sides and snatched me away to another dancer.

A wolf. A hawk. A lizard. Soon they surrounded me. The music became a frenzied blur in my ears, and the world a dark and bright smear on my eyes.

They tossed me about like a butterfly in a gale. I spun from hands to hands so my hair whipped into my eyes. Ribbons and flowers fluttered, and my mask strained to fly off. I pinned it against my cheeks, lost and dizzy with energy and fear.

There were so many strangers. So much noise.

Feet stepped on mine, and my arms ached where too many hands gripped. Every piece of me was sore and shaking. When I tried to flee, the wolf seized me again, ignoring when I screamed. The music was loud, and others shouted with joy. The din swallowed my voice whole.

I jabbed my elbow into the wolf's chest and kicked the lizard's shin, tried to run again. A swan caught me, but before they recaptured me in their circle, a new dancer stepped in and fitted himself between the others and me.

My heart raced, but he caressed my cheek and shot the others a fierce look as he drew me to safety. Wings strained as he spun me away, before I got a look at his mask. I caught only a flash of gray and black and a streak of white, and then my back pressed against his chest. His arm around my waist kept me from facing him, but his embrace was gentle.

His fingers brushed my cheek, down my neck. The entire masquerade stretched out before me, but my focus tunneled to the man behind me. Hands eased toward my hips and held tight as we spun; my feet lifted off the ground, but even when I thought the wings might carry me into the breeze, he held me tight.

My new captor, or rescuer, guided us toward the edge of the crowd. He kept me so close no one could come between us. His hands stayed on my hips and stomach. The music turned slower and deeper, and his fingers curled against silk-covered flesh. I couldn't breathe.

The whole dance shifted. Heavy seductiveness replaced the fear, and the gaiety before that. My new partner smoothed my dress down my stomach, down my thigh. When I tilted my head back against his shoulder, warmth billowed against my throat where he kissed.

I stiffened and gasped, almost darted away. But his arms tightened, somehow conveying apology, and I remembered he hadn't hurt me, only saved me from the others. I relaxed again and closed my eyes. We'd moved beyond the worst of the crowd, and I trusted him not to let us run into anyone.

Music filled the space around us, the slivers of air between us. Strings sang, long and warm as gold. Flutes sounded like silver, and clarinets like forests.

This almost wasn't real. It was almost a dream when I tilted my head back again; his mouth lingered just over my skin, and I managed a slight nod. His hesitation lasted a life-time, but finally his lips brushed the tip of my ear.

I shivered deeper into his embrace, pressed my hands over his so he wouldn't let me go. I'd waited my entire life for this.

Eternities passed between kisses down my neck. His free hand traced patterns on my hip and thigh and back up, around my wing. He touched my face and hair, restraint evi-dent in the way he trembled and tried again.

A waltz began. His breath caught as he took my hand, spun me away, and then drew me back so we faced each other.

His mask covered the upper half of his face. Not a hawk or falcon, in spite of the hooked beak; the markings weren't right. Dashes of black under his eyes, gray hood and feathers, and a white ruffle at his throat. The shrike.

He didn't give me a chance to study him further, just drew me close so I leaned against him. His arms circled my waist, careful beneath my wings. As we danced, his heart pounded over the music. I could feel the tension in his arms and chest, trying to hold me, trying not to break me. I wanted to say something, reassure him that I trusted him, but if I spoke, the moment might shatter.

He felt good. Familiar. My body knew where his hands would slide before he moved, and where we'd breathe together. He knew the music as well as I did, anticipating the strong beats, letting the others linger.

Shrikes were songbirds; he ought to know.

We danced forever, and not nearly long enough. Now that I faced him, I could touch him, too, rather than self-consciously drip through his fingers. I explored his back, fingertips discovering ridges of his spine, muscles, a place below his left shoulder blade that made him writhe, as if struggling not to laugh. I tickled him again, devouring the sensation of his chest against my cheek.

When the song ended, he drew back and angled behind me as we looked up at the stairs. There, a sparrow and a lizard—not the lizard who'd trapped me—navigated the arches, hand in hand. One tugged, the other followed. Through the pine, flowers, obsidian, silver, stone— The couple made it through every archway, even with the silken blindfolds over their masks. Gold cloth streamed behind them like banners.

262

They'd really done it. Whether because one knew the route, or their true love drew them down the correct path, maybe it didn't matter. They *did* love each other.

Framed by the columns of the Councilhouse facade, the sparrow and lizard embraced, kissed, and tore off their masks and blindfolds. Everyone cheered as the masks went flying into the crowd; Sarit would have explained that to me, but she wasn't here.

Meuric stepped up to the microphone again and began another speech. Ugh. Meuric. No thanks.

I turned back to the shrike, but the beak of his mask grazed up my neck and warm lips brushed my ear. Thrills coursed through me, but I didn't move until he started away. I caught his hand. "Wait."

He'd felt right. I knew who I needed him to be, even if the way we'd danced was not how— That kind of passion he reserved for music. Not me.

A cold breeze made me shiver as I tightened my grip on his. Stepped closer. Searched his eyes.

His lips tilted up at one corner, like amusement. I'd known, but still, the familiar expression stunned me so much I almost didn't act.

I kissed him.

Rather, I pressed my mouth against his and hoped he wouldn't run. It would probably kill me.

Three long seconds and he only gasped and tightened his hands on my back. Then, with a soft moan, he opened his mouth and kissed me. It wasn't an easy, sweet kiss like I'd imagined my first would be, but frustrated and hungry. That was good, better than easy and sweet, because after everything, I was frustrated and hungry for him, too.

His beak scraped my cheek, but I ignored it while the tip of his tongue danced over my lips. Everything he did was magic, but when he deepened the kiss and the moaning came from me, I held my palms over his mask and nudged until it slipped off and dangled around my wrist. I needed Sam, not the shrike.

He jerked back, surprise and embarrassment flickering across his face. I licked my lips and pretended like my cheeks weren't hot, my insides weren't melting, and I didn't want everything his kiss had promised. "Hi." Hand shaking, I held out his mask.

He didn't take it. "You knew."

"I'll always know." My entire body was still on fire from his touch, from his legs brushing mine, from his mouth. I wanted him to kiss me again.

Meuric's speech must have stopped. Around us, others were removing their masks, greeting one another. They didn't pay attention to us.

"You knew the whole time," Sam said. "While we were dancing?"

264

"Yes." As soon as he'd touched me. The way he fit against me, and the way his mouth had hesitated over my neck. It was a very Sam thing to do, hesitating. "Didn't you know me, too?" There was an unsettling thought. What if he'd hoped I was someone else?

He took my hands like he feared I'd fly away. "Of course."

"Oh, good." That might have sounded desperate. "I mean, I wouldn't have danced with you like that if I didn't know who you were."

"You danced with a lot of people."

"Not like that." I forced myself to keep his gaze. All the places he'd touched me, I could still feel him. Maybe it hadn't meant much to him, but it had been important to me. He needed to understand. "Why were you trying to run away?"

"I wanted—" His cheeks were dark as he shook his head. "I'm sorry about today. I want to tell you everything, but mostly"—he tucked a loose strand of my hair behind my ear—"mostly I want to tell you I lied to Stef."

And I wanted him to kiss me again. Less talking. More kissing.

"She knew, I think. We're not very good at lying to each other after so long." He inhaled sharply. "Ana. I want you to know I'd choose you. If it were up to anyone, if what I wanted counted for anything, I'd have chosen you."

I felt like I had the night he'd first played for me, like I wanted to drop to the ground because my legs weren't strong enough to hold me. Instead, I used his shoulders for balance and stood on the tips of my toes to whisper by his ear. "Let's go home, Sam. No more thinking. These wings are heavy."

He kissed my neck and murmured something that sounded like assent.

22

WINGS

AS MUCH AS I wanted to go straight back to Sam's house, the ceremony wasn't quite over. Several of Tera and Ash's friends made speeches, going on about how happy they were to see another successful rededication. Many people had brought gifts, which required oohing over, and photos, and thanks.

The crowd pressed closer so everyone could look, and it was obvious with the way people cheered: the ceremony was important to them. Even if few people actually believed in matching souls, it was hard to deny that Ash and Tera fit together. They practically glowed when they looked at each other. After more than three thousand years. Incredible.

We stood another hour, and then the *entire* population of

Heart was supposed to get in line to congratulate Tera and Ash on their rededication. I noticed a few people skipping out, but that just made people around us mutter.

Sam clutched my hand, as if I might fly off, and at last we had a turn hugging Tera and Ash, congratulating them.

Mission successful, we wove through the lingering revelers in the field, who were chatting and laughing, comparing costumes. To my relief, we didn't stop to speak to anyone. We barely spoke to each other. I couldn't fathom why he didn't have anything to say, but I'd just experienced my first kiss, not to mention a billion other things I'd be dreaming about tonight. I was a little stunned, and fire burned inside my chest, inside my stomach, and lower.

We didn't take the long way back, the way I knew, but the shorter way that involved a dozen smaller streets. I wished we could fly back.

"Ana," he said, once we were alone on the moonlit road.

Nighttime hid anything farther than an arm's length away. We might have been the only people in the entire city. Just us, the dark, and cold. Air prickled across my arms and face, making me shiver. "Sam." His name became mist.

Our masks dangled from his fingers, swaying with his steps. Darkness obscured the bright colors of my butterfly, which I'd spent so long cutting and painting. "I shouldn't have danced with you like that. Or kissed you."

My heart stuttered. "Yes, you should have."

"Not in front of everyone." His voice sounded like icicles crunching underfoot. "I lost control."

He'd seemed plenty controlled to me. "You acted on passion." I'd assumed. I was less certain now, what with the way he was insisting it shouldn't have happened. But he'd *kissed* me. Hard. "There's nothing wrong with that."

"What do you think everyone will assume?"

"I don't care." I bit my lip and followed him around a corner. The cold ached worse now. Why couldn't he need me as much as I needed him? "Okay, I do care a little what they think, but mostly I care that you meant it."

"It?"

"Dancing. The way you kissed me." I didn't want to have to ask or clarify. I wanted him to take me in his arms and kiss me until I couldn't breathe. Now I simply couldn't breathe for other, far less pleasant reasons. "Did you mean it?"

He stopped walking and turned on me. "Of course! Why would you think otherwise?"

If he didn't remember when *nothing happened* in the kitchen, and then pretty much all of today, he was stupid. "You tried to run away, and now you're saying you shouldn't have kissed me. What do you expect me to think?" My voice betrayed me; it caught and trembled. "I can't do this in-between stuff. Either we kiss or we don't. If we do, then no more running away or saying we shouldn't. Because I can't—" I swallowed hard and tried again. "It's

269

too confusing when you change your mind."

The masks hissed as they fell to the cobblestones. Sam made a noise almost like my name, then took my shoulders and kissed me. Not as passionately as before, but my insides clenched up just the same. I struggled to mimic everything he did, but relief and rage were stronger. I jerked back, kicking the masks with my heel.

"That wasn't an answer." Maybe it was, but I needed to hear the words.

He drew a sharp breath as he scooped up the masks. "I've wanted to kiss you since we met. Never out of pity. Only because I think you're amazing and beautiful. You make me happy."

I hugged myself, blinking away tears and bitterness. "It's hard to believe that."

"Never doubt it." He cupped his hand over my cheek, sharing faint warmth. "I hope you'll forgive me."

"You can make it up to me." I wanted to touch him, but in spite of the ease of dancing, and the way he stood close now, it still felt off-limits. The masks were gone. "And you don't have to care what anyone else thinks. Much."

"I have to care what the Council thinks. Technically, you're still—" He glanced toward the center of Heart, templelight shining on his face. "They won't understand."

About a five-thousand-year-old teenager and a nosoul? I didn't understand it, either, but that didn't change what I wanted. "I'm doing everything they've ordered. We'll worry about them if they complain."

He faced me again, but it was too dark to see the subtleties of his expression. "Earlier you said, 'Let's go home.' You've never called it home before." There was a pause where I could have responded, but I left it filled only with starlight and misted breath. "Do you"—he shifted his weight—"want this relationship? You and me?"

"Do you remember what I told you in the cabin before I knew who you were? How I'd always felt about Dossam?" I was dizzy with hope and cold and need.

"Not like I could forget." He stepped closer, blocking the wind. "I was so nervous after. I was afraid you'd be disappointed when you found out I'm just me."

"I liked *you* before that. The piano was extra." I waited, breath heavy in my chest, until finally I whispered, "You didn't say whether you wanted this."

He slid his fingers through my hair, arranging it over my shoulders. "Do you remember when I kissed you? I felt like a starving man given a feast."

If we weren't in the middle of a dark street, I'd ask him to refresh my memory, but I couldn't feel my nose and fingertips anymore, so I echoed, "Not like I could forget."

His hands drifted down my arms. "Well then. Good. I'm relieved."

"As if I'd have said no." I turned up my face and gasped

again when he brushed a kiss across my mouth. So casual, like this was how life would be from now on. Sam would kiss me. I'd kiss him. "Let's go before I freeze. I didn't plan for a meandering walk home."

"Home, then." Sam threaded his fingers with mine. His fingers were cold, too. "I regret I didn't wear a jacket, or I'd give it to you."

"I still have my wings. It wouldn't fit."

"I'd carry them for you."

"They're attached to the dress. It was the only way I could get them to stay."

He squeezed my hand, tone mischievous. "In that case, I'd be especially happy to carry the wings."

"Sam!"

"It wouldn't be the first time I've seen you without clothes."

"Sam!" The blush warmed me as I searched for something to tease him about in return, but just as I remembered a few of his embarrassing missteps during dance practice, a blue light flashed across the street. I blinked away stars.

Sam dropped to the ground and choked on a wordless shout. "Ana." He clutched his left arm, face twisted with agony. "Ana, run."

Another dagger of light cut across the night, and the cobblestone just in front of my toes sizzled.

Someone was trying to kill us.

23
THUNDERSTORM

I LUNGED FOR Sam. Either our attacker had bad aim, or they weren't really trying to *kill* us, just make us think they were. Still, I didn't want even a graze.

"We need to run." I tugged on his right arm; he kept his palm clamped over the left, which undoubtedly meant bad things, but another spear of light stabbed my wing and there was no time to fret over him. The burning silk smelled like ash. "I'm not going anywhere without you."

His expression twisted, but he hauled himself up with a grunt. "It's okay," he said. "Not even bleeding."

Shadows concealed our attacker, but it looked as though the shots had come from between two fir trees near the intersection. That was behind us, so they must have followed us from the masquerade. The same person who'd followed me the other night?

I freed my knife from my hair. I'd loathed it before, but they'd shot Sam. They'd get a hole in them if I had a chance.

Our footsteps pounded on the cobblestones as we ran. My stupid wings caught air and slowed me, so when I had both hands free, I clutched the wire frame and stabbed my knife through the silk, cutting gashes. I did the same to the other wing.

I led Sam along the left edge of the street, where starlight wouldn't silhouette us and moonlight wouldn't shine. If I'd been more confident, I'd have cut through yards, but my sense of direction was even worse in the dark. I wouldn't recognize whatever street we came to.

The attacker continued shooting, bright bursts to our right. I glanced over my shoulder, but our pursuer hid in the shadows across the street, somewhere behind us.

"This road!" Sam cried. We turned left, onto another tree-lined street. I took a fistful of his shirt and, as soon as we were around the corner, dragged him into the brush. Pine needles rustled, and the sudden shift must have twinged his arm because he cursed, but we took cover behind a bush and kept as still as possible.

Mindful of my knife and his injury, I put my arms around him and drew him close. His heart sped beneath my hand, and his breath hissed in quiet gasps. I petted his cheek while we waited for our attacker to run past, but the street remained empty.

My fingers stiffened around the knife handle as I began to shiver again, both with fear and adrenaline. By Sam's ear, I whispered, "I'm going to look."

"Don't." He clutched my waist. "You'll get hurt."

"You already are. We have to get to safety." I slipped from his grasp, easy when I was covered in silk. "I'm just going to check if they're gone."

He shook his head but didn't try to stop me again.

Before I left, I bent the wires of my wings closer to my body, out of my way. Shredded silk dripped from ruined wings.

I tiptoed onto the road, straining my ears for noises that didn't belong, but the thud of my own heartbeat was distracting. Couldn't ignore it, either, or the rustle of evergreen boughs.

Wood snapped. I searched for the source, but shadows dusted the street like charcoal. One shadow moved, darker than the others.

I froze, stupidly obvious in my silly dress and tattered wings. Moonlight leaked across the street; I could half feel it on my skin, like a breath no warmer than the night. "Who's there?"

Behind me, Sam let out a string of curses.

"There's no harm in asking," I muttered. "They've already shot at us."

I shouldn't have spoken. A targeting light came from the shadow that had moved, and hit my left wing. Wire melted. I yelped and started running, shoes pounding on the cobblestones. Crashing sounds in the bushes signaled Sam coming after me, but when I looked, a new person emerged.

A large figure barreled onto the street, easily catching up to me. I pushed myself harder, but I was cold and tired. He grabbed my wing and jerked me around. I stared at a white mask that covered his entire face.

I struggled in the direction I'd left Sam, but my attacker seized my arm and threw me to the ground. Stinging raced through my elbow and thigh; my knife, which of course I'd forgotten about, skittered away. Warmth oozed as I scrambled to my feet.

He shoved me again.

I crawled toward my knife, just two steps away. Before I could reach it, my attacker plucked me off the ground and hurled me in the opposite direction. I screamed as limbs banged against stone. Blackness gripped me as I rolled onto my back, groaning at sharp fires everywhere.

Something dull hit my ribs. His shoe. I let out two weak *oof*s, and footsteps retreated. A pair of them, perhaps, but I couldn't look to see. My whole body rang with numbness, cold, and heat from forming bruises.

I had to find Sam. My arms shook as I lifted myself to my elbows. Pain flared where the skin had scraped off, but it drove me all the way to sitting to avoid more stinging. "Sam?" I sounded like a frog as I lurched to my feet.

The knife was where I'd dropped it. I stumbled, retrieved it in case our attackers returned, and shambled toward the bush. My whole body felt like a bruise.

Sam was prone on the dead grass. I dropped to my knees, sheathed my knife, and touched his throat. His pulse beat steadily beneath my questing fingers. "Wake up." I cupped his cheek; his skin was cold.

He moaned and opened his eyes, but couldn't seem to focus. "Someone hit me."

"Let's go. They might come back."

"Are you okay?" He sat up and swayed. "I don't think I am."

"You'll live." We helped each other limp toward safety. If our attackers had returned, they could have killed us both and we couldn't have done much about it.

It seemed like it took hours to get back to the house, and the streets of Heart were such that you could wander that long without ever meeting anyone until the market field, so there was no one to help us. Not even Stef, who lived next door. Though since we didn't know who attacked us, it was probably better that we didn't see anyone.

Sam flicked on the lights as we staggered inside. We winced at the brightness, but that pain was minor compared to everything else.

"You look awful." Before I remembered, I leaned on the wall for balance while I kicked off my shoes. The white stone, the same that ran around the city and doorless temple, chose that moment to pulse like a heartbeat. I recoiled and tripped over my half-off shoes, then landed on my butt next to a piano leg. My tailbone ached. "Ow."

"So do you." Dirt and blood streaked his face, and his sleeve hung open to reveal a nasty burn on his arm, blistered and red in the middle and black around the edges. He saw where my gaze landed, and grimaced. "It will heal."

"We should call someone. A medic. The Council." I dragged myself to my feet. "They need to know, right?"

He nodded. "I'll call Sine while I check that the house is empty. Stay here."

"Nope. Going with you." One advantage of our condition: he couldn't stop me. "Why Sine, not Meuric?"

"I trust Sine." He drew a ragged breath and braced himself on the wall as he headed for the stairs. The shelves groaned protest, but they held until he reached the banister. His ascent was slow—the blow to the head must have disoriented him worse than he let on—so I went behind, ready to catch him should he lose his balance. Well, I could soften his landing when we hit the floor. Maybe.

After he made a quick call and we checked all the rooms, I followed him into his washroom.

"Sine said she'll look for a medic to send over," he said,

"but it's late and people are still hard to contact after the rededication."

"At this point, I'd rather just take every painkiller in the house and go to sleep."

He gave me a weak smile. "Yeah."

While he reached behind the curtain and turned on the spray, I fished out a handful of pills for him and filled a glass of water. He took them without comment; I took a handful myself.

"Are you going to stay in here while I shower?"

"Oh, no." I glanced at his arm. "We should put something on that. The water will hurt."

"Right." He slouched on the edge of the tub and didn't complain when I helped him pull off his shirt, careful of the blisters. I placed gauze over his burn, then wrapped it in a waterproof bandage and moved to leave. "Hey."

I waited at the door where steam billowed out.

He met my eyes, suddenly focused. "Don't go far." When I nodded, he closed the door halfway, enough that I couldn't see him, but I could see his shadow in the steamy mirror while he undressed and then vanished behind the shower curtain.

After he finished, he helped me clean and bandage my scrapes before I headed into the other room for my turn. Hot water soaked through my muscles, easing some of the strain from hours of dancing, and getting thrown around the street. Some, but not nearly enough.

Nightgown-clad, I emerged to find him asleep on my bed. My painkillers had kicked in while I squeezed water from my hair, so I hoped that meant his had, too. I sat next to him. "Wake up, sleepy."

"I am awake."

"Prove it."

He opened his eyes and managed a smirk. "See?"

I touched his chin. "No one mentioned that you get beat up after the masquerade. Seems counter to all the romance."

Sam pushed himself vertical and sat next to me. Our socked feet hung off the edge of the bed. "That wasn't part of the plan."

"You had a plan?" From where we sat, my butterfly dress was visible on the washroom floor, bent and shredded wings and all. Cheeks hot, I remembered what he'd suggested just before someone shot him.

His eyes found the dress, too. "I was teasing about that. Unless you were looking forward to it. Then I meant every word."

"Ask me tomorrow." The painkillers had numbed the aches across my body, but my mind felt ready to explode from today. "Do you know who attacked us?"

Sam shook his head, then groaned and rested his face in his palms. "I think this is going to hurt for days. No, I don't know. I have suspicions, but I didn't see anyone. Did you?"

"I think there were two. One shooting, who I didn't see,

and then a big man with a mask covering his entire face."

"That could describe a lot of people."

"He probably knocked you out so you wouldn't be able to identify him." Sam might have figured it out, based on other physical clues and who was currently what age and which gender. I was the only one in the world who wouldn't be able to even guess. A thousand emotions I thought I'd moved past came rushing back.

"Other than scrapes and bruises, you're unhurt?"

"Sure." But the whole situation infuriated me. There was Sam with his experience and the way he kept alternating between friendly and more than friendly; I'd been attacked somewhere I should have felt safe—creepy white stone walls notwithstanding—and then I was constantly reminded that I was the only nosoul in existence. The only person who didn't see the beginning of Heart, or know everyone, or have something to contribute.

The butterfly costume had been the real me. Like me, it hadn't lasted long. Wouldn't be there in the morning.

I marched into the washroom and scooped up the silk and wire shreds. Futilely, I yanked at it as though I could rip it in two, but it was too strong, even destroyed.

With a wordless shriek, I flung it across the washroom, picked it up and threw it again. Wire clattered across stone and wood, but no matter how many times I hurled the costume remnants, I didn't feel better. It was too light, too easy, but there was nothing heavier I could throw, nothing that was mine, anyway.

Everything here was Sam's.

Costume included.

"Ana?"

"What?" I yelled, and spun to face him.

He stood in the washroom doorway, wearing confusion and something I couldn't identify. Pain? His head hurt. My fit probably made things worse.

I swallowed back tears. "Sorry. Maybe, since we don't know who did a bad job of trying to kill us, we should just go to bed." That would be better than subjecting either of us to this, and if I accidentally cried, only my pillow would witness it.

His gaze traveled from me to the costume, and the line between his eyes said he'd figured out why I was so angry. "I want to tell you something."

"I don't want to hear it." I wanted to scream and kick things, but I couldn't do that if he tried to make me feel better.

No, I *wanted* to be back at the masquerade, so close I could hear his heart beating over the music. I *wanted* that moment when there was no question who he was and I had a brave impulse—and I kissed him. I *wanted* him to need me like that again.

"I want to feel real." The words escaped before I realized,

and I'd have fled the washroom in horror if he hadn't been standing in the doorway. Instead, I turned away, leaned on the counter, and squeezed my eyes shut. Warmth trickled out.

His good arm circled my waist. "You feel real to me." When he tugged me toward him, I went. I didn't know what else to do. "I can't imagine what's going on inside you now."

"Everything." I mumbled into his nightshirt. "There's a thunderstorm inside me, swirling everything around."

He kissed the top of my head and didn't let go.

"Can't you make it stop?" My throat ached with struggling not to cry more. I hated this, halfway hated him, except how I wanted him as much as I wanted music.

"I'd give anything to make things right for you." He caressed my cheek, my hair, my back. Everywhere he touched, the angry fires cooled. I wished he'd touch my heart. "But I can't. I can help, but the hard work is all up to you. If you don't feel real, no one else can do it for you. I promise, though, you've always felt real to me. From the moment I saw you jump off the cliff."

"Sometimes I still feel like I'm jumping off the cliff."

He nodded and kissed my head again. "Can I tell you something?"

If he felt that strongly about it, I had little choice. "Okay."

"Come out of the washroom." He nudged me toward the door. "It won't make your thunderstorm stop, but maybe it will help. Proof you're real to me. Important."

I looked up and sought his haggard face, his eyes. How could I be important? I was an afterthought, five thousand years later. A mistake, because Ciana was gone. I was the dissonant note on the end of a masterpiece symphony. I was the brushstroke that ruined the painting.

"Come on," he urged, and I allowed him to guide me back into the bedroom, where he draped a thick white blanket over my shoulders. We curled up in the top corner of the bed, by the headboard and the wall. "Are you comfortable?" he asked, when I was leaning against him.

"Are you?" If I twisted, I could see his face from the corner of my eye.

He rested his cheek on my head. "When I went north in my last life, I was searching for inspiration. I hadn't written anything new in a generation. I felt empty. I didn't find anything, no matter how far I traveled. I just died. That was autumn of the Year of Darkness, three-twenty-nine."

I waited.

"Usually, it takes a few years to be reincarnated, but it took just over a year for me to be reborn." From the way he said it, I should have understood what that meant.

"And?"

He sighed, but his tone was endlessly patient. "That was the three-hundred-thirtieth Year of Songs. That's your birth year, too. When we met eighteen years later, that was the first time in a generation I felt inspired, the first time I felt music in me again."

I couldn't move. A million emotions flooded me—awe, joy, fear—and what did he expect of me now? I was raw inside, too much back-and-forth today, not enough just . . . happiness, like it should have been. So I didn't move or speak, because I couldn't.

His voice lowered, as though to cover hints of hesitation. "I think I died to be reborn with you. To find you in the lake. I found my inspiration."

"But you had to die for it." What a dumb thing to say. My mouth hated me.

He turned his head slightly, so his whisper came by my ear. "If I'd looked like a ninety-year-old man when we met, would you have wanted to be with me?"

I wanted to be able to say yes, because I'd known him at the masquerade, and in all the photographs and videos from other lifetimes, but *this* was the Sam I wanted to kiss. As much as I felt for him, I couldn't imagine being attracted to a ninety-year-old, at least not while I was eighteen. Maybe when I was ninety, too.

He gave a soft chuckle. "I thought not. I'd worry if you had said yes. Even people who've loved each other for lifetimes aren't always attracted to each other when their physical ages are so different. It *does* matter, at least some."

Like what Armande had said about Tera and Ash

arranging to be reborn as close together as possible. "That's sort of a relief." I wished it didn't matter. It didn't change that he was five thousand years older than me, just made it easier to forget sometimes. "So it doesn't bother you that I don't have four digits in my age?"

"Saying I never thought about it would be a lie, but it doesn't change how I feel. Ana, you make me ache in places that aren't even physical." He held me tighter, and for a moment I didn't understand what that meant. Then I remembered how I'd felt while we were dancing. That *yearning*. "Does it bother you that I do have four digits?"

"Well, you don't look fossilized. And it's helpful that you like girls your physical age." I bit my lip. "But it is sad that you had to die to get back here."

"Well, I'm glad about it. I've never been particularly attractive, but at least this way I have youth on my side. I don't know how I'd have convinced you to stay with me if I was ugly *and* half-fossilized."

"Sam?" I twisted around, freeing myself from his arms.

He tilted his head. "Hmm?"

"You think too much." I took fistfuls of his shirt and kissed him, somewhat more confident now that we had a little practice, still nervous because I felt like we balanced on a razor blade. One wrong move and we'd slice apart.

His fingers curled against my back as I faced him, careful of scrapes and bruises, of jabbing each other with knees

286

or elbows. "You were amazing tonight, the way you danced. Beautiful." He brushed his fingertips across my cheeks, chin, and lips. Down my throat, across my collarbone.

I splayed my hands across his chest, unable to move while he touched me like echoes of dancing. Softer, more delicate than before, but heavy with tension and—too amazing to believe—desire. How could he desire *me*?

Sam continued his mapping of my face and arms, completely engaged in his study. I took in his captivated expression until I couldn't anymore, and closed my eyes, willing him to touch everywhere.

I didn't have to understand why he felt this way. I could be grateful for now, and enjoy it.

Hands stopped above my breasts. He hesitated, and chose a path down the sides of my body. He made me tremble, made me ache inside. My heart wasn't big enough to hold everything I felt, but I couldn't bear the thought of asking him to wait while I caught up.

He traced patterns on my stomach. I held my breath, waiting.

"Ana?" A mere whisper.

"I'm nervous." I kept my eyes closed and hoped he'd understand everything I couldn't say. "I don't know what happens next."

"Only what you want." He rested his forefinger on my chin until I met his eyes. He looked like he balanced on a razor, too, one side patient as ever, and the other— He looked like I felt, ready to burst from pressure.

"What I want." I slid my hands over him until cloth folded between my fingers. "I don't even know what that is. It feels like too much, but I'll fall apart if I don't get it."

"You won't fall apart." He lowered his eyes, smiled. "I won't let you."

"You're truly kind." Now that he wasn't caressing me, I could breathe. I could think straight. "There's a lot I don't know." Such as, anything beyond what had just happened. No, I didn't even know what just happened, just that it felt *good*. "Will you show me?"

"A thousand things, whenever you're ready."

There was a heartbeat where I could have been resentful of his experience, but I decided to be grateful instead. One of us would always know what we were doing, rather than both of us fumbling and messing up. "Not all at once. I don't want to rush."

"I'm sure we can pace ourselves." His mouth turned up. "What do you think? One thing a day?"

I considered, then shook my head. "Maybe two. A thousand days is a long time."

He laughed. "If you say so."

I withdrew from him and lifted an eyebrow.

His breath caught. "Okay, suddenly it seems like eternity. Two it is." While I struggled to figure out exactly what I'd done to make him react that way, he went on. "Unfortunately, I think we've used up our two—or ten—for the day."

"Did we? It's after midnight." Using the shelf-wall to keep from falling, I stood on the bed and arranged my blanket over my shoulders again. The white cloth rippled like wings. "I think we have time for you to kneel down and worship me."

"Number two on the list." He sat on his knees and gazed up. "Number one was convincing you to like me."

He made it impossible not to smile. "Kiss my hands and feet, and you will be worthy of my liking."

"But those were five-ninety-six and five-ninety-seven."

I offered my hand that wasn't keeping me balanced against the wall. "You were going to wait that long?"

"You're the one who said not to rush." He took my hand in his, pressed his mouth against the back. "Oh." His breath warmed my skin. "I just thought of a hundred more."

"Maybe three a day." As I sat, he held my hips to steady me. "Maybe ten," I whispered, kneeling with him. He held me so close; I rested my hand just beneath the bandage on his arm. "How does this feel?"

"Like a burn. It's okay." He kissed me, not deep like before, but just as sweet. A sleepy kiss while he struggled to stay awake. He so often guarded himself; it was startling to see him like this. "How's that thunderstorm inside you?"

"Already forgot about it." I didn't want the hour to end.

The Sam I always imagined was here, holding me. He liked me. I wouldn't forget the moody Sam after the dragon attack, the Sam who'd been sneaking around every night, or the Sam who thought we shouldn't have danced and kissed, but for this moment, with this Sam, I enjoyed the sensation of happiness. "Want to know a secret?"

"Yes." He sat down, and I followed. If I pulled back the covers, maybe he wouldn't leave. After today, I couldn't stand the thought of being away from him. I had to keep him like this, the sweet Sam. The Sam who kissed me.

"Aside from the parts where we fought and were nearly killed and then I threw things," I whispered, "today has been the best day of my life."

His brown eyes drew me in as he said, "Mine too."

I was about to tease him about how this life must have felt so short, but something banged downstairs. We stiffened, both of us poised to listen when it came again. "Someone's at the door." It was so late. "A medic? Or whoever attacked us?"

He slipped off the bed and nodded. "Keep your knife with you, no matter what happens." Without so much as a last glance, he left the room.

I struggled into real clothes and tucked my knife into my waistband before creeping after Sam. From the balcony over the parlor, I could just see him at the door, blocking whoever had called.

"I don't understand," he said.

"You're under arrest." The high, youthful voice was familiar. Meuric? It was dim downstairs, but I could just make out another shadow in the doorway, maybe two others. I couldn't tell. "There's nothing confusing about that. I just hope you won't make a fuss."

"But *why*?"

"For conspiring to murder Ana, the newsoul."

24
OBSESSION

"NO!" I SPRINTED for the stairs, drawing everyone's attention. "No, he didn't. He wouldn't."

Before I'd reached the middle step, three more people shoved into the house. One was Li, just as angry and formidable as she'd been the day at the market, and the day I left Purple Rose Cottage.

I rocked back on my heels and clutched the banister so hard my hand went numb. "What is she doing here?"

"She's here to take you home," said Meuric. The other two people, Corin and a woman I didn't know, stepped toward Sam. "Your guardianship has been transferred."

"No." I pried my hand off the banister and hurtled down

the rest of the stairs. I couldn't go with Li. Not again. I was supposed to be free. "Sam, don't let them."

Li swore. "Ana, he's been tricking you. Haven't you noticed him sneaking to the library every night?"

"Liar!" I couldn't breathe from all my anger and fear inside. She wasn't completely a liar.

Sam stretched his hurt arm toward me, but Corin yanked him back, heedless of the bandage. "Don't touch her," shouted Corin. "Not after what you've done."

"What did I do?" Sam drew himself away from Corin but didn't reach for me again. And I'd stopped because Li blocked my path. "I'd never harm Ana. We were attacked tonight. It was Li."

"It's true!" My support went ignored, of course.

"Get him out!" Li roared, pointing at the guards. "Corin, Aleta, get him away from my daughter."

I wanted desperately to move, to run, but I couldn't abandon Sam.

"Do it." Meuric opened the door wider while Corin and Aleta jostled Sam.

"Don't!" Freed from paralysis, I pushed past Li and lunged for Sam. Hands dug into my sides; Li ripped me away with a grunt, inserting herself between us again. "Sam!" I strained, and he struggled against the guards, but they were stronger, and soon he was outside.

"It's for the best." Meuric shut the door. Though muffled, the grumble of an engine starting came, and quieted as the batteries kicked in. They took him away.

I stood in the middle of the parlor, Meuric between the door and me, and Li blocking the stairs. I was trapped, a butterfly under glass. Muscles and bones ached, and my head was heavy with shock and fear and exhaustion. If I didn't speak now, I'd never be heard. "I don't want to go with Li."

"You have the right to refuse that, but remember, you're only permitted to stay in Heart if someone agrees to watch over you."

"Li was a bad guardian. She didn't do anything right. Call Stef. Or Sarit, Orrin, or Whit." I edged toward the piano, the opposite direction from Li. "Just not her."

"We have evidence that suggests they were working together. Stef and Orrin are already in custody for attacking you tonight."

"They wouldn't—"

"Both Sam and Stef came to my house today," Li interrupted. "Sam accused me of trying to murder you, and then he hit me when I suggested his intentions toward you weren't pure." True to her word, a bruise darkened her cheek.

"Sam wouldn't have done that. Stef and Orrin wouldn't have attacked us." My legs hit the piano bench. I sat down, hard. "I don't believe either of you."

"Sam and Stef confronted me while their friends went

sneaking around my house and the guard station." Li sneered. "I don't know what they were looking for."

"We need to search upstairs," Meuric said. "All of Li's and Menehem's most recent diaries are missing from the library. Evidence—which Whit and Orrin tried to hide, by the way—suggests Sam had taken the books. Personal diaries, professional—everything."

If I hadn't been sitting already, I would have now. "They're free to anyone who wants to read them." Wasn't that the line I'd been given? "That doesn't mean anything." But it did. I'd asked Sam about the books in his room, and he'd said they were about dragons.

"Someone obsessed with you might search for anything related to you, including your parents' diaries." He motioned toward the stairs. "I expect you'll want to see."

He didn't want to leave me by myself; we both knew I would run. But if I refused to go up, he'd tell Li to watch me. I didn't want to be alone with her. One glance at the front door, and I made my way upstairs again, shaking with a new thunderstorm inside me. "Sam wouldn't hurt me."

The words came out strong, but he *had* left this morning, and had been talking to Stef about something Li said. I hadn't noticed swelling on his hand from hitting Li, but even if he had, there was nothing wrong with *that*. I wanted to hit Li. Not that I would ever have the courage.

Every step up brought a new layer of dread. I couldn't

live with Li. Couldn't. She marched up behind me. Any minute now she'd do something terrible.

And if I didn't go with her, I'd be exiled from Heart. From Range. Even if I didn't die within the first week—early death being most likely—I'd never see Sam or my friends again. I'd never have music again, not like I did now, and I'd never have a chance to learn the truth of my existence.

Which left obeying Meuric's orders my only choice. I hated him.

"I saw the way you danced together." Li's voice was dark as dusk. "He was so upset when I suggested he might be taking advantage of your naïveté, but if he does that with you in public, what are we supposed to assume happens in private?"

Just like he'd feared they would think. I kept my face down, as if that would hide my secret longings. "He wouldn't hurt me." She wouldn't believe me no matter how many times I said it, but if I stopped, she'd think she won.

Li gave a hoarse laugh. "I think he'd do anything to gain your trust. You don't know him. Not the way everyone else does. He focuses on what he wants—in this case, someone who practically worships him—and doesn't let anything get in his way."

The house was cold as we reached the top of the stairs, and Meuric started toward Sam's bedroom. As much as I tried, I couldn't forget the other night, when I'd helped Sam up to his room and had to kick aside books so neither of us tripped. Books that had been gone in the morning. There'd been so many. Had they *all* been about dragons and sylph?

"Watch her," Meuric said, and flicked on lights until the entire upstairs was blinding bright. He rummaged around Sam's belongings while I waited with my back against the balcony rail. Li guarded me.

"Why are you doing this?" I flinched away, but she didn't hit me. She wouldn't with Meuric in the next room. "You didn't want me before. Why now?"

"You're my daughter." Li flashed a benevolent smile. "And you've been living with a man you know nothing about. I was under the impression you'd be on your own, and I thought you could handle that. But Dossam isn't safe for you."

"You gave me a broken compass. Sam pulled me out of Rangedge Lake."

"The compass worked when I tested it. I can't help it if you broke it." She shrugged. "At any rate, it's come to my attention that your education has been neglected, and I've been given good incentive to rectify that."

What did that mean? Someone had bribed her? It must have been for something good, if she'd agreed to endure my presence again.

She went on. "I didn't do a good enough job teaching you before, and Sam's idea of educating you seems to be— Well, you need to know more than music and dancing and whatever else he's been doing to you."

"We haven't *done* anything."

"After what I saw earlier? I doubt that."

I grasped at anything, any accusation. "You followed me home the other night."

She scoffed. "I have better things to do. What makes you think it wasn't one of Sam's tricks? It could have been a friend of his, trying to scare you so you'd trust Sam more. That Stef. They're always so close." Her voice lowered. "You should hear about the things *they've* done together."

"It was you. I know it."

Meuric emerged from the bedroom, a stack of books in his arms. "I've found the missing diaries. It seems you were right about Sam. He's been studying everything he can about little Ana."

I clenched my jaw; he was just as *little* as me. "So what? It doesn't prove anything." Except that he'd lied. Maybe lied. Avoided the truth, anyway. Omitted important information. Wasn't that just as bad?

Meuric gave a long sigh. "Remind me why you're scraped up."

"Li attacked us on the way home." My whole body trembled. I needed to run, needed to get free. I had to find Sam and ask why he'd been researching Li and Menehem, and why he hadn't told me.

"Someone attacked you, clearly, but it wasn't me." She shook her head, as though I should be ashamed for thinking badly of her. "What is that, Meuric? This one isn't a diary." She plucked a book from the middle of the stack, not fast enough to keep those on top of it from falling. A dozen books thumped on the floor.

"Oh, that's worrying." Meuric squinted as Li turned pages. "There were more books in there. Hang on." He went back into Sam's room while Li kept flipping through whatever had caught her attention.

I squatted by the pile of books, my knife jabbing a bruise on my stomach when I moved. I suffered the pain; if I drew attention to the weapon, Li would take it away.

Mostly, there were diaries on the floor. Several were marked with Li's name, but most were Menehem's. His were thick, with bits of paper sticking out of them as though he'd tried to fit more information in at the last minute. From my angle, I couldn't see what Li held, but her face was cold and rigid.

Not much scared her, not that I'd ever seen, but she didn't react well to threats of humiliation, which I clearly remembered from Soul Night thirteen years ago. I'd been too young to leave behind, and she'd wanted to go to the celebration being held near Purple Rose Cottage while the main one went on in Heart. I'd tagged along while she explained that some of her friends had come down because they knew she couldn't make it to Heart, not with me in tow. When some of them had teased her about the nosoul, her face had gotten like that: cold and rigid.

This wasn't the same, not exactly, but whatever she felt, she tried to hide it. I imagined it was fear.

Then she noticed my stare, and she sneered. "Get off the floor. None of those are your business."

"The Council said I could look at anything I wanted."

"The Council said a lot of things because Sam convinced a few persuasive voices to let you roam free through the library. Sam isn't here anymore, and I'm going to be more strict about your education. Now stand up."

I did as she ordered. When we left, I would escape. Go to Sarit's. She'd hide me. But she'd also be the first person Li would suspect. Maybe Armande would help.

Meuric came out of the bedroom with another stack of books, which he placed on the floor. "I found these, too. This is very upsetting."

Li's expression shifted again as she crossed her arms, tucking the book against her side. "I can't imagine what he wanted with all this. So much about sylph."

I shuddered. Neither were looking at me, at least.

"Not only sylph." Meuric picked through the books. "This one is on dragons. Sam hates dragons."

No matter Sam's real reason for taking these books, the Council would find a way to make this look bad.

"I wonder how long he's been doing this," Li mused. "He's got a lot on Menehem here, and you remember what Menehem was researching?"

"Sylph," Meuric muttered. "Ana, weren't you attacked by sylph on the edges of Range? Twice?"

They didn't wait for me to nod.

"Menehem was experimenting on sylph, trying to find out if he could control them with some kind of chemical." Li glanced at Meuric. "He was close to discovering the right mix of hormones, if I recall. Do you think Sam—"

"Sam wouldn't." I couldn't stop the tremors inside me, the way my heart raced and ached. It had to have been Li. Sam couldn't have known about the experiments until after we met, because he didn't associate with Li or Menehem. Right? "Li knew about Menehem's research. I bet she figured out how to control the sylph and send them after me."

Li looked at me like I was the stupidest person she'd ever met.

"Sam just happened to be in the area both times you were attacked?" Meuric shook his head. "I'm sorry, Ana, I know you wanted to trust him, but this is all very incriminating. You may have to realize that, while his feelings for you might be real, they aren't healthy or safe."

"Not feelings," Li said. "Obsession. What he's done is unacceptable, beyond what anyone would do to someone they claim to have feelings for. He followed her into the woods, coerced the sylph into chasing her, and *rescued* her so she'd trust him. He's been doing variations of the same thing ever since."

"No, he wouldn't—"

"Now, Li, that's quite an accusation. You're assuming a lot about what Sam can do, and some things may be coincidence." Meuric almost sounded reasonable, but his words were clipped. If they hadn't planned all this ahead of time, he already believed her. "I do find the timing eerie, though, considering the dragon attack on the market, and"—he glanced at me—"other things."

"What other things?" I asked. "Me?"

He actually did look worried for a second. "If you've read as much history as you claim, you know what inevitably follows these small attacks."

Big attacks. It hadn't happened in a long time, but dragons always returned. They hated Heart. Hated humans.

He didn't give me a chance to respond. He snapped photos of everything on the floor, the bruises and scrapes on my face and arms, and then announced we were finished. He didn't care how much I pleaded.

Li held fast to my wrist as we marched downstairs and outside. I barely had time to put on shoes, let alone get any of my things.

The moon had fallen below the wall by now, leaving only dull starlight to illuminate the yard. I searched for a place to hide, but as soon as I looked interested in my surroundings, Li's grip tightened.

"Don't even think about it." She squinted as lights darted

across the lawn and reflected off the cold stone of the house. Wheels ground over cobblestones and stopped.

Corin exited the vehicle and motioned all of us in. "Sam's in with the others. None of them are happy about it."

"No," said Meuric, "I imagine they're not."

"I don't want to go with Li." It was futile to keep protesting, but the minute I stopped was the minute I started thinking about all the things Sam had been keeping from me. He'd left the house after I went to bed so often, and was always so secretive about whatever he was working on . . . "Please, Corin. Sam said you weren't bad."

He herded me into the backseat of the vehicle, everyone blocking my way so I couldn't escape. Li slid in on one side of me, and Meuric on the other. Trapped.

We drove down the walkway and through the twisting cobblestone streets of Heart, away from Sam's house. Aside from when I'd been an infant, this was my first time riding in a vehicle, and I couldn't even enjoy it. I was a prisoner, as surely as Sam had been. We all knew I'd have run if they'd tried to make me walk to Li's house.

"I know you're worried, Ana." Li's voice was heavier in the confined space. "I realize I neglected your education before. I'm going to do a better job this time."

Whatever Meuric had offered her—I was sure he was responsible for this—she must have really wanted it. "Sam and I had it covered."

She kept talking as though I hadn't spoken, listing all the plans she'd made for my life. When we drove by the Councilhouse, eerily lit with remnants of the masquerade and the glow from the temple, I caught a light go out near the base of the building, in an otherwise dark corner I'd never been. The prison?

Li would never let me out of her sight now, but I was certain that was where they were keeping Sam.

25
TRAPPED

LIFE TUNNELED ON my new focus: guarding myself from Li.

There was no music in her house; she'd removed all recordings in preparation for my arrival, insisting such nonsense would only distract me.

Every morning, she woke me before dawn, rushed me through breakfast, and had me running laps around the house by the time the sun crested the city wall. Fifteen the first day, and twenty when I got through fifteen without trouble. A few more laps left me winded to her satisfaction, but after a week, she decided I should run thirty. Only my loathing kept me thrusting foot before foot when I couldn't see straight anymore. The sulfuric reek from a fumarole on the other side of the wall didn't help.

After I caught my breath, I worked on strengthening exercises until lunch. As far as I could tell, she just liked to watch me struggle. I'd never thought of myself as weak or out of shape, but after meeting Sam and his friends, it had become apparent I was smaller than average. I'd never be as tall as Li or as muscular as Orrin—not in this lifetime—so there was no point in making me strain.

She explained about working at the guard stations and showed me the equipment, but I wasn't allowed to touch anything. She taught me nothing about weapons or how to defend myself.

Maybe she was afraid I'd use my training against her, but I was more concerned about the attack Meuric had hinted about. If a hundred dragons descended on Heart, I didn't want to be the only one without a laser.

Sam's knife stayed under my pillow where Li wouldn't find it.

After lunch, I got to study fascinating subjects like plows, irrigation systems, and the first efforts to install sewers beneath Heart, made even more challenging by the caldera and geothermal *everything* around the city. Most days, I fell asleep across my books, and woke to Li's smirk and declaration that I'd never be a productive member of society.

I was not permitted to continue the training Sam had scheduled for me, let alone visit Sarit or Whit. I didn't dare ask about Orrin or Stef, and mentioning Sam earned me a sharp slap on the wrist. Apparently that didn't count as harming me, because when Meuric was present, he didn't care.

"Can I see Sine?" I tried one evening. "She's on the Council. Hardly a corrupting influence."

"Keep your sarcasm quiet." Li finished her soup and slid the bowl aside. "You're not fit for company until you can hold a conversation that doesn't revolve around what you want."

Not counting Sam and his friends? I wanted music and dancing, to translate little dots and bars into something unimaginably gorgeous and real. I wanted to know why I'd been born, to understand this mistake that gave me someone else's life. I wanted to know if I'd be reborn after this life, allowed to continue everything I wanted to begin.

"I hate you," I whispered.

Li slammed her palms on the table, making spoons and bowls clatter as she stood. Her glare darkened. "Whatever you think you feel? It's not real. You're a nosoul. You don't feel. You barely exist. In a hundred years, no one will remember you were ever alive."

"You're wrong." I knew I shouldn't have spoken, but my muscles shook with the strain from a fortnight of physical exhaustion and emotional torture. "People will remember. Sam made sure of it."

The rage cooled from her eyes. "Is that so?" Dread cut me deep as she crossed the kitchen and reached into a drawer. "Paper is so temporary, don't you think? Many of our oldest records have been copied dozens of times, simply because the pages don't last. Like someone else I know."

I kept my eyes on the bundle of pages she carried. "What is that?"

"The other problem with paper is if you spill something on it, or burn it, whatever you kept on there is lost." She dropped the pages on the table; they spread out and settled without order. Even so, I knew what they were. Music. Bars and notes and tiny doodles in the margins. AI-4, AI-10: they were pages of a longer piece.

My hand was as heavy as a brick as I reached for the title page and turned it toward me. "Ana Incarnate," it read, no fancy flourishes or underlines with it, just a tiny butterfly in the corner.

It was the waltz Sam had written for me. My song.

"Don't hurt it," I whispered.

"Paper is so temporary," she repeated, looking pointedly at the fireplace.

"No!" I threw myself across the table and scooped up pages, but Li was faster.

She ripped the pages from my hands and tossed them at the fire. Paper fluttered, some into the flame, and some drifted to the ashy hearth.

308

I lunged across the room and rescued as many sheets as I could, but fire singed my hands. No matter how many I saved from the flames, Li balled up more pages and threw them in, laughing.

When she was bored, she wiped her hands on her pants and headed for the door. "Go to bed. You have a long day tomorrow."

I patted out the last of the embers with a dish towel and struggled to put the pages in order. My hands stung as I sifted through the delicate sheets. Some were salvageable; others were burned so badly they hadn't been worth rescuing, as black blotted out the bars of music.

Those pages went in back. Maybe Sam would know how to save them. Determined to see him try, I eased the pages of my song into a stiff notebook for safekeeping.

Forget Li. Forget the Council. If this was life in Heart, I would give up my quest. I'd rather never know where I came from than let Li destroy everything that mattered to me.

I went upstairs to get my knife.

There wasn't much to pack. My song fit inside my backpack, along with a few other necessities. For the last two weeks I'd been too scared to escape. There were guards—Li made sure I saw them every morning—and I'd been afraid of what would happen if they caught me. Now I was more afraid of what would happen if I didn't try.

I waited until the sun dipped behind the wall, casting the city in hazy indigo. Within minutes, it would be full night.

Dressed in the darkest clothes I could find, I tied and tucked my hair into a cap and picked the lock on the window. Stef had taught me, saying I shouldn't be the only one in Range who didn't know how; Sam had called her a miscreant.

Clouds covered the sky, threatening some kind of unfortunate weather. In the inky-dark yard, I found only fir trees and bushes, a small garden. Normal things. Most people had what they needed to be self-sufficient between market days, even Li.

Bored-sounding voices came from the north side of the house. No footsteps or swishing brush accompanied them, so they were standing still. Chances were they faced my window, hidden at an angle so I wouldn't be able to see them unless I leaned out. And then they'd see me.

I hurled an old shoe outside. It landed inside a thick copse of conifers. Two pair of footfalls followed, and I hauled myself out of the window, turned to catch my toes on a ledge, and reached for a bare cottonwood branch. I hung two stories up as the footsteps came toward the house again.

Frantically, I swung myself into the tree, which obliged me with silence. I stayed huddled on the thick branch until the guards were settled. When they went around to the house—discussing whether or not I'd tried to escape, or just

310

wanted to tease them—I scrambled down the tree and into the brush on the far side of the yard.

When everything was quiet, only a breeze and night birds singing lullabies, I crept around to the walkway. As much as I wanted to run, I made myself stop and listen every few steps.

Past the walkway and onto North Avenue, I sneaked through the city, keeping to shadows. When I had to cross intersections, I held my breath and sprinted, hyperalert for sounds other than that of my shoes on cobblestones. Sleet pattered to the ground. I was almost grateful for the noise to blot out my footfalls, but it blotted anyone else's, too.

The city seemed bigger with every step I took, and the temple farther away. I ran down North Avenue and stopped short at the market field. So much empty space. I imagined a shadow of me streaking across the field and my stupid black clothes pressed against the white buildings.

Great.

Sleet tapped harder on the city, glistening under the iridescent light. If I didn't move, I'd turn into an ice statue right here.

I searched the gray-lit area and listened as long as I dared. I still had to get around the Councilhouse, not to mention find some kind of entrance into the building, and a way to get Sam out. Just because I could pick the lock on my window didn't mean I knew anything about the soul-scanners used in the more secure parts of the city.

"No more stalling," I whispered, and pushed myself across the market field. Too loud. My shoes slapped the cobblestones. My breath hissed and whitened the cold air. I held the straps of my backpack to keep it from bouncing, but that didn't stop the contents from jostling. Forget someone seeing my stupid black clothes against the building; they'd hear me coming first.

After an eternity, I slipped on wet stone and landed against the Councilhouse wall, bounced off, and crumpled to the street as breath whooshed from my chest. I coughed and gasped into my sleeves, waiting for my vision to clear before I tried sneaking around the building.

Black clothes. White building. Sam would have anticipated this. Anyone would have. Anyone but me. I hated being new.

Once again confident in my ability to breathe, I searched the field. Sleet glittered on the cobblestones, making the road slick. But the weather came from the north, so as soon as I was on the south side of the Councilhouse, I'd be out of the worst of it. I hoped.

I started around, keeping low, but the building was twice the length of the market field; it would take forever if I insisted on creeping. I made a run for it. Cobblestones slid under my boots, but I didn't stop. Up one side of the half-moon stairs, behind the columns that guarded the doors, and down the other side of the stairs. The market field stayed clear.

Meuric's house loomed on the corner of the southwest quarter. Lights burned upstairs, but no silhouettes stood in windows, waiting to catch me misbehaving. Li and the guards wouldn't check on me until morning. By then, I'd be out of the city.

Thunder rumbled in the north. Worse storms were on the way.

I slipped around to the south side of the building and brushed ice off my clothes and backpack. Shivering, I checked Meuric's house one more time—nothing—and crept around in search of the window I'd seen before.

The temple shed just enough light to see by. As much as I hated the strange patterns that shimmered across its white surface, I was grateful for the light as I looked for a way into the Councilhouse, like the side doors that led into the library.

Yellow light came from a window only hip-high, sliced with iron bars. I knelt and peered through the glass as more thunder growled.

The room was mostly belowground, lit with old-fashioned bulbs like Purple Rose Cottage. I couldn't see much from my vantage point, but bars divided the room into several sections with cots and toilets. Cells. One sat just beneath my window, but I couldn't see anyone in it. In the next cell over, Sam slumped on a cot, facing away and talking with someone I couldn't see. Glass muffled their low voices.

I tapped on the window. Sam's back straightened, and a face appeared in the window right in front of me. Startled, I fell to my butt and smothered a yelp in my mittens. Stef grinned and fiddled with latches. The window slid up, and warm air billowed onto my face.

"Whew." Stef shivered. "Cold out there."

"It's sleeting." I wrapped my mittens around the bars.

"Ana!" Sam stood against the bars between his cell and Stef's, reaching one arm toward me. "What are you doing? Are you okay?"

When Stef stood away from the window, I tore off one mitten and slipped my hand through. Our fingers scraped and caught, but my shoulder was already pressed against the bars; I couldn't stretch farther. Resignedly, I pulled my arm free and held my fingers against my chest. "I'm leaving."

He dropped his arm. "Leaving?"

I nodded. "Leaving Heart. Range, if I have to."

Stef glanced between us. "Did something happen?"

The mixture of cold and heat made my eyes water. "I can't live with Li. Not for a few years, not even for a few more days. I have to get out, even if it means letting go of everything I was trying to find."

Sam bit his lip. His face was dark and shadowed in the uncertain light, like how I'd first seen him by Rangedge Lake. "Did she harm you?"

"No. Just—" I shook my head. "She tried to burn your song. She's going to keep doing things like that until—I don't know—until I break. They'll never let me see any of you again."

"It's going to be hard to see anyone if you leave." Stef gave a one-shouldered shrug.

"That's why I'm here. I came to free you all." I met Sam's eyes and hoped more than anything he'd say yes. "I thought you'd come with me." It hadn't occurred to me that he might not, but now, it seemed more likely he'd stay with his friends.

"Okay." Sam leaned his forehead on the bars. His gaze stayed on mine.

Stef raised her eyebrows. "You know that when you're reborn, you'll be turned over to the Council. Your next life will be in here. And yours, Ana, if you're reincarnated."

I sucked in a sharp breath. Seventy or more years in this room, bars separating me from the world? It might not be my fate if I just vanished when I died, but it would definitely be Sam's if he went with me.

"I don't care." Sam reached again, so I did too, and when our fingertips touched, he said, "It will be worth it."

My shoulder hurt from pushing it against the bars. "I don't know how to get you out." Maybe I should have changed my mind now that I knew the price, but I couldn't stay here, and I couldn't survive outside Range by myself.

Not just that. Memories of the way he'd kissed me heated

my insides. I'd always needed him, for music and refuge and reasons not to hate *everything* about my life, and now because he made my chest tight and he'd promised a thousand things. He was Sam.

"No." Stef shook her head. "I'm not going to let this happen. Sam, you're smarter than that. Ana, if you really cared for him, you wouldn't sentence him to a lifetime of imprisonment and sewer maintenance."

"He's five thousand years old, Stef." I pulled my hands off the bars in case she slapped my knuckles like Li would have. "Let him make his own decisions."

Sam smirked, but the hint of a smile vanished when Stef turned on him. His voice deepened. "What Ana said."

"Idiot." She marched away from the window.

Sam frowned and turned back to me. "I'm sorry I didn't tell you about the diaries. I *was* trying to hide them from you, but only because I didn't want you to worry."

"I don't care about that anymore. I think I understand." A quick glance over my shoulder revealed no one had found me yet, but it was only a matter of time. My knees ached, and my chest itched from pressing against the white stone. "How do I get to the prison from the Councilhouse? Or is there another door?"

"Li was trying to kill you." His expression was earnest. "I was searching for proof that she wanted to murder you using sylph. Menehem was working on something that might affect sylph, but I couldn't find anything else about it. I went to her house the day of the masquerade, but she hid any information she had. She, and whoever she's working with."

We'd been doing the same research all along. He wanted to prove Li tried to murder me, using sylph so she wouldn't be imprisoned for it. And I— I'd stumbled onto it, though I'd never quite recognized the threat as he did.

"I know about all that." I pushed myself up to my knees again and held on to the bars. "It's okay. Just tell me how to get you out."

He flashed a hopeful smile. "Go around to the—"

Footsteps. He must have heard them, too, just louder than the wind around the building. And before he could order me to hide, thunder rumbled again and his eyes widened. Stef and Orrin—who was out of my line of sight—swore loudly.

"Go, Ana. Hide anywhere, and don't come out until the thunder stops." When I didn't leave immediately, frantically trying to sort through my thoughts and emotions, he shouted, "*Run*, Ana. Dragons."

I lurched to my feet and hurled myself in any direction. Meuric had said they'd come. History books said the same thing—sometimes hundreds of dragons. So I ran until I hit a white wall with a door. Shivering, I twisted the handle and glanced over my shoulder—no one yet—and threw myself into somewhere dark and still and heavy.

The air pulsed.

I spun, heartbeat thudding in my ears. No, not my heartbeat. The air. The walls. White light shimmered across a vast chamber. This wasn't the Councilhouse. It was the temple.

New panic surged through me, and I darted for the door to escape. I'd rather deal with dragons.

But the door was gone.

26
IMPOSSIBLE

I BANGED ON the wall until pain knifed through my palms. I yelled until my voice became shards of glass whistling through my throat. I kicked the wall until numbness raced up my toes and feet.

The door was gone. How was I supposed to escape if the door was gone?

My legs quivered as I strained not to crumple to the floor. There was never a door into the temple, not until ten minutes ago, and it hadn't even lasted. This shouldn't be possible. Not just the door, but me being the one to find it. Me, who shouldn't have been born. Me, who was supposed to be Ciana.

There were too many impossible things.

"Calm down," I whispered, again and again, hoping eventually it would work. "Breathe." The air was heavy, like inhaling dry water. My head throbbed with the weight and pressure. My thoughts tumbled: how to get away, how to get free.

I drew away from the wall, but the pulsing air didn't ease its grip on my head. It was like pressing my entire body against the city wall. Being inside Heart didn't do this, nor did being inside the white-walled homes or Councilhouse.

But this was the temple without doors, the very center of Heart. On clear days, the temple's shadow swung over the city like a sundial. Thousands of years ago, they'd used the temple to tell time.

I hated the temple. Instinctively, the first time I saw it and felt it was *looking* at me, and then when I felt the pulse through the city wall. Rock shouldn't have a heartbeat.

There was no sound, not even ringing in my ears, like quiet often did. I hated the silence and throbbing and weight, the absence of temperature. Not cold or hot, but not just right, either. It simply . . . didn't feel like anything.

I squatted in front of the wall and squeezed my eyes shut, waiting for something to happen. For the door to magically reappear. I didn't want to call out—no matter that I already had—and risk anything coming to eat me. Or, worse, risk the marble-thick air squashing my voice before it was ever out.

320

The chamber's faraway white walls glowed in the same eerie way the outside did, wearing no ornamentation. There were no paintings, pottery, or statues. There were no shadows, hardly any depth thanks to the everywhere-light.

There was only me.

Sam hadn't said much about the temple. That it was empty, yes, and that there were words on the outside, which Deborl had deciphered. They spoke of an entity named Janan, who'd given everyone souls and an eternity of lifetimes, maybe even built Heart to protect them from dragons and sylph and the like. They were to worship Janan, though they didn't know how, and he never appeared to claim what they owed.

"Janan?" I left a mitten where the door had been, then rested my hand over Sam's knife as I sidled along the wall, careful not to touch the stone more than necessary.

After ten steps, I glanced at my mitten for reassurance— not that it mattered if the door never reappeared—but the mitten was gone, too.

Ugh. In the unlikely event I escaped, my hand would be cold.

I focused on that so I wouldn't think about where it might have gone. What might have taken it. Nor did I want to think about Sam, or dragons, or what would happen if he were killed.

An archway appeared ahead, almost invisible with the white walls and even light.

If I'd thought it might work, I'd have tried to lay a trail so I could come back this way, but when I checked, my mitten was still gone. Anyway, considering how the door had vanished, I didn't trust the archway to stay where I left it.

The dragon thunder, which had been growing louder outside, was nonexistent in here. The walls blocked the noise completely, but I wished I could hear what was going on. I kept imagining Sam trapped in prison while dragons rampaged through Heart.

Last time they'd come through, they'd gone straight for the temple, which I was now inside. If I didn't get out and dragons breached the wall—

I gave up on stealth and threw myself through the archway, tripped, and landed on my hands and knees, top side higher than my butt.

Stairs.

Because there were no shadows, I hadn't seen the stairs. My eyes ached from the constant white, from trying to discern definition when everything looked the same distance.

With more caution, I groped until I figured out the height and depth of the steps as they descended before me.

Odd. I'd tripped as though the stairs went up. If they went down, then I'd have fallen to the bottom and broken my neck. Nevertheless, they felt as though they went down. I slid my hands over the stone, trying desperately to ignore the temple's heartbeat.

I stood again, but when I tried to slide my foot down, my toe hit stone. Adrenaline still made my head fuzzy, but I forced myself to crouch and feel again. They definitely went down when I slid my hands over the stone, but as soon as I tried to descend, I bumped into them as though they headed up.

Lying stairs.

Fine. I went up, and my eyes gave up trying to adjust to the everywhere-light and lack of shadows.

The stairs seemed endless, and the opposite effect remained disorienting. I felt as though I climbed, but every time my gaze fell on my feet, it looked like I should be descending. My thighs burned with exertion. Definitely up.

Twice, I stopped to rest and breathe, and to fight the sensation of walls simultaneously near and far. When I reached, there was nothing to either side of me. It was difficult to tell how wide the stairs were. I could crouch and extend one leg all the way without running out of floor, and do the same on the other side, but I'd also been able to feel the stairs going down, so I didn't trust anything.

I should have stayed back in the big chamber down—or up—stairs. I wouldn't have known what to do there, but at least I wouldn't have been so blind and confused, straining all my senses for a hint of anything else in this empty temple. What if I was trapped here forever? Alone?

Surely there was a way out.

At last I reached . . . somewhere. The floor leveled out, and the light was dimmer on one side of a long room, which made it easier to see, but didn't cure my headache. And, even though I knew better, I checked on the stairs. They were gone. I doubted I could trust anything to stay where I'd left it.

Fifteen darkened archways led out of the new room, which was about the size of Sam's parlor. Books sat on the floor at the opposite end. Dark leather covers, shiny as if freshly bound. I almost ran for them—a sign of *something* other than me and a lot of emptiness—but the last thing I wanted to do was meet an ugly death because I hadn't exercised caution.

"Hello?" The air and walls smothered my whisper. What if there were others trapped in here, caught in the white nothingness?

I listened, but there was only the absence of sound.

Biting my lip, I inched across the room, making sure to test the floor before I trusted it to bear my weight. Or stay there. The stairway hadn't dropped me, but it had probably thought about it.

The temple's heartbeat continued. Steady. Drumming. I clutched my knife. It was useless here, but the smooth rose-wood handle sent a ripple of comfort through me.

There were only a dozen or so books at the far end of the chamber, but they cast eye-friendly shadows. My headache retreated as my hand hesitated over the blood-red cover. No title. No indication of what was inside.

No dust, either.

Holding my breath, I laid my palm on the front and waited.

"Janan?" I whispered. "Are you there?"

No answer but the rhythmic heartbeat in the air.

My hands shook as I slid the book off the stack. It was thin, but had a good weight to it. Cloth paper, leather cover. The binding creaked when I opened it, but the stitches held. The faint scent of ink tickled my nose.

That had been another thing missing from the temple: odor.

I pressed the paper to my face and inhaled, stupidly grateful for something so simple I hadn't noticed it was gone. Then, embarrassed even though no one was there, I cradled the book in one hand and flipped pages in search of writing. Answers.

Dashes of black spread across the papers, as though the writer had tapped his pen to make ink splatter everywhere, or a squirrel had gotten ink on his claws and used the paper to clean them. The markings weren't left to right like the words I knew, or even music.

I tried another book. Same nonsense scribbles. No matter how many pages I flipped, the markings never made sense.

I'd felt this before, knowing that something should work, but unable to see how. I'd been ten years old. Li had taken one of Cris's books and skimmed through it, hmmed like she understood the ink splatters, and repaired the septic system with ease now that she'd read how to do it.

After she'd gone to bed, I had sneaked into the library and opened the book she'd read, but it didn't make sense. It was just ink on paper.

But then I'd placed the book on the table and squinted right, and suddenly saw the way everything made lines and spaces.

It had taken another year to figure out all the letters and words, but I'd known they *must* work somehow. I'd trusted that they did.

I needed the same kind of trust with these. Spending a year in here deciphering them was out of the question, but perhaps it would be wise to look for anything useful—like a map—before heading off through any of the archways leading from the room.

Before I could settle on the floor to sort through the books, the temple heartbeat paused. The temple *gasped*.

Murmurs snaked through the temple. That didn't help the heaviness of the air or the general discomfort now that the heartbeat was back, but it was the first sound other than mine, and it sent shivers along my back.

When the whispers grew louder, I pulled off my backpack and tucked a few books in with my clothes; it was hard to say if I'd find this room again. Then I crept away, head cocked like that would help me figure out where the sounds came from. But, like the light, the whispers came from everywhere.

I wanted to call out and find out who was here. The words were out of my throat before I realized, but I trapped them behind my lips before they could fully escape. If it was Janan, if he was real, I wanted at least a second to prepare. Observing him before he saw me was probably impossible, but this was the place for impossible things.

It was just, this Janan had demanded worship and then left. Even if he did give people souls and eternal lives, he'd abandoned them to figure everything out on their own, defend themselves from dragons and sylph and a hundred other creatures that regularly tried to destroy Heart. If Janan *was* real, the most he ever did was protect the temple when dragons wrapped their bodies around it.

And the dragons must *hate* Janan if they went right for the temple every time.

The whispers softened. Some sounded like weeping.

I chose the nearest archway, knowing it might be foolish and I might never get back to the book room. But if something was happening, there might be a way out.

The archways had been dark before, like light simply wouldn't touch them, but their light shifted as I stepped through, into a hall. The darkness had been an illusion. The walls were black and slick as oil, but glowed eerily. The illumination pulsed in time with the heartbeat.

The hall seemed impossibly long; the light at the other

end was so tiny. But when I blinked, I stepped through another archway and had to cover my eyes at the blinding white.

It was as big as the first chamber, and as bright, but it wasn't the same. A brilliant pit lurked in the middle of the room, its walls white as far down as I could see. I tried not to get too close to the edge; someone—Janan—might rush up behind me and push me. The new weight in my backpack took adjusting to, also.

Murmurs hissed again, rippling like a sheet flaring over a bed. The sound still came from everywhere at once, like the heartbeat and pressure.

I lurched away from the pit as the room twisted. Blurs ran up one side of my vision and down the other, a giant circle of shadows as the ceiling fell to the floor, and the floor rose to the ceiling. The pit climbed the wall like an enormous spider. The room turned upside down. The walls groaned and grumbled as though in pain.

The stone under me stayed put. Probably. It was hard to tell. When everything stopped grinding, I was on my knees, palms pressed against my eyes so hard my cheekbones ached.

The temple's heartbeat steadied. Light beyond my fingers eased, and when I peeked, the room had turned completely upside down. Hesitantly, I stood and tried to decide between looking up at the hole, or fleeing this room. The archway was still there, and on the floor. For now.

"Here," the temple whispered. "Newsoul."

I didn't move.

Was it talking to me? Was that Janan? I could hardly breathe for all the questions gathering in my throat.

"You know what I am?" I bit my tongue as soon as the words slipped out. I couldn't trust the temple to tell me the truth. It made me queasy inside, and the whole place was weird and upside down. There was so much emptiness, and the books made no sense. But I needed to know. If this was Janan, maybe he could finally tell me what had happened to Ciana. "Why was I born?"

"Mistake." The word dripped through the stones like sweat. "You are a mistake of no consequence."

The absence of temperature hadn't changed, but I shuddered and hugged myself. I'd always known I was a mistake. Always been told I didn't matter . . .

"Ana?" Not Janan. This second, higher voice belonged to a real human.

I spun on my heel to find a boy standing in the black archway. Short brown hair, thin cheeks, and eyes that held millennia of experience. He only *appeared* as if he was fifteen years old.

"Meuric."

27
SPEAKER

THE COUNCIL'S SPEAKER stood in the doorway, frowning. "What are you doing here?" He stalked toward me.

I backed away.

"Not too close." His gaze flicked upward, at the reverse pit. "Don't want to fall in."

Right. Because the stairs that went down actually went up, and the hole that went up might actually go down. I planted my feet on the ground and glared at him. "What are *you* doing here?" My heart thudded against my ribs so hard I waited for bones to break. "What's going on outside?"

"I saw you run in here. I came to help."

That was unlikely. I'd been here at least an hour. Unless time ran differently in the temple.

He continued to creep closer, cautious like I was a wild animal. I felt like one; my legs itched to carry me away, but I stayed and fought the adrenaline flooding my system. He shook his head, kept his voice soft and even. "It's chaos out there. Dragons and sylph. They arrived shortly after you vanished."

Dragons *and* sylph? My hands tingled with memory.

"It's never happened before, both together." He stopped directly in front of me, his gaze never leaving mine. "Do you know anything about that?"

How far could I back up before I fell? I couldn't tell.

"Ana." He spoke gently, like that would change anything. The temple still had a heartbeat. The air still smothered sound. Everything we said was flat, barely audible. The only thing that echoed was Janan—maybe Janan. "You should be at home with Li. You'd be safe there. Dragon acid can't hurt the walls."

So I'd seen during the market attack. Janan's doing?

"What about the sylph?" I scratched at the backs of my hands. The burns had itched like mad when they were healing, and Sam always threatened to bind my hands forever if I didn't stop trying to ease the sensation of something crawling beneath my flesh.

"Sylph . . ." Meuric's eyes lifted to the pit again. "They can't go through the stone."

That didn't mean they couldn't use doors or windows.

Li's house was no safer than the market field when it came to sylph.

"Why aren't you at home?" he asked again.

I edged toward the wall to keep from being trapped between him and the hole. My voice shook. "I heard the dragon thunder and I ran." Sort of true. "I lost track of where I was going, I was so scared. Then a door appeared and I darted inside, but I've never seen this part of the Councilhouse."

His expression flickered as though he was reevaluating me. Hopefully he'd decided I was an idiot.

When I had a clear view of both Speaker and pit, I stopped edging and lowered my voice. "Are we in the temple?"

He narrowed his eyes—I'd probably been too dramatic—but gave a curt nod. "Yes, that's what your door led to."

"I thought there was no way in." I glanced at the pit. He might underestimate me if he knew how afraid I was. Still, it was humiliating to be caught when I felt so panicked. "Why is everything backward?"

"I don't know."

This room made my skin crawl, but I couldn't figure out which way to go. Other archways appeared and disappeared in the corners of my vision. Any of them might lead to freedom, but more than likely they would take me somewhere worse. "Before you got here, I heard a voice." I pressed my hands over my heart. "Was that Janan?"

Meuric's mouth pinched. "Yes."

I kept my eyes on him, trying to search the rest of the room with my peripheral vision. There was nothing, save the pit and occasional dark archway. "He said I was a mistake. Do you think he meant I wasn't supposed to be born?"

The Speaker said nothing.

"I know about Ciana. I heard Frase tell Li that she never came back. Half of Heart believes I replaced her. That's why they hate me."

Meuric winced. "I'm sorry, Ana. I wish I could answer your questions. I just don't know. I was as mystified as everyone else when you were born. All I can tell you is that the words on the outside of the temple are true: Janan gave us life. All our lives. Maybe something went wrong when Ciana didn't come back, but Dossam believes you're a gift. Surely you can take heart in that."

Sam. I tried not to think about Sam out there with the dragons and sylph. Better to keep asking questions, no matter how much I wanted to remind Meuric that he was the one who'd taken me from Sam. Take heart in that indeed. "But Janan gave everyone life, and he said I'm a mistake. How can he make mistakes?"

His expression was dark as thunderclouds. No idea what he'd do if I kept pushing, if he could do anything, but I'd have bet Sam's piano that Meuric knew more about the temple than he was letting on. I just had to find the right questions.

"What are you looking for?" he asked. "To be told you're a mistake? Would it make a difference if I tell you that you're not? You already know I believe in Janan, and this is his temple. He *is* the temple. He doesn't speak often, but he never lies. If he said you're a mistake, then you are. I don't know where you came from, but I know *Janan* had nothing to do with you. Your answers aren't in here."

The words landed like fists. I could only nod. It certainly wasn't the answer I wanted, but I'd learned long ago I didn't need to worry anyone would lie just to keep my feelings from getting hurt.

Really, I just wanted to know what had happened. I couldn't change what I was or wasn't. I lowered my gaze. "Do you know the way out? I want to find Sam."

"Yes, we can do that." His hand brushed his coat pocket, so quickly I wasn't supposed to see. I feigned interest in my sleeves, in the dark cloth over white skin. "Come with me."

Too easy. And at some point, he'd given up pretending he knew nothing about the temple. That could only mean that he wanted to lead me somewhere I didn't want to go.

"Okay." I straightened my clothes and hitched my back-pack, heavy with the books I'd stolen. "Yeah, I'd rather not stay here any longer. You can't see anything, and nothing is what it looks like." I strode toward him, stopping just out of arm's reach. I kept him between the upside-down pit and me.

"Unsettling, isn't it?"

334

I hesitated, desperately wishing I were as brave as Sam claimed.

Before I could act, Meuric noticed *something* about me—maybe posture or accelerated breathing—and said, "It will be easier if you behave."

"What will?"

"Getting lost in here. You won't get hungry or thirsty. You'll never get tired. Janan doesn't want you, and I won't kill you, but you cause too many problems in Heart. You ask too many questions. I'd hoped you'd grow out of all that if I gave you back to Li. This wasn't what I wanted for you."

"Sam won't let you—"

"Sam will assume you died. Lots of bodies are never found when dragons or sylph attack. He'll be sad, but he'll get over it. Unless he dies, too. And even then it's unlikely he'd be reborn before Soul Night."

"What happens then?" Soul Night wasn't until the spring equinox in the Year of Souls, more than a year away.

He showed teeth when he smiled. "Nothing you need to worry about."

I didn't move.

"Birth is never pretty, Ana. It's painful. Trust me, you will be happier in here." He gestured around the chamber as though it was the grand concert hall in the Councilhouse; I saw only cold, unforgiving white. "And you'll live forever. Isn't that what you want?"

"I *want* to go home. I *want* people to stop telling me what to do, insisting progress reports are the most important thing in my life, and assuming I have some nefarious plan for newsouls to replace everyone. I don't. For some reason, I've been given a chance at life, and I want to make the most of it."

Meuric just shook his head. "You honestly don't know the trouble you have caused." He stepped closer, his eyes on mine. We were exactly the same height, so neither of us had to look up or down. He still seemed so much bigger than me. "I understand," he said. "You're young. Your world revolves around you. Or, like your father, you are simply incapable of considering others. He was always asking questions, too, trying to figure out why people are reincarnated."

"There's no crime in curiosity."

"Your questions make my life difficult."

"Fortunately, as you said, I'm self-centered enough that I don't care." I checked the pit but couldn't judge the distance; the everywhere-light made depth perception impossible. "I've decided not to go with you. I'll find my own way out."

"Then you'll never leave."

No, I had a pretty good idea of what I needed. Or, at least, where to find it. I tackled Meuric, the weight of my backpack making that more awkward than it needed to be.

He was young and fast enough that he could have darted away, but maybe he'd forgotten. Changing bodies must get confusing. Instead, he dropped to the floor and dragged me with him, his nails gouging my arm through my sleeve. "What are you *doing*?" He stood and hauled me up; he was strong for his size.

I dove for his pocket and whatever was in there.

With a grunt, he grabbed my shoulders to fling me across the room, but I caught the cloth of his pocket—not its contents—and he fell with me. I elbowed him, trying to find some kind of advantage, but he was stronger and his elbows were pointier.

We wrestled, both of us trying to get his pocket and keep away from the upside-down pit. When we came close to it, he shoved me, but I threw myself aside just before I stumbled beneath the opening.

My shoulder jammed against the floor, shooting pain all down my arm. My foot, which had landed under the pit, hung upward as though gravity had reversed. I pulled it down—it was as heavy as if I were lifting it out of the pit—and scrambled away as Meuric attacked.

He hit my sore shoulder, which sent waves of numbness to my fingers. With my free hand, I drew Sam's knife and thrust it, not caring where it hit, as long as it hit somewhere.

Flesh squished and popped.

Blood squirted and dribbled from his eye.

His expression flickered to shock, then to a dull nothing as I withdrew my knife and gagged at the metallic odor of blood and salt. I avoided looking at his youthful face as I found a thin, SED-size device in his pocket. It was made of silver. His other pockets were empty, so this had to be what would get me out of here.

Meuric groaned and clutched at his ruined eye. I couldn't imagine how he was still alive, but the knife wasn't long; perhaps I hadn't gone deep enough to puncture his brain. Acid boiling in my stomach, I wiped my blade clean on his coat, then kicked him underneath the pit. It sucked him upward as quickly as though he'd fallen.

My head spun, and I needed to throw up.

I'd *killed* him.

When he was reborn, he'd spend his life trying to kill me. He might even tell the Council what I'd done. I could show them what I'd found in his pocket, tell them what had happened before he returned, but it was unlikely they'd believe me. I was the nosoul.

Jammed shoulder aching, I hauled myself into a sitting position and studied the device. It gleamed silver in the everywhere-light, and had five pictures engraved in the metal. They were a horizontal line, a vertical line, a square, a circle, and a diamond. None of them looked like a door, and I couldn't tell if touching one would activate anything or not. They weren't buttons.

For a moment, I feared I'd made a mistake—hadn't I? I'd killed him—but this was Meuric. He wouldn't have come in here unprepared. He'd probably been the one to create the door in the first place, just to get me out of the way. There'd been nothing else in his pockets, so everything necessary to activate this device must be here already.

Or not. What if this was tied to only Meuric's soul, the same way the scanners in the city could detect which soul was which?

"Janan?" I whispered, just in case he was still there and inclined to help. Only the temple heartbeat pulsed in reply.

The last thing I wanted to do was lock myself in here, but wasn't I trapped already? I had to take a chance and hope I escaped. Then I could raid Meuric's house for some kind of instructions.

The horizontal line was first; I touched that.

Nothing happened.

Same thing with the vertical line and the square, so perhaps that meant I had to do something else to them. But *what?* Frustrated, I squeezed the device and considered throwing it into the pit.

Something shifted inside the device. With a soft *snick*, the pictures all rotated and the metal slid into itself, as if one half was hollow.

I had no idea what I'd done, but as soon as I looked up, the wall shimmered and groaned. In the same dizzying way the room had turned upside down, a gray blur appeared on the white stone, expanding into a door-size hole. I couldn't see anything beyond.

339

Stay here, or go through the mysterious door? I drew in a shaky breath and found my feet. Before I made it halfway, the edges of the door flickered and whitened.

My entire body hurt, and fire stabbed my shoulder every time I moved my arm, but I sprinted for the door before it closed and I was forced to repeat whatever I'd done to the device.

I stepped through.

Icy wind battered my face, and sleet obscured my vision. My first instinct was to run as far from the temple as possible, but—I swayed and pressed my backpack against the now-smooth wall where the door had been—I'd emerged on a ledge, high above the ground. If not for the weather, I'd have been able to see everything. I'd never been so grateful for sleet before.

Carefully, I tugged off my backpack. I considered letting it go—I had the door device and my knife in my coat—but this had the books from the temple, as well as the charred remains of Sam's song. If it came to it, I could drop it, but for now, I put the backpack on in front of me. Balancing would be awkward, but I would compensate.

Just as I steadied myself to get my bearings, a dark shape formed in the gray: long and slender, huge black wings.

A dragon.

28
RAGE

THE TEMPLE THROBBED against my back as I pressed harder against it, trying to become invisible. My door was gone, and too easily, I could recall how Sam had described the dragon acid. I could imagine myself burning and itching, my skin boiling until I saw bone. I didn't want to die. Not in the temple, or by falling off, or by dragon.

I considered opening another door only for a heartbeat; there was no telling what I'd find inside, or if I could get back to the ground level to create a new door. I couldn't risk it.

Thinking invisible thoughts, I planted both palms on the warm stone and tried to calm my vertigo and terror. The dragon's wings spread wide, glittering in the strange temple-light.

Right. Warm stone. That would at least keep ice from making me slip, but there was still water. The ledge was only a foot deep, which didn't leave much room for me to keep my balance.

The dragon's jaws gaped as it flew nearer, but before it speared me with teeth as long as my forearm, blue light shot from the ground, piercing the roof of its mouth. With a roar, it veered and dove at its attacker. Wind from its wings nearly forced me off the ledge, but I dug my heels in and clenched my jaw, as if that would keep me from tumbling to the market field.

The Councilhouse roof wasn't far to the left—which meant I faced north, and all the incoming dragons—and that seemed like a safer place to be stranded. It was still at least a one-story drop, and I couldn't tell if my ledge went that far, but it was better than staying here.

I inched toward the roof. The glow helped when it was right underneath me, but anything beyond arm's reach was hazy with sleet and numinous light. And even with the warm temple, my face and fingers were numb. My backpack tugged awkwardly on my shoulder, making fire shoot through it. Something was out of place, or maybe broken.

Dragons snaked through the air, diving into the streets. There were hundreds of them, shrieking and making thunder shake the world. Their cacophony drowned any screams my fellow humans might make. They'd never hear mine, either.

I clutched the temple harder, inching faster.

A mistake. My heel slipped in water, sending me weightless for a split second as my other foot followed. I threw my weight back, hoping beyond reason I didn't overcompensate and push myself off. My tailbone thudded against stone, sending shocks through my spine.

My legs dangled off the ledge. The stone cut at my thighs, revealing exactly how much room I didn't have to move. Trying to stand again would get me killed, so I pressed my hands to the ledge and scooted like that. Water soaked the seat of my pants. Chills surged through my legs and stomach.

The temple shuddered as a dragon latched onto it far above me. I didn't look. If what I'd seen during the market attack was an indication, the claws wouldn't even scratch the stone.

Meuric had said there were sylph. I couldn't see any through the blinding lights and sleet, but no doubt they were out there. They were creatures of shadow and air; did that mean they could fly?

I focused on scooting without falling, and fought the urge to look down. I'd see the Councilhouse when I was over it. Roof first. Ground later.

The view of the north half of the city was frightening enough without adding dizzy to that.

I couldn't discern the cannonballs through the distance and misty light, but the booms rattled the air and made dragons scream. Dark shapes wove through the sky, pursued by laser blasts. Lights shone off city walls, Councilhouse walls, and all along the main avenues. Heart would have been as bright as day, if not for the sleet and clouds and pressing darkness.

At last, a white expanse appeared under my ledge. It was still difficult to tell how far a fall it would be. Too far. I'd shatter every bone in my legs and arms. As far as I could tell, the temple wall beneath me was sheer, so that ruled out dropping from ledge to ledge.

Claws shrieked against stone. I looked up just in time to duck a swinging tail. A dragon flailed, struggling to keep its hold on the temple. It scraped and tried to scramble up again, lashing its tail for balance. The end of the tail was close.

I grabbed the dragon's tail and jumped.

Screaming, I wrapped my legs around the tail and squeezed as hard as I could. The backpack over my stomach made it difficult to keep my grip, but I ducked my head down and didn't let go as the tail whipped through the air, flipping me upside down and stopping just short of smacking me into the wall.

Bad idea. Bad idea.

The instant the tail was close to the Councilhouse roof, I let go.

My back hit first. Air whooshed from my lungs. I gasped and coughed as I turned over, barely quick enough to keep from puking on myself. Then I spit until the acidic taste faded.

Above me, my dragon smeared gore across the temple wall, still thrashing as lasers speared its stretched-out wings. It gave a last deafening roar as it fell, making the Councilhouse shake when it landed, draped from the roof down.

It had just given me another way to the ground.

I switched my backpack again. My shoulder twinged, but the shooting pain had faded. Whatever had come out of place must have been jarred back when I landed.

Thanking the dying dragon for three things now, I trotted to where its tail and hind legs hung on the south side of the roof. I couldn't see whether it went all the way to the ground. Regardless, I had to hurry before it slipped the rest of the way; with ice making everything slick, the beast wouldn't stay here long.

Twice, I skidded on the roof and scraped my palms catching myself, but I reached the dragon's hind legs just as the body began to shudder. Hoping it was dead, I climbed up its talons and leg, then up the side to its back. The scales were sharp and cold, wet with sleet. But it was a lizard—albeit a huge one adapted for the tundra—and cold-blooded, so cold scales should be normal. Maybe.

I scrambled onto its back and used scales like a ladder over the edge of the building. My hands froze and ached, but I didn't stop moving.

The body convulsed when I was halfway down, near the stretched wings. Everything slipped. I held on tighter, but when it didn't stabilize again, I leapt onto the wing and slid the rest of the way down, jerking and stumbling over bones beneath the thin, smooth scales.

Wind cut at my face and up my sleeves as I sped down. Finally the slope eased at the wing tips resting on the cobblestones. Momentum threw me onto the ground just as the dragon crashed behind me.

Someone running by stared at me and swore, then tossed a laser in my direction as he headed north. My hands were too cold and stiff to catch the weapon, but I grabbed it off the ground, then tried to decide where I was in relation to Sam's window. Not far. I scrambled over the dragon's corpse. The building and beast created a narrow gorge, sheltered from wind and noise.

I found the prison window easily enough, and they hadn't shut the glass. "Sam?" I knelt and peered inside the dim room.

Empty.

I sank to my heels and rested my forehead against an iron bar, trying to figure out what could have happened. It was possible he could have escaped, but he barely remembered how to use a data console. Disabling the soul-scanners was beyond him. Orrin had been in there, but he was as hopeless as Sam. Stef would have been able to do it, but it probably required tools she didn't have.

The other possibility was that Li had discovered my absence and known where to find me. She wouldn't have hesitated to kill Sam.

Then I would avenge him. Li would come back, and like Meuric, she'd hunt me for the rest of her lives, but at least she'd suffer the same soul-ripping pain as Sam.

My stomach twisted. When had I become so blasé about killing? My knife was still wet with Meuric's blood, and I was already thinking about what to do to my mother? I wanted to throw up again, but there was nothing left in me.

Keening and moaning jolted me from my thoughts.

Tall shadows drifted about the dragon's remains, charring scales. I scrunched my nose at the ashy reek and bolted away from the sylph. They weren't interested in me yet, and I didn't have sylph eggs.

I sprinted into the stinging night, battle din rising as I pulled away from the Councilhouse. Airborne drones roared around dragons, shooting lasers every chance they got. The dragons spat globs of acid. I pulled my hood on tight. If anything fell on me, I'd hear it sizzle and I could throw off my coat. It'd work only once, though.

My muscles ached, but I ran as hard as I could, avoiding anything shadowy or glowing green. I wished I had a flashlight or SED—mine had been confiscated—but my knife and laser were better than nothing.

I searched the faces of everyone I passed. Most everyone else was running, too, but they looked like they knew what to do. More than I did, at any rate. None of them were Sam, or my friends. I pushed on, hiding my fists inside my sleeves for warmth.

People and lights and acid globs packed North Avenue. I wished I could duck into the residential quarter, but I didn't know my way around that maze well enough. Li's house was right by the guard station, anyway.

I wished I were cowardly enough to hide in someone's house until everything was over.

Heart's north wall loomed ahead, brilliant as it reflected light across the guard station. I pushed my weak legs harder. What if Li wasn't at her house? She was a warrior. No doubt she'd be single-handedly killing half the dragons, not waiting for me to confront her.

I focused on rage. She *always* hurt what mattered to me. Collections of things I'd found in the forest, the purple roses, and Sam's song. She'd done nothing in my entire life to give me a reason to trust that she wouldn't kill Sam just to spite me.

Lungs and legs burning, I darted around a trio of children firing lasers into the sky, and skidded to a stop near the guard station. Everything was so bright it made my eyes water. My nose ran from the cold. It seemed like, if I was going to face my mother, I should at least look like I could take care of myself.

I wiped my nose on my sleeve and clutched the laser. The path there was familiar by now, though the dead dragon and acid-marked cobblestone were new. Shadows lingered everywhere, but none made sylph songs.

Shivering, I stood at the end of her walkway and stared down the front door.

It swung open, framing Li.

She seemed bigger. Angrier. "Where have you been?" She didn't move. Li always waited for me to go to her.

I flexed my fingers around the laser grip. "What did you do to Sam?"

She cocked her head. "Sam?"

"You heard me." I stepped forward. She wasn't holding anything but the doorknob. I could fire before she could. Maybe. I'd never used a laser; my aim was probably terrible. "What did you do with Sam? He's not there anymore."

"I don't know what happened to him." She checked over

her shoulder. Distracted. Agitated. It was natural, considering the war going on around us, but not for Li. She liked
conflict. She liked opportunities to see me hurt, and here I
was without the one person who meant everything to me,
worried he was dead, and she was *distracted*? "Is that where
you went?"

"He was in prison. Now he's not." I stopped halfway down
the walk and straightened my shoulders. The sore one stung,
but I tried to make my expression frozen with anger, like she
did. I didn't want her to know how much I hurt.

"Why do you think I'd do something to him?" Her familiar sneer returned.

"You always do things. It's what you are." I lifted my laser
and let my free hand rest on the rosewood handle of Sam's
knife. "You tried to make my life miserable, make me believe
that no one could ever care about me. But you're wrong. Sam
does. Sarit, Stef, and the others do. I'm not a nosoul." My
hand shook as I took aim. "Now tell me what you did to him."

Her mouth dropped open.

At first I thought it was shock because I'd finally stood
up to her, but then her expression went slack and her eyes
focused on nothing. One last flicker of rage, and she crumpled.
Dead.

I staggered backward. A dragon wouldn't fit inside, and a
sylph would have been more obvious. I hadn't done it.

A man stepped out of the shadows, over my mother's body,

and lowered a handheld laser like mine. "You must be Ana." Odd that it took only one small man with a laser to kill her. He didn't look like much. Short. Clipped auburn hair. Pale.

Oh. I knew those features, though I'd never seen him before.

"I'm Menehem," he said. "We should talk."

29
DARKNESS

I KEPT MY laser aimed at his chest. "You killed her."

"Yes." He raised his eyebrows. "Wasn't that what you were here for? I thought I'd get it over with. You weren't going to stop accusing her of murdering Dossam, and she wasn't going to admit to it. She didn't, by the way. She's been here with me."

My jaw ached from clenching it as he strode toward me. I held my ground. "But the battle—"

"Yes, that's where she was going. And she could have done a lot to help people, but honestly, I didn't want her to."

This, too, was like drowning. My questions were like drops of water, enough to fill an ocean. "I don't understand."

I hated feeling stupid. I hated having to ask. And I hated

being delayed, kept from finding Sam. If Li hadn't killed him, he was somewhere in the city. With dragons.

I steeled myself. "Tell me everything or I'll shoot holes in your arms and legs." As if I had that kind of skill.

But he didn't know.

"Okay." He headed inside the house, stopping just before he hit shadows. "Aren't you coming?"

I nodded toward his hand. "Your weapon."

He rolled his eyes and tossed it on the walkway. "I have no plans to harm you."

"You've given me no reason to believe that." I didn't lower my laser as I followed him to the door. Li was motionless on the doorstep, ice already collecting on her face. If I touched her, she'd be cold. "Are you working with Meuric? Did you attack Sam and me after the masquerade?" He was smaller than the man who'd tossed me around the street, but I'd been terrified then. I was terrified *now*, but at least I was armed.

Menehem grabbed my laser and flung it out the door with his. "No, I'm not working with Meuric or anyone else. I didn't attack you, and I didn't send sylph after you. If I'd wanted to hurt you, you'd be dead now. Never take your eyes off the person you're threatening."

My heart stuttered and tried to catch up with itself, but I nodded, using the door frame to hold myself up. The cold stone chilled my hands. I jerked back. "All right. You've made your point. I'm a lousy interrogator. Now are you going to tell me why you abandoned me, why you killed Li, and why you want people to die?"

He motioned me to sit. Li's parlor was sparsely furnished, holding only a few chairs and tables. Once, she'd had swords and axes displayed on the walls—hers were real walls, not like Sam's—but she took down the weapons when I moved in.

We left the door open, both of us angled toward it. And Li on the ground, a clean hole in the back of her head. "When she comes back," I said, "she's going to kill you. Probably several times."

"She won't come back."

I jerked around. "Of course she will. Everyone comes back." Except Ciana. Maybe except me, too. We couldn't know unless I died, but it didn't seem likely.

And there was that thing Meuric had talked about, something that was supposed to happen next Soul Night. . . .

He shook his head. "I've been working your whole life to redo what I managed only once. I stopped a reincarnation."

"What?"

"Several years ago I was experimenting on the market field. It was the only open area I thought was safe enough if anything should go wrong. I couldn't go outside Heart, either. I didn't want gases interfering. I'm sure you know how terrible it can smell out there. Imagine that when you're trying to focus on other flammable chemicals—"

"Menehem." Just like the diaries I'd read, he really liked to explain things. "Your point."

He rolled his eyes. "Anyway, as things so often do with experiments, something went wrong, but it was mostly unexpected in that it went *right* when I'd originally assumed otherwise. That was the night Ciana died."

"That doesn't make sense." And if Li wouldn't come back, like Ciana hadn't, what about everyone else who died tonight?

He smiled, not cruel or calculating like Li, but not one I wanted aimed at me. "I know it's hard for you to understand. Here's the truth. Anyone who dies tonight is dead. Gone forever. Like you replaced Ciana, I suspect other newsouls will replace tonight's casualties. I've poisoned Janan, Ana. He's responsible for reincarnations. Tonight, he's incapable of fulfilling his duty."

I couldn't fit it in my head. Janan was real, I was certain now, but poisoning him? Janan seemed to live within the walls of the temple. I couldn't imagine a way to poison stone. If I hadn't been born—proof that what Menehem had done had worked—I'd have called him crazy.

"The effects won't last more than a few hours, but it will be enough to bring more newsouls into the world."

"Why? Why would you want your friends to die? And Li? And maybe you?"

He lowered his voice, almost sounding hurt. "I thought

you'd appreciate that Li won't be back. She was nothing but awful to you. At least that's what it sounded like."

"That's not the point. She's *never* coming back. You destroyed her completely."

"And everyone else who dies tonight. I only chose Li for your sake. Nature will choose the rest. The strong will live. They will be reborn. Newsouls will replace the rest."

I bolted for the door. "Sam is out there. Dragons *always* kill him." I stepped over my dead mother and scooped up both lasers. "If he dies tonight, so do you."

Menehem kept up with me easily and didn't appear upset by his lack of weapon. "If dragons or sylph kill me, so be it, but you won't. Not even if Dossam is dead."

"You wouldn't say that if you knew me." I waved for him to go first. If something attacked, I'd prefer it ate him while I had a chance to run away. That, and I wasn't over the way he'd disarmed me earlier.

"I think I know you well enough. Your need for knowledge is insatiable. I have answers you want. Isn't that what you were doing at the library so late at night while you were living with Sam?" He glanced over his shoulder. "I've been following your progress since you arrived in Heart, and mostly managed to keep my return a secret."

So he'd been the one following me that night? I shook my head and kept moving. It didn't matter anymore. "Is that why you came here tonight? Looking for me?"

"Exactly." He smiled over his shoulder. "You're the one person I wanted to save tonight. You haven't had a full life yet. Or dozens of them. It wouldn't be fair if you died so soon."

"Will I be reborn?"

We turned onto the road, lights and sleet shining again. Drones and dragons swarmed overhead, and we could see North Avenue from here, where sylph chased people, burning corpses as they went. I was morbidly glad we didn't have sylph eggs; I would have been compelled to stop and help people. Since I didn't, I focused on finding Sam.

But something was different. Unusual darkness caught my eye.

In the center of Heart, the temple was dull. Exterior lights illuminated the building, but its pearlescent glow had vanished. Stone screamed as dragons wrapped around it, straining to crush it or—

Jagged black lines appeared on the temple.

I'd stopped walking. Menehem stood next to me, gazing at the temple that rose above the treetops and other buildings. "Huh," he said. "I wonder what will happen if they rip it down." After a moment's contemplation, he shrugged. "Well, maybe no one will be reborn."

"You never said whether I will be."

"I can't. I'm sorry. I mean, you're here now, so maybe it will happen. It's impossible to say for sure until you die.

Same for all the other newsouls who'll be born after this."

That was not comforting. If we replaced people Janan had been reincarnating for millennia, why would he bother reincarnating us? Or would he know the difference?

"Don't be angry," Menehem said. "Aren't you glad you had the chance to exist? Don't you want others to have the chance, too? There could be billions more like you, waiting to be born."

Maybe he was right. I had to come from somewhere, so maybe there were other souls waiting for their turn to live, too. But that didn't make his actions moral. "So you're killing your friends out of benevolence?"

"No. Well, I suppose. Really, it's for science. I had questions. I wanted to know if my theories were right."

"Were they?"

"More or less. I've proven that Janan isn't all-powerful and worthy of worship, like Meuric and his friends keep saying." He glanced at me. "Don't you hate them? I can't stand listening to them argue about how we're here for this or that purpose. Now, even though I think I've proven Janan is real, I've also proven that whatever he is, he can be stopped."

I didn't want to think about Meuric. My stomach twisted, remembering the way I'd thrust my knife into his eye. "So that's what you've been working on these last eighteen years? How to halt reincarnation?"

Menehem nodded.

"I thought it was about sylph. And controlling them."

"No. Well, yes, it started out that way. But I never discovered a way to control sylph."

Which meant Li couldn't have stolen his research and used it to send sylph after me. Menehem wouldn't be able to tell me why there'd been two sylph attacks in as many days, back when I left Purple Rose Cottage.

"I thought you wanted to find Sam." He waved me toward the avenue again. "I saw him earlier, heading toward the north wall."

Of course he knew what Sam looked like if he'd been following me. I shuddered.

Targeting lights streaked across the air, lasers piercing dragon flesh. We splashed through chemicals—probably Menehem's concoction—meant to neutralize the dragon's acid, and darted around dead beasts littering the ground. The creatures provided cover for humans and sylph alike, though the latter seemed more intent on finding a way out of the city. They wafted toward the wall, then jumped and *fled* when they saw Menehem.

I grabbed the nearest stranger. "Have you seen Sam?" He shook his head and started to pull away, but I didn't release his coat. "Don't die tonight. You won't be reborn. Tell everybody."

The stranger narrowed his eyes, but nodded. "Good luck finding Sam."

I shouted for Sam as loud as I could, but my voice was useless under the din. When I asked people about him, some of them pointed to places they thought they'd seen him; most of those places were in opposite directions. Nevertheless, I told everyone about Menehem's plan, pointed at the darkened temple for proof, and followed their leads through the press of people. Five said they'd seen him in the northwest quarter.

My shoes squelched in mud. The crops were ruined from the acid and neutralizing chemicals; the ground was safe to walk on, at least.

"Sam!" My throat ached with cold and screaming. I ducked behind a dead dragon and shot at another as it swooped through the air, homing in on a nearby section of the wall. The beast shrieked as I shot it again. I ran for a ladder. Maybe someone on the wall had seen Sam.

I'd lost Menehem. Didn't matter. I'd find him if he lived. If not . . .

He wasn't my concern. I hauled myself up the ladder, aching bone-deep now, and paused only to shoot at the enormous wing as the dragon landed on the wall. The structure shuddered, and my ladder trembled, but I leaned all my weight forward and it held the rest of my ascent.

The wall was thick enough for ten people to stand abreast. It was still too small for a dragon to perch on, but this one tried. It hooked its front talons on the wall, hovering over a prone figure. Lights glared, making me squint as I took aim and fired.

A lucky shot; I hit its eye. With a deafening roar, the dragon spewed acid in my direction, but its depth perception was gone with its eye. My ladder sizzled as the dragon fell backward, clawing at its face. It flailed, its wings scooping air so hard I couldn't breathe, but I didn't think it would attack again, at least for a few minutes.

I ran for the man who'd nearly been dragon melt. He wasn't moving.

"Ana?" Stef was just beyond the man I crouched over. Blood streaked her face and matted her hair as she struggled to her feet. "What are you doing here? Is he okay?" She swayed and dropped to her knees on the other side of . . .

Sam. He was on his stomach and wearing a coat I didn't recognize, but shifting lights illuminated his profile. I touched his throat, searching for a pulse. His skin was cold, and for a moment I thought he was dead, but then I found the flutter of blood through arteries. Sam coughed and tried to pull his elbows in so he could push himself up. "Not dead yet?"

I choked on a sob. "Not yet."

He moved quickly, pushed up and onto his knees, and stared at me with wide eyes and disbelief. "Ana."

More than anything, I wanted to hug him. I didn't.

"No time for 'I missed yous.'" I found my feet and grabbed

my weapons. "Menehem did something to Janan. No one who dies tonight will be reborn. We need to be elsewhere until it's safe to be dead again."

Stef looked dazed. "What?"

"The wall doesn't have a heartbeat." Sam frowned at it. "Wait, Menehem?"

They both had concussions, no doubt. Nevertheless, I jabbed a finger toward the temple, illuminated by flood-lights. Three dragons had wrapped themselves around it while others flew in wide circles, spitting at people on the market field. "And the lights aren't on there. Let's *go*, both of you. Is Orrin around? Whit or Sarit?"

Sam shook his head. "They were somewhere else."

I didn't know whether to be relieved or afraid as I helped Sam and Stef to their feet. They were both taller than me, so I wasn't much use for keeping them upright as we staggered over debris, but I tried.

On the way to the north guard station, where there'd be medical help, we told anyone who'd listen that they'd be gone forever if they died tonight. Several came with us, but even more didn't believe us and kept fighting. Some who hadn't been hurt yet went to spread the word.

Sam had sylph eggs in his coat pockets. When sylph got too close, I trapped them, but mostly the shadows seemed to be looking for escape.

Finally we made it to the guard station, where people

shouted orders and others ran to obey. I led Sam and the rest to the medical station tucked in the left side, the cots on wheels all brightly illuminated and surrounded by machines. I helped everyone onto cots while medics and less-injured patients rushed to help.

"What happened to them?" a girl asked. She looked about nine years old, and her trying to sound authoritative in her tiny voice might have been funny in other circumstances. She climbed onto a stool and eyed me distastefully. "What happened to *you*?"

"I don't know. Sam and Stef were on the wall. I think they were both unconscious." I couldn't watch while the girl and her assistants took care of my friends, so I ran to the window and stared at the temple, willing the light to come back on.

Menehem staggered across my view. I shouted his name, but when he looked my way, half his face was blackened and blistered.

"What happened?" The question of the night.

"Sylph," he said. "Mad at me for bringing them here. In eggs, if you were curious."

I was too exhausted to be surprised. "Did you bring the dragons, too?" I'd read a lot about the old wars, but none had ever had both dragons and sylph. Nothing in or out of Range liked the sylph, no matter how powerful an ally they'd be.

"No." He coughed and squinted beyond me. "That was just good timing. I see you found Sam."

I wanted to leave Menehem to suffer on his own. But I couldn't. "Come inside. We'll get a medic to look at your face." I took off for the door as the fighting waned outside. The whine of vehicles and bang of cannons dimmed. Shrieks of dragons grew and faded as they fled over the guard station and north, chased out of Heart and Range by a flight of air drones.

When Menehem was safe in a cot, medics shooed me away so they could work. I lingered, listening to groans and curses, catching only glimpses of him between the medics' bodies while he confessed his sins. At last they stood back, blood soaking their white smocks, and said there was nothing more they could do.

His shirt had been cut away, and gauze covered most of his exposed skin. The rest was angry red. He grimaced, but painkillers ran through a tube into his arm. "Sorry, Ana," he rasped.

"Tell me what you know." Not what I wanted to say, but he looked ready to die, and I couldn't ask whether he ever cared that he had a daughter. I wasn't sure I wanted to know the answer.

"It's too late." Menehem gave a weak smile as the guard station walls crackled and a loud pulse filled the room, then dulled into white noise. "See you in another life, butterfly."

I shivered. How did he *know*?

He died before I had a chance to ask.

I stayed for only a moment longer, a miasma of emotions tumbling inside me. Then I turned away and wove through the mess of patients to find Sam.

His eyes were closed, but machines beeped comfortingly and he murmured, "Hi, Ana. What was that noise?"

"Janan is back." From the corner of my window, familiar templelight filled the sky. I touched Sam's wrist to feel his pulse, just for reassurance. Blood had been cleaned away from his face and arms, revealing bruises and the laser burn from a couple of weeks ago. The latter was still bandaged, and fluid dripped through a tube into his near arm. I couldn't find anywhere burned by acid, but when I blinked, I saw the huge dragon head hovering over him. If I'd been just a little slower . . . "But don't die just because it's safe."

"And leave you alone with my piano? Not a chance."

Mindful of cuts on his face, I leaned over and brushed a kiss across his lips. He smiled wearily.

"What about me?" Stef mumbled. "No kiss for me?"

"Sorry, Stef. I'll hold your hand, though." The aisles between the cots were narrow enough for a small chair and nothing else. I slipped one hand into Stef's as she fell asleep again, and leaned my head on Sam's pillow, next to his.

When I awoke, all my muscles creaking, daylight illuminated the ravaged city. Search parties went out for the missing, but they'd never find Meuric. I kept waiting for someone to blame me for his disappearance, but when Sine came by,

she just told me that Sam and his friends had been exoner-
ated and I could live with him again.

As our vehicle drove over debris and through the market
field, I peered up at the temple. The crack the dragons had
made mended itself while I watched, and I could almost hear
the echoes of Janan's words in the rumble: "Mistake. You are
a mistake of no consequence."

I hugged my backpack and tried not to listen as the driver
talked about the seventy-two people who'd died while the
temple was dark.

Seventy-two people who'd never come back.

30
AFTER

MORE THAN ANYTHING, I wanted Sam to myself for a few days, but Stef invited herself to stay with us. She didn't want to be alone.

I didn't blame her, and I didn't protest. She'd been his best friend since the beginning. I couldn't comprehend how deep their feelings for each other ran, but I knew what it meant. When the driver stopped in front of Sam's house, I helped Stef out, too. She took my room and I took the parlor.

While they recovered, I did what I could to put their homes back in order. Li and the Council had ransacked Sam's house, and dragons had marauded through every quarter, spitting acid. Though the exteriors had healed themselves once the temple began to glow again, the interiors and out-buildings were wrecked.

I took care of what I could on my own, starting with gardens and cavies and chicken coops, other things that would provide food during the last month of winter. I swept shattered glass and dragged off useless wood boards for recycling. I cooked and cleaned, did anything I could to keep myself busy while search parties found more survivors and the Councilhouse hospital sent medics around to check on everyone.

I did anything to keep from thinking about Templedark, what they called that night, and all the people I hadn't saved. I tried not to think about Menehem, either. Sylph fires had killed him—medics said it had been very painful—but he'd be reincarnated, since he'd hung on until the temple lit itself again. A hundred others had managed to wait to die, too.

But seventy-two would be gone forever. Probably more. There were a lot of people they weren't sure about.

Sam and Stef rested and ate when ordered, and did various exercises to regain strength. After a week, Stef thanked me and said she was going home. She promised to look in on us; her expression, behind the mask of fading bruises, was filled with worry. I just nodded.

After she left, I sat on the stairs and hugged my knees. Pieces of me felt hollow. No amount of putting Sam's house back together would fill them.

I'd killed Meuric. He might come back. There was a good chance he'd been dead before the temple went dark, but what if he'd writhed in pain for hours before finally dying? What if I'd destroyed him as Menehem had Li?

Sam sat down next to me. "I know you must live here, because things move when I'm not looking."

"This is living?" Everything inside me wallowed in numbness, like I had leapt off the top of the temple and was still falling. Like I'd never again have a thunderstorm inside me. At least thunderstorms involved feeling.

"You told the medics you weren't hurt. Did they miss something?"

"I wish I hurt." I slid one hand up to my shoulder and massaged the muscles around it. Still tender. The wise thing to do would have been to let them look at it, but they'd have taken me away from Sam. Not that I'd hung around him once we got here.

I kept my gaze on my socks.

"Can you tell me what happened after you left the prison window?"

"Will it help?"

He hesitated, and I imagined the line between his eyes while he considered the best way to tell the truth. "Maybe. If you don't want to talk about it, there's nothing wrong with that decision. I'd like to know. It would help me to know what we'll be dealing with."

"What will happen to Menehem when he's reincarnated?"

"It's hard to say. I imagine he'll be imprisoned for at least one lifetime. Probably more, considering . . ." Sam stared down into the parlor. "I'm sure they'll want to know how he did it."

"He was going to tell me."

All those people, gone forever. Where did they go?

My voice sounded as hollow as the rest of me. "He thought I'd appreciate what he'd done, sacrificing Ciana so I'd be born. Sacrificing oldsouls during Templedark for more newsouls. But I don't. I mean, I guess I'd rather be here than not, but I only have that opinion because I'm here."

Sam touched my hand. "Yesterday, Sarit dropped off an envelope. She'd gone to Li's house to find your things before the Council took them."

"What's in the envelope?"

"I didn't look. It has your name on it. Menehem's handwriting." Sam's voice was soft. "Do you want to see?"

Definitely not. But I stood and followed him into his room. He fetched the large envelope from a bookcase.

Inside, there were slim leather-bound journals, filled with notes and chemical formulas, drawings and photographs of sylph, and a map of somewhere east of Range; it was the place he'd done all his research, I supposed. I put everything away. It would take time to study, but Menehem had told me how he'd destroyed so many souls after all.

And how I'd been given a chance at someone else's life.

I set the envelope aside and stepped toward Sam. He put his arms around me, kissed the top of my head, and whispered, "You didn't have to sleep downstairs all week."

"Stef was here."

He gave a one-shouldered shrug.

Maybe he couldn't understand how awkward that would have been, knowing his best friend and sometimes-lover was three rooms over. After lifetimes of awkwardness, they probably got desensitized. I pressed my cheek on his chest and listened to his heartbeat while he ran his fingers through my hair.

"I can tell you what happened," I said at last. "No one else, though. Not yet." I traced his fingers, his hand holding tight to my waist. "They wouldn't believe me. I don't want them to know about Meuric, either. I'll have to figure it out eventually, but for now . . ."

"Okay." He guided me to his bed so we could sit. "Whatever you're comfortable saying, that will be enough."

I told him everything.

The everywhere-light. The stairs and books and uncaring voice. And Meuric. When I slept, I dreamt about my knife, the pop and spray and slurp, the way I'd kicked his flailing body into the upside-down pit.

I'd killed him, been willing to kill Li and Menehem. Only eighteen, and already I felt a thousand years old. I should have been happy Li would never come back, no matter how many lifetimes I lived, but I wasn't. It didn't make any sense, but when I thought about it too much, the hollow chasms inside me only gaped wider.

Sam hmmed when I was finished. He didn't ask questions or urge me to *do* anything about it, just breathed into my hair and tucked the subject away for a time when we could both deal. "So I guess we're not leaving Range?"

"Guess not. Sine is the Speaker now. She convinced the Council it was Li who attacked us." Li and someone we didn't know yet. I doubted it was Menehem. Maybe one of Li's guard friends, or someone Meuric paid. "But when you said you'd have come with me, that helped. It still helps."

He gave me a light squeeze. "I'd go anywhere with you."

My heart thumped, sending waves of realness through my limbs. I wasn't alone. I wasn't, to Sam, a mistake of no consequence. He'd never thought I was a nosoul.

I didn't realize I was crying until Sam brushed tears off my cheeks.

"Ana," he murmured, leaning his forehead on mine. If he tilted, or I did, our noses would bump, and then our lips would. I wanted to kiss him, but not while I felt so soggy. "Where's your backpack?"

"Huh?" Not what I thought he'd ask. "Did you want the books?" We'd have to look into them soon. I wished I'd grabbed more, now that I knew there was something coming on Soul Night. We were in the beginning of a Year of Hunger now; Soul Night fell on the spring equinox of the Year of Souls. That was next year. It didn't seem like enough time to prepare for the unknown, especially with so much work already piling up: figuring out Menehem's notes, helping to rebuild sections of Heart, and preparing for potential newsouls.

In a year, I might not be the only one.

"Let's leave the books for another time." Sam slid off the bed, taking my hands in his. "You said some papers met with a fire. I thought we'd go down to the piano and start restoring your music."

"Both of us?" The last time I'd touched the piano had been before the masquerade. It felt like ages ago. "I can't—"

"You must." Sam tugged me to my feet and swept me into a tight hug. "You're the only one who can help me restore it." He was serious. He wasn't going to surprise me with a fresh, unburned stack of papers in the morning, music already written.

"I don't know."

"You can do anything." He said it with such conviction, and I wanted to believe. I *had* to believe. I *would* believe, or I'd never be free.

I let go of my wings.

Not a nosoul. Not a butterfly.

A thousand years from now, even if I was never reborn, people would remember me: Ana Incarnate.

ACKNOWLEDGMENTS

INFINITE THANKS TO:

(Princess) Lauren MacLeod, my agent, who must have read this fifty times, yet her enthusiasm never waned.

Sarah Shumway, my editor, for her encouragement, wisdom, and overall superfantasticness.

The entire team at Katherine Tegen Books, including Katherine Tegen herself; Amy Ryan, Joel Tippie, and the art department, for my *amazing* cover and the most beautiful insides of a book a girl could ever ask for; and marketing and publicity.

Christine Nguyen, who fangirled even my first drafts, especially when I was stuck in a rut.

Corinne Duyvis, for many things, including our butterfly collection.

Gabrielle Harvey, for patiently explaining the whole "music as a job" thing, and who kept this book from leaving the house with musical toilet paper stuck between the pages.

Gwen Hayes, who's not just a critique partner, but a Cheese Pact sister. Cheese forever!

Jaime Lee Moyer, who said, "This is the one."

Jillian Boehme, whose friendship and encouragement kept me sane.

Wendy Beer, who, like any true friend, encouraged me to treat my characters badly.

Thanks to Adam Heine, Beth Revis, Bria Quinlan (cheese!), Elizabeth Bear, Holly McDowell, Jamie Harrington, Julie Klumb, Kathleen Peacock, Lisa Iriarte, Maggie Boehme, Maigan Turner, Michelle Hodkin, Rae Carson, Ricki Schultz, Sarah Heile, Shawna Thomas, and Tami Moore. Without your support, encouragement, challenges, and research assistance, this book would not be what it is. All failings are my own.

Thanks to the Apocalypsies for such a fantastic support group, and to all the kind folks who read the first few chapters on the Online Writing Workshop.

Thanks to my husband, Jeff, who worked hard so I could pursue my passion and who listened to my book-crazed ramblings all hours of the day.

Thanks to God, who deserves more gratitude than I can ever give.

And thanks to you, the reader, for taking a chance by picking up this book. I hope you enjoy reading it as much as I enjoyed writing it.

ASUNDER

1
MEMORY

MY LIFE WAS A MISTAKE.

As long as I'd been alive, I'd wanted to know why I'd been born. Why, after five thousand years of the same souls being reincarnated, my soul had slipped through the cracks of existence and burdened the people of Heart with such *newness*.

No one could tell me how I happened, not until the night I'd found my way into the temple with no door, trapping myself with the entity called Janan.

"Mistake," he'd said. "You are a mistake of no consequence."

I knew, as I'd always known, that I was a soul asunder.

Outside the temple, the night had spiraled into chaos. Sylph burned, and dragons rained acid from the thunder-torn sky.

The numinous light of the temple had vanished. The father I'd never known appeared and told me the same as Janan: I was an experiment gone wrong.

My life might have begun as a mistake, but I wouldn't let it end as one.

Spring slipped across Range, a verdant blanket stitched with new life. Trees blossomed and young animals peeked from the forest, and the people of Heart cleared a stretch of land north of the city, just beyond the geysers and mud pits that steamed and bubbled as winter eased its grip on the world.

Instead of crops, they planted dozens of black obelisks, each carved with loving words, achievements, and the name of a darksoul: a soul who wouldn't be reincarnated; a soul lost during the battle of Templedark.

Every citizen of Heart took on a task. They gathered physical reminders to place by the obelisks, combed through records to find videos of darksoul friends, or assisted in the construction of the Templedark Memorial.

Sam and Councilor Sine combined their efforts, composing music and writing laments. They created different melodies and lyrics for every darksoul. I wanted to help, though I didn't know most of the darksouls well enough to contribute.

When spring bowed to summer and the memorial was finished, everyone in Heart met on North Avenue and formed two lines.

2

Two by two, we passed beneath the Northern Arch.

Two by two, we filed out of the white city.

Two by two, we entered the Templedark Memorial.

Our lines split there, and we followed the iron bars of the fence. Wind gusted through, making the whole place smell of roses and tinges of sulfur from a nearby geyser. Steam drifted through the cerulean sky.

The procession took ages. By the time we all arrived, people stood three deep around the field of high monuments. Everything was silent, save rustling leaves and the gasp-heave of weeping. Next to me, my best friend, Sarit, squeezed my hand tight and blinked tears off her dark lashes. Our dresses tugged in the wind while we waited.

A bell tolled in the center of the memorial, one peal for each soul lost.

What happened after death? Where did you go? What did you do? The scariest possibility was that we might. just. stop.

After another moment of aching hush, Sine pulled away from the perimeter and took a microphone. "Today, we gather to remember those who fell during Templedark. We come to honor their lives and deaths, and begin the long process of healing not only our bodies and city, but also our souls. . . ."

Most people kept their heads down, the weight of grief so evident in their slumped postures I feared they might collapse. Others stood stoic, blank, as though their minds were somewhere very far away.

3

But here and there I caught eyes seeking mine; I exchanged sad smiles with almost-friends. Most were people I'd warned about dying during Templedark. There wasn't much to say about it, but they were nice to me, and our encounters were always cautiously hopeful.

Sine finished her speech.

One at a time, someone stood for each darksoul to recount lifetimes and memories. Sam and Sine performed the music they'd written. Small screens went into the base of each obelisk, set to play a video of the darksoul, or play a recorded copy of the music written for them.

Then we turned our attention to the next darksoul.

At the end of the day, we filed out of the memorial, same as we'd come in. Friends stayed at Sam's house with us, but everyone was so raw with sadness there was no joy in the companionship, and the next morning, we walked back to Templedark Memorial.

It took four days to remember the lives of almost eighty souls, and as we left the field of black obelisks for the final time, people kept glancing at the empty places in the back: room for more darksouls, because we couldn't be sure about when a few people had died. Some might still come back.

Over the next weeks, some people went on like it never happened, but there were rumors of people sleeping in the market field or destroying everything in their homes. Others supposedly didn't leave their houses for weeks at a time.

4

I went back to my lessons—what lessons were still being offered—and tried to find happiness with my friends and music, but the strangeness of the community's behavior smothered me. No one seemed to heal.

As summer hurtled toward autumn, the mood sagged from melancholy to disconsolate, and the pulse in the walls grew unbearable. The city wall. The Councilhouse walls. Even the exterior walls of everyone's homes. The slow throb of life inside stone made my skin try to crawl off.

I couldn't take it anymore.

"I have to get out," I told Sam. "I need to get away. Will you go with me?"

"Anywhere," he said, and kissed me.

We left Heart just before summer faded into memory.

"You've been quiet," Sam said as we left behind the geysers and mud pits, the fumaroles and rime-whitened trees.

"Nothing's wrong." Oops. We hadn't gotten to that part of his questioning yet.

He snorted. "Okay. What's on your mind?"

I lengthened my strides to keep up with Sam and Not as Shaggy as His Father, the pony that bore most of our bags. We called him Shaggy for short. My backpack straps dug into my shoulders, but I carried only a few essentials—in case we somehow got separated—plus the temple door device, and my notebook. Sam had taken to calling it my diary, but I didn't keep track of my days in there.

"Nothing in particular, I guess." I glanced back at Heart, from here just a seemingly endless expanse of white ripples and curves over the plateau. The immense central tower stood partially obscured by late-summer foliage. The city looked peaceful from far away. "I feel better getting out of there."

"The walls?" He said it like he understood, but the walls didn't feel bad to anyone but me.

"Yeah." I slipped my thumbs beneath my backpack straps, relieving some of the pressure on my shoulders. "Did you see Corin when we went through the guard station?"

"Corin?" Sam raised an eyebrow. "He didn't do anything."

"No, he didn't." I kicked a fallen branch off the road. Pine needles scraped the cobblestone. "He just sat there at his desk. He didn't say anything. He didn't acknowledge us. He barely moved."

"He's grieving," Sam said gently. "He lost souls very close to him."

"Then why does he go to the guard station every day?"

"What else should he be doing?"

"I don't know. Staying home? Staying with a friend?"

Sam's eyes were dark as dusk, and his voice deep with a hundred lifetimes. "It doesn't always make sense, the way others grieve. I can't imagine what I'd be like if I'd lost you, but it would probably seem very strange to others."

6

Because I was the newsoul, and why would anyone grieve that much over me?

Then again, I knew how I'd behaved during Templedark. Fearing for Sam's life, I'd hurtled through fields of dragon acid, dodging sylph and laser fire. I'd felt like someone other than myself, like I might do something crazy if I didn't find Sam, because how could my world be right without him?

"I don't like the way grief feels," I said at last. "And I don't like the way it feels when other people grieve." Which sounded like I thought they should avoid the emotion because it made me uncomfortable. No, what did I really mean? "After the dragons attacked the market, I wanted you to feel better. I wanted to do anything I could to help, to make you stop hurting, but I didn't know how. I tried and . . ."

Sam nodded. "It makes you feel helpless."

"I don't like that."

"Me neither." He pushed a strand of black hair from his eyes. "I've felt like that about you, helpless to make you feel better."

"Really?"

He flashed a strained smile. "When we first met. You trapped the sylph in an egg, letting your hands get burned so you could rescue me."

Sylph. Just the word made me shudder and check the woods for unnatural shadows. Too easily, I could remember the inferno racing through my hands, up my forearms, and the red-and-black skin all bubbling with blisters.

"You tried to be so strong after that," Sam said. "And you *were* strong, but I knew how much it must have hurt. I wanted to take the pain from you, but I couldn't. I felt helpless."

"Even though we'd just met?"

Sam only smiled and touched my hand, and we shifted to the safer topics of music he wanted me to learn, and debating whether or not Sarit would actually make good on her threat to come after us if we didn't return to Heart before winter.

Late summer bathed Range in shades of green. Clouds drifted across the sky, catching and tangling on mountains like gauze. A hawk careened in from above, calling his territory, and a family of weasels startled at the sound. They tumbled to hide in the brush, even though the hawk was far away.

When night fell, we set up a tent and sleeping bags and discussed music over dinner, then went outside to take turns on the flute he'd packed. I liked waking up across the tent from him; seeing his messy hair and sleepy smile first thing chased away my lingering fears and sadness.

We made good progress across Range, and finally we reached our destination: Purple Rose Cottage.

The last time I'd seen Purple Rose Cottage, the roof bore daggers of ice, and the path uphill had been slippery with snow. Li had stood in the doorway, tall and beautiful and fierce, and she'd given me a broken compass so I'd lose my way and fall prey to sylph.

Now Sam and I stepped out of the forest shade and trudged up the hill. Sunlight warmed my face and arms and made the cottage glow brown and almost unfamiliar with how welcoming it looked. Rosebushes huddled around the wall, indigo blooms just fading as summer came to a close. Vegetables lay half-eaten and rotted in the garden; no one had been here to harvest and put them away for winter.

We spent a couple of days getting the cottage cleaned up, arranging our things in the bedrooms and kitchen, and not discussing anything more difficult than who was in charge of coffee each morning. It was nice living with Sam without the heartbeat-filled walls boxing us in.

Our third evening in Purple Rose Cottage, Sam asked me to wait for him outside.

The cool air gave me goose bumps, but I waited on the grass by a bush of indigo roses. Low sunlight shot around the cottage, casting the forest in shadow and gold-green and hints of russet. The door shut, and Sam walked over carrying a large basket.

"Help me with this?" he asked. Together, we spread a blanket on the grass to sit, and his eyes shone in the dimness. "I want to give you something." From the basket, he removed a long wooden box. Faint light from the window made the polish glisten. When had he packed that? "This is for you."

"You didn't have to get anything for me. I have everything I need."

He smiled and regarded the box, his hands covering the gilt latches. "It's a gift, like friends gave Tera and Ash for their rededication ceremony."

That had been a special occasion, celebrating their eternal love. Today was nothing, as far as I could remember. Still, the idea of a gift delighted me, and I tried to squeeze my fingers between his to look. There were patterns carved into the wood, but I couldn't see them. "What is it?"

His hands trembled as he pulled up the latches, and the box was soundless as he turned up the lid.

Light glimmered across two lengths of silver, catching on a row of keys and delicate swirls engraved into the metal.

It was a flute, one I'd never seen before.

A rush of wind stirred the trees and stole my quiet "Oh" as Sam pulled the flute from its case and pieced it together. His eyes were dark, wide with anticipation and something else as he offered the instrument with both hands. "It's beautiful," I whispered.

"I hoped you would like it." The flute nearly vanished in his hands, though it seemed normal-sized when I rested my fingertips on the cool metal. "Take it," he urged. "It's yours."

"Why?" My question didn't stop my fingers from wrapping around the flute, from pulling it to my lips. My breath hissed over the mouthpiece as my fingers found their places on the keys.

The heat of his body warmed me as he leaned closer.

"Here." He nudged my right thumb farther down the tube. "And your chin." He tilted my face up slightly, his fingers lingering over my skin.

Our eyes met, both of us suddenly aware of his other hand flat on my ribs, unconsciously adjusting my posture. "Better?" I breathed.

He watched my mouth and nodded. "Play for me."

Play what? He hadn't brought out music. But as sunlight began to fade, making the indigo roses turn ink-dark and early snow glow on the mountaintops, I played a long, low note that filled the cottage clearing with a haunting reverberation.

The note created a bubble of warmth around us. It tangled around vines, caught in rosebushes, and pushed out toward the mountains that rose like distant walls. I found a breath, and my fingers climbed a half step up.

The flute stretched its sound. It fit me as precisely as though it had once been part of my body and now we were reunited. My hands and mouth and lungs knew this flute, and I knew this flute would do anything I could ask of it, and more.

I climbed notes until a pattern emerged, as sweet and haunting as the flute's sound. The melody took shape and flew on sure, steady wings. Music filled me until it seemed I might burst.

When I lowered the flute, Sam leaned toward me, a

satisfied smile on his lips. "It suits you."

"It's perfect." I caressed the silver, engravings sharp and new beneath my fingertips. They looked like ivy, or something delicate and twisty. "Did you make it?"

"Some. I had a friend do a lot of the work. How was I going to hide it from you otherwise?"

The metal was warm from my playing, and I couldn't stop staring at the way it looked in my hands. It was *perfect*. "I want to play it all the time."

"Good." Sam grinned widely. "Because you will." His tone turned conspiring. "I wrote some duets for us."

My heart stumbled over itself. "Really?"

"I want to keep this moment forever, the way you're smiling right now."

"You may." I placed the flute in my lap and brushed my hands over my mouth, pretending to grab my smile as though it were bits of wool or clouds. "Here." I pressed my imaginary smile into his hands. "This is for you."

He held his fists against his heart and laughed. "It's just what I always wanted."

"I have more whenever you want them."

"All I have to do is give you new instruments?"

I shrugged. "We might be able to find other things worthy of smiles."

He cupped my cheek and kissed me. "Ana, I . . ." The way his voice had softened, deepening with emotion, made me

12

shiver. He pulled back. "I'll get you a jacket."

Whatever he'd been ready to say before faded into the cool night. "No, you know what would help me warm up? If you got the other flute and music."

"You're ready to start now?" He lifted an eyebrow.

"You can't give me a pretty new flute and expect me just to put it away." I clutched the instrument to my chest.

"Then I'll be right back." He kissed me again, then got up and vanished into the cottage, turning on the front light as the door shut behind him. Good idea, if we were to read music.

Alone but for the trees and roses and a few birds settling in, I lifted my flute and found a simple melody. Somewhere in the woods, a bird repeated a few notes. I smiled and played again, and the bird sang back.

Strange, but I couldn't identify the bird. It didn't sound like a shrike or mockingbird. A thrush? No, the voice was too otherworldly.

Peering into the darkness, I played a few measures of my minuet—the one I'd written not long before Templedark—and the bird . . . something . . . sang it back. It wasn't a bird.

"What are you doing?" Sam came outside again, his arms filled with a stand, a book of music, and his flute.

"There's something out there." I couldn't see. The front light stretched and vanished only halfway down the path, and the trees huddled beyond its reach. Rosebushes shivered in a cool breeze, and in the woods, someone moaned long and mournful.

My stomach dropped. I knew that sound.

"Sylph." The light made harsh shadows across Sam's face. "Is that a sylph? Here?"

"It didn't sound like a sylph before. I thought it was a bird. It was mimicking my playing."

Shock flickered in Sam's expression as he squinted into the dark. "Surely they wouldn't be this far into Range. Or— mimic you."

I licked my lips and played four notes, and the repeat came from closer. Just beyond the light, a shadow writhed. Then another, to the left, and a third still in the forest. There were so many, maybe as many as there'd been the night they chased me off a cliff, into Rangedge Lake.

Sylph burned, reeked of ash and fire, and they were without substance. The lore was complicated and contradictory. Some said they were shadows brought to a terrible half-life, thanks to fumes and heat from the caldera beneath Range. Skeptics maintained sylph were simply another of the planet's dominant species, like dragons or centaurs or trolls; people should be cautious, but not assign them any special history or powers.

Whatever they were, I'd had more than enough experience with them for one lifetime.

"Sam." I hardly recognized my voice, so opposite the storm

of fear building inside me. "Get all the traps you can find."

Several more sylph picked up the notes, singing as though it were a short round of music. The sound grew, pressing closer, and abruptly stopped.

A sense of *waiting* grew heavy in the air. A heartbeat later, a sylph whistled a scale.

Sam touched my elbow. "You need to get inside. The walls are protected."

"Protected. Not sylph-proof." I lifted my flute. "I think—" My breath hissed across the mouthpiece and made all the sylph tense, push closer. I retreated until my skirt caught in a rosebush; thorns pricked through the cloth. "I think my playing keeps them distracted. Get the eggs. Set the traps. If the sylph attack, I'll go inside."

And hope I was fast enough to reach the door before they burned me alive.

"I'll hurry." Sam vanished into the cottage.

Heat billowed from all sides as the sylph swarmed closer. Heart pounding, I began to play.